ALSO BY RACHEL HAWKINS

Rebel Belle

Miss Mayhem

Lady Renegades

ROYALS

Rachel Hawkins

G. P. PUTNAM'S SONS

G. P. Putnam's Sons
an imprint of Penguin Random House LLC
375 Hudson Street
New York, NY 10014

Library of Congress Cataloging-in-Publication Data
Names: Hawkins, Rachel, 1979– author.
Title: Royals / Rachel Hawkins.
Description: New York, NY : G. P. Putnam's Sons, 2018.
Summary: "When Daisy's older sister gets engaged to the Crown Prince of Scotland,
Daisy makes the royal rulebook all her own"—Provided by publisher.
Identifiers: LCCN 2017041444 | ISBN 9781524738235 (hardback)
Subjects: | CYAC: Conduct of life—Fiction. | Publicity—Fiction. | Dating (Social customs)—
Fiction. | Princes—Fiction. | Kings, queens, rulers, etc.—Fiction. | Scotland—Fiction.
Classification: LCC PZ7.H313525 Roy 2018 | DDC [Fic]—dc23
LC record available at https://lccn.loc.gov/2017041444

Printed in the United States of America.
ISBN 9781524738235
1 3 5 7 9 10 8 6 4 2

Design by Marikka Tamura. Text set in Fournier MT Pro.

*For Kathie Moore, who got up at 5 a.m. to watch
William and Kate's wedding with me via text. Love you, Mama.*

Ever since Prince Alexander of Scotland was spotted with the blond American beauty, we've been nuts for all things Ellie! But do you know everything about this maybe-princess-to-be? We bet at least a few of these will surprise you!

1) Eleanor Winters may have the same la-di-da accent as her boyfriend, but she was born in Florida to British parents!

2) Clearly a love of the spotlight runs in the family since Ellie's dad was once a musician and her mom writes mystery novels set in Ellie's very own cozy small town.

3) Born on September 9, our Ellie is a Virgo (no jokes about how princes only marry virgins)!

4) Valedictorian, National Merit Scholar, and captain of her local swim team, Ellie has clearly been overachieving since forever! Hmmmm, not seeing any crowns on that list, though. But why be a prom queen when you can be a REAL queen!

5) Ellie attended the très exclusive University of the Isles in her boyfriend's home country—one day to be his kingdom—where she studied English literature!

6) Her favorite color is blue, as you can probably see from some of the killer outfits she's worn!

7) For the past year, Ellie has been working for a small press located in Edinburgh, editing children's books about Scottish history. Maybe brushing up on some lessons for herself?

8) A vegetarian since the age of twelve, Ellie has Prince Alexander—a longtime outdoorsman—giving up some of his old hobbies, like fly-fishing and hunting! (Something that has made her not too popular with certain members of his circle, we hear!)

9) While "Eleanor Winters" is definitely a fancy—dare we say regal?—name, Ellie's middle name is the decidedly less posh "Berry"! Apparently it's a family joke!

10) Or maybe plant life is just really popular in the Winters household—Ellie has a seventeen-year-old sister named Daisy!

Chapter 1

"SOME OLD LADY JUST CALLED ME THE C-WORD."

I glance up from the magazine I'm paging through. Isabel Alonso, my best friend and fellow cashier at the Sur-N-Sav, leans back against her register and snaps her gum. Her dark hair is caught up in a messy braid, black against the green of her apron.

"Just now?" I ask. The store is more or less deserted, which has been the case since the giant Walmart opened up on the other side of town, so Isabel and I are the only cashiers working today. I haven't had anyone in my line in over an hour, hence the magazine. Still, I can't believe I was absorbed enough to miss something actually exciting—if super rude—happening.

Isabel rolls her eyes. "It's my fault the price of sour cream went up."

"That seems fair," I tell her with a solemn nod. "You are a fabulous dairy heiress, after all."

Isabel turns back to her register, punching buttons at random. "We have got to get new jobs, Daze. This is humiliating."

I don't disagree, but when you live in a small town in north

Florida, your options are kind of limited. I'd wanted to get a job at the library last fall, but that hadn't worked out—no funding—and one summer of helping out at Vacation Bible School had cured me of the desire to work with little kids, which meant babysitting or working part time at the local preschool was out. So it was all Sur-N-Sav all the time.

Although now, looking at my phone where it's propped against the register, I see that my time at Sur-N-Sav is up.

"Ah, three o'clock, the most beautiful time of day," I say happily, and Isabel groans. "Not fair!"

"Hey, I've been here since seven," I remind her. "You wanna leave early—"

"You have to take the early shift," she finishes, waving a hand at me. "Okay, Mrs. Miller, got it."

Mrs. Miller is the manager of the Sur-N-Sav, and Isabel and I have gotten very used to her lectures over the past year.

Sighing, Isabel leans next to her register, chin propped in her hand. Her nails are painted three different shades of green, and a simple beaded bracelet slides down one slender wrist. "Four more weeks," she says, and I repeat our favorite mantra.

"Four more weeks."

At the end of June, Isabel and I are bidding a not-so-fond farewell to the Sur-N-Sav life and heading out to Key West for Key Con, then plan to spend a week bumming around the town. Isabel's brother lives there with his wife and Isabel's ridiculously cute baby nephew, so we have a free (and parent-approved) place to stay. To say my entire life is revolving around this trip might be something of an understatement. Not only will we get our geek on, but we will also get to do fun Key West things. Snorkeling,

2

the Hemingway House, all the key lime pie a gal can hold . . . yes, this trip is going to make my entire summer, and Isa and I have been planning it for almost a year now, as soon as the con was announced. Our favorite author, Ash Bentley, is going to be there talking about her Finnigan Sparks series, plus there are at least twenty different panels Isabel and I want to check out—on everything from women in space operas to cosplay design. It is geek heaven, and we are beyond ready.

"You need to come over this weekend so we can start planning outfits," Isabel says, straightening up and punching random buttons on the register as Whitney Houston wails about the greatest love of all over the sound system. "I still haven't decided if I'm cosplaying as Miranda from *Finnegan and the Falcon* or Jezza from *Finnegan's Moon*."

"Ben would probably prefer Jezza," I say. Ben is Isa's boyfriend, and has been for roughly eleventy billion years. Okay, since eighth grade. "Lot less clothes on Jezza."

Isa screws up her face, thinking. "True, but Ben's not even going to be there, and I don't know if I'm ready to show a quarter of my butt cheeks to all of Key West."

"Fair," I acknowledge. "Besides, being Miranda means you get to wear a purple wig."

She points a finger at me. "Yes! Miranda it is, then. Who are you going to go as?"

Smiling, I start shutting down my register. "Cosplay is your thing," I remind her, "so I'm just going as me. Boring Girl in T-Shirt and Jeans."

"You are a disappointment to me in every way," Isa replies, and I shake my head.

The doors slide open, another senior citizen shopper strolling in as I finish with my register and take the cash drawer to Mrs. Miller's office. At most grocery stores, clerks count the money themselves, but years of working with teenage employees has given Mrs. Miller trust issues, and to be honest, I'm happy to leave that chore to someone else anyway.

That done, I make my way across the store, noticing as I pass the magazine racks lining the register lanes that a bunch of them have been turned around, the ads on their backs, rather than the covers, facing the customer.

This has to be Isabel's doing. I walk up to a rack and turn the nearest backward magazine to face me. I see a quick flash of blond hair and bright teeth, and then my eyes land on the headline, printed in bold yellow script: "TEN THINGS YOU NEVER KNEW ABOUT ELLIE WINTERS!"

I wonder if any of the ten things would surprise *me*. I doubt it, though.

My sister has lived a life pretty free from the scandalous, almost as if she knew she'd end up on the cover of magazines. I'm almost tempted to flip through, but then decide that "A," it would be weird and "B," Isabel *did* go to the trouble of trying to hide the magazines from me in the first place.

"It was nothing bad this time," she calls out now. "Just figured you didn't need to see!"

Giving her a thumbs-up, I continue toward the door at the far side of the store.

My stuff is in the break room, a truly tragic space made up of orange walls, green plastic chairs, and a scratched laminate table. At some point, someone had carved "BECKY LOVES

JOSH" into the top of it, and every time I sat there on my break, reading or studying, I wondered what became of Becky and Josh. Were they still in love? Had Becky been as insanely bored here as I was?

Although, hey, at least Becky was never confronted with pictures of her sister on the front of tabloids.

Or being in the tabloids herself for that matter.

Ugh.

The whole prom debacle is still this mix of anger and hurt, a thorny ball lodged right in my chest, and thinking about it is like poking a sore tooth. You forget just how much the tooth aches until you focus on it, and then suddenly it's all you can think about.

Which means I can't risk thinking about it now, or I might start crying in the break room at the Sur-N-Sav, and there is nothing on earth more depressing than that scenario. That's like movie-where-the-dog-dies levels of pathos, so yeah, not doing that.

Instead, I heft my beat-up patchwork bag onto my shoulder and head out the door.

The blinding brightness and heat of the late-May afternoon is intense as I walk outside and into the parking lot, and I squint, reaching in my bag for my sunglasses, my mind already on what I'm going to do for the rest of the afternoon. Mostly, it involves draping myself over the AC vent in my room and reading the new manga I picked up from the bookstore yesterday.

"Dais."

And there's that sore tooth.

Great.

Michael is leaning against one of the yellow-painted concrete pylons in front of the store, one ankle crossed in front of the other, dark hair falling in his eyes. He's probably been practicing that pose. Michael Dorset is a *champion* leaner, one of the best, really. In the Olympics for Cute Boys, he'd take the gold in the Hot Lean every time.

Lucky for me, I am now immune to the Hot Lean (trademark pending).

Sliding my sunglasses onto my face, I hold up a hand at my ex-boyfriend.

"Nope."

Michael's face curls into a scowl. He has these really soft features, all round cheeks and pretty brown eyes, and I swear he's taught his hair to do that thing where it falls juuuuust right over his forehead. A month ago, I would've been a puddle of melted Daisy at that face, would've reached out to push his hair back from his forehead. Michael Dorset had been my crush since ninth grade. He'd always hung out with a way more popular crowd than I had (I know, shocking that my glasses and *Adventure Time* T-shirts didn't make me a bigger draw), and then last year—*finally*—I'd gotten him.

"I screwed up," he says now, shoving his hands in his pockets. He's wearing the skinniest jeans known to man, jeggings if I'm being honest, and he's got one of my ponytail holders around his wrist. The green one.

Fighting the kindergarten urge to rip it off, I shift my bag to my other shoulder. "That's an understatement."

It's *hot* in the parking lot, and I suddenly realize I'm still wearing the little green Sur-N-Sav apron that goes over my clothes. Michael is all in black, as per usual, but doesn't seem to be sweating, possibly because he's like 0.06% body fat. This is the last place I want to have this discussion, so I move past him and toward my car.

"C'mon," he wheedles, following. "We need to at least *talk* about it."

The asphalt grits under my sneakers as I keep walking. Even though we're not that close to a beach, sand magically appears here, pooling in cracks and potholes in the parking lot.

"We did talk about it," I say. "It's just that there wasn't much to say. You tried to sell our prom pictures."

Fun part of having a famous sibling—you yourself somehow become *kind of* famous.

But it seems like you just get the annoying parts of fame, like, you know, your boyfriend selling private stuff to a tabloid.

Or trying to.

Apparently the royal family had people on the lookout for that kind of thing and shut it down pretty quickly, which, honestly, just made the whole thing ever weirder.

"Babe," he starts, and I wave him off. I'd *liked* those stupid pictures. Thought we looked cute. And now every time I look at them, they're just another thing that got weird because of Ellie.

I think that's what pissed me off most of all.

"I was doing it for *us*," Michael continues, and that actually makes me stop and whirl around.

"You did it to buy a 'super-sweet' guitar," I say, my voice flat. "The kind you'd talked about forever."

Michael actually does look a little sheepish at that. He shoves his hands in his pockets, shrugging his shoulders up and rocking back on his heels. "But music was *our thing*," he says, and I roll my eyes.

"You never liked the bands I liked, you would never let me play my music in the car, you—"

Fumbling in his back pocket, Michael cuts me off—another habit of his I wasn't that nuts about—saying, "No, but listen." He pulls out his phone, scrolling through it, and I'm just about to turn away and walk to my car when there's a sudden cry from the Sur-N-Sav.

"NO BOYS!" a voice warbles across the parking lot.

I turn back to the store to see Mrs. Miller, my manager, standing on the sidewalk just in front of the sliding doors, hands on her hips. Her hair is probably supposed to be red, but it's faded to a sort of peachy hue, and thin enough that you can see her scalp through it.

"NO BOYS ON SHIFT!" she yells again, wagging a finger at me, the skin under her arm wobbling with judgment.

"I'm off the clock," I call back, then jerk my thumb at Michael. "And this isn't a boy. It's a sentient pair of skinny jeans with good hair."

"NO! BOYS!" Mrs. Miller hollers again, and seriously, Mrs. Miller's hang-up about her female employees having boys around them is both psychotic and ridiculous. I'm not sure why she thinks the freaking Sur-N-Sav is a hotbed of sexual activity, but the "no fraternizing with the opposite sex" rule is far and away her strictest.

"THERE IS ZERO EROTICISM HAPPENING HERE IN THE PARKING LOT!" I shout back, but by now, Michael has found what he was looking for.

"I wrote this for you," he says, touching the screen, and a tinny blast of music shoots out of his phone. The quality is crap, and I can't really make out any of the lyrics over the shriek of the electric guitar, but I'm pretty sure I hear my name several times, rhymed with both "crazy" and "hazy," and then Michael starts actually *singing along with it*, and please, god, let me die of sudden heat stroke, let a car take a turn and mow me down here in the parking lot of the Sur-N-Sav because between my ex warbling "Daisy's driving me crazy" and Mrs. Miller beginning to march across the asphalt toward us, I'm not sure this afternoon can get much worse.

And then I look up to see the black SUV parked at the edge of the lot, window rolled down . . .

With a telephoto lens pointed directly at me.

Chapter 2

I HUSTLE TO MY CAR NEAR THE BACK OF THE LOT, keeping my head down, my bag tucked close to my side. I can't hear the clicking of the camera over Michael's stupid song—he's trailing behind me still, the phone held out like an offering—but I imagine it anyway, my brain already racing ahead to what these pictures will look like, what the headline will say. Whatever it is, it will totally paint me as the bitch. In the past year since Ellie started dating Alex, I've learned that there's basically nothing that's not the girl's fault in tabloid stories. Two months ago, Alex and Ellie went to some ship christening in Scotland, and Alex frowned and winced through the whole thing, which led to all these stories about how my sister was making him miserable, and that her demands for an engagement ring were tearing them apart.

The truth? Alex had fractured his toe that morning tripping down some stairs. The pained look on his face had been *actual, literal pain*, not sadness because his evil girlfriend was bumming him out.

Yay, patriarchy, I guess.

That's what's so weird to me about Ellie buying into the whole royalty deal. It's *built* on crap like that. If she married Alex and they had a daughter and *then* a son? Guess who'd rule.

Yanking my car door open, I turn to face Michael. The song is ending now, and he pauses there, looking back down at his phone. I have a feeling he's about to start the song over, and that obviously cannot happen, so I put my hand over his. His head shoots up, dark eyes meeting mine, and, ugh, he's doing The Smile, which is almost as potent as The Hot Lean, which means I need to nip this in the bud right now.

"Is that your doing, too?" I ask, jerking my head toward the SUV, and he glances over. Michael is cute and all, but he's a terrible liar—I still remember the social studies test incident five years ago in middle school—so when he looks genuinely surprised and shakes his head, I believe him and sigh with relief.

He's still a douche who sold our prom pictures, but at least he's not actively calling the paparazzi.

"Look, Michael," I say now, painfully aware of the lens still pointed at us, at the sweat dripping down my back, at how my hair is sticking to my face, and how any makeup I put on this morning is a distant memory.

"We talked, okay?" I continue. "I get why you did it, and I hope the guitar is awesome and all you hoped it would be. But we're done. Like. Really, really done."

With that, I sling my bag into the car, slide into the driver's seat, and shut the door on him. He stands there, phone in hand, and I look at my ponytail holder on his wrist again, wondering if I should ask for it back.

No, that would just make this whole thing sadder, really, and given that Mrs. Miller has finally reached Michael, he's being punished enough. Her hair is trembling with righteous outrage, and as she shakes a finger at him, Michael—despite being a good head taller—actually cowers.

Which is fun to see.

I drive out of the parking lot, not bothering to look back in the rearview mirror.

The drive home doesn't take long since our neighborhood is only a few miles from the store. It isn't exactly the most scenic of routes, either. When my parents first moved to Perdido, it was actually kind of a cool place. I mean, as cool as a town in Florida that's nowhere near the ocean can be. It was quirky and eccentric, full of artists and writers and old houses that people had painted nutso colors. Lime green, turquoise, a shade I thought of as "electric violet," all slapped on these dollhouse-looking Victorian mansions and cozy bungalows.

But over the years, a lot of the cooler people moved out, and eventually beige started making its way back into Perdido. There's a country club now, too, complete with a golf course— something that made my dad threaten to move. But while Perdido might not be the idyllic little artist community it once was, it's still a nice place. Quiet, dull, and, as Mom was always pointing out, far enough away that it isn't really worth visiting. Today's photographer was the first one I've seen in months. There were better targets for the paps to go after.

Like, for instance, Ellie.

Beige had moved into Perdido, all right, but it still hasn't crept into our neighborhood. My house is actually one of the more subdued on the block, a cheerful yellow instead of magenta or indigo. Tucked back from the street, it's surrounded by banana trees and bougainvillea, the pink blossoms pretty against the sunshine-y paint. Wind chimes dangle from the porch, glass ones, wooden ones that sound like flutes, and the tacky shell-covered ones they sell in gift shops around here. Mom has a thing for wind chimes.

But it isn't the wind chimes that catch my eye as I pull into the driveway. It's the big SUV parked behind my mom's.

Suddenly, the photographer back at the Sur-N-Sav makes sense.

Chapter 3

I PARK MY CAR OFF TO THE SIDE OF THE SUV, AND when I get out, I give a wave to the security guys. It's always the same two when El and Alex come to the States, so I've gotten used to them. "Hi, Malcolm!" I call. "David, how's it going?"

David, the younger of the two guys, lifts his bottle of water in acknowledgment while Malcolm just nods. As always, they're in serious black suits, and I imagine that even with the air-conditioning in the car going full blast, they're still dying. The heat is no joke, but Alexander doesn't like bringing body-guards into my parents' house, so it's the driveway for Malcolm and David.

"Still disappointed you guys don't wear plaid suits," I tell them as I pass by the car, and while Malcolm just keeps staring at the house through his shades, David cracks a smile.

My keys rattle in my hand as I jog up the steps of the porch to see the front door is open, but the glass door is closed. That means I get a second to see my sister and her boyfriend sitting on the couch, their posture perfect, before I come inside. They look as gorgeous and polished as ever, Ellie with her ankles crossed demurely, Alexander sitting on my mom's floral couch like it's a throne.

He always sits like that—maybe he's practicing.

I think again about the guy taking pictures at the Sur-N-Sav and wonder if I need to mention that right off the bat. Ellie wasn't thrilled about the prom pics thing (which, I mean, hi, neither was I, and honestly I think *I'm* the one with cause to complain), and I'm not sure if I want to get into all that on top of dealing with this surprise visit from El and Alex.

Today's Michael thing probably won't even make the papers.

As soon as I walk into the house, El—who hasn't seen me since Christmas—takes one look at my head and says, "Oh, Daisy, your *hair*." Her voice, as always, takes me by surprise. Even though we have British parents, neither El nor I picked up the accent. Then Ellie went away to university in the UK and came back sounding like a character from *Downton Abbey*.

I lift a hand to tuck the bright red strands behind my ear, but then decide to heck with that, my hair is *amazing*.

Luckily, Alexander agrees (or at least pretends to) because he immediately says, "Personally, I approve, Daisy. Redheads, very popular in my family."

He tousles his own reddish-blond hair with a smile, and I'm reminded why everyone in the world is pretty much in love with him. Prince Alexander James Lachlan Baird, Duke of Rothesay, Earl of Carrick, next in line to become King of the Scots, is both cute *and* a surprisingly nice guy. Definitely nicer than El.

"It's her Little Mermaid hair," my mom says, coming in from the kitchen with a full tray in her hands, complete with teapot and our nicest china cups. Before Ellie and Alexander happened, we didn't even own nice china. Or a teapot for that matter. We made tea in mugs with water from the electric kettle.

But I get it—once their oldest daughter started dating a prince, fancy china seemed like the least they could do.

Mom sets the tray on the table, but no one makes a move to actually pour any tea, probably because while Alexander—and now El—live in cold, misty Scotland, this is Florida in May, which means the idea of drinking hot beverages seems insane, if not masochistic.

"Wasn't it purple for a little while last year?" Ellie asks me now, and I raise my eyebrows at her.

"Did you really come all the way from bonny Scotland to interrogate me about my hair choices?"

Ellie's nostrils flare a bit and she laces her fingers together between her knees. "It just seems like there's always something new with you. That's all I'm saying."

I shrug. "I like trying different things."

This is one of the major differences between me and Ellie— she's been Princess Barbie since birth, pretty much. Me? I'm still . . . figuring things out. When Michael said music was "our thing" in the parking lot, he wasn't wrong, exactly. When I'd dated him, I'd been super into learning to play the guitar, almost as intense about that as I'd been about origami lessons the year before. Or the art classes I took freshman year. But honestly, how are you supposed to know what you like unless you *try* stuff?

Ellie says it's "flighty," but I think it's fun, and before she can get going on that train of thought, I change the subject back to her, where it always ends up anyway. "I didn't know y'all were coming."

Mom is sitting in her wingback chair, so I flop in Dad's recliner, and Ellie frowns a little.

My sister has always been one step away from having mice make dresses for her, but ever since she met Alexander, her Disney Princessness has been dialed up to eleven. While we both got Mom's light hair, El's was always shinier, more golden. Right now, it falls in soft waves to her shoulders, held back with a pair of sunglasses that probably cost more than my entire wardrobe. She's wearing jeans, as is Alexander, but even those look fancy on them, probably because they've paired them with expensive leather loafers. Alexander is wearing a white button-down with the sleeves rolled up, and El has on some kind of drapey navy blouse with little white polka dots all over it.

Basically, they look like they belong on a yacht, while I am wearing a T-shirt that says, "EVE WAS FRAMED."

"It was a surprise!" Ellie says brightly, and Alexander flashes me and Mom a smile.

This is the unsettling thing about Ellie and Alexander. They spend so much of their life being public people that sometimes they act that way in private, too, so it can make you feel like they're holding the world's smallest press conference in the living room.

"And a lovely one, too," my dad says, coming into the room. He's wearing a pair of khaki shorts that started their life as pants, a few stray strings hanging down to his bony knees. El's forehead creases a bit as she looks over his graying hair, which is pulled back into a ponytail, and the paint that's splattered all over his Pink Floyd T-shirt. Dad fancies himself an artist these days, although he's not very good at it. But he gave up music ages ago, and as Mom points out, it's good for him to have something that keeps him busy.

And for all that Ellie is clearly not impressed with Dad's appearance, he's kind of the reason she even met Alexander in the first place.

Here, let me give you the *Star Magazine* treatment.

"10 THINGS YOU NEVER KNEW ABOUT ELLIE WINTERS (OR, MORE ACCURATELY, HER FAMILY!)"

1) Ellie's dad, Liam, was famous for eleven months in 1992! According to Liam, that's the worst amount of time for a person to have fame—not long enough for anyone to remember you, but just long enough to ruin your life.

2) Liam was in a band called Velvet! It was every bit as embarrassing as the name implies, and full of more gelled hair and skinny suits than his daughter Daisy would like to talk about.

3) Velvet had exactly ONE HIT SONG, "Harbor Me," and while that title sounds pretty sweet, "harbor" is being used in a metaphorical sense, and the video was banned in seven countries. The less we say about it, the better.

4) Their second song only went to #22 ("Staying the Night," less gross than "Harbor Me" but with way too many references to sheets and skin for anyone's comfort), and the third never even cracked the top 100 ("Daisy Chain," surprisingly not offensive, but also not listenable).

5) By that point, Liam had a flat in London he couldn't afford,

a fancy car he'd crashed twice, and a pretty significant drug problem. It was all very *Behind the Music*!

6) He moved back to his hometown, a tiny village in the Midlands, where he started working at his father's garden supply shop, only to meet a lovely journalist by the name of Bess Murdock, who was working for some hip London newspaper and came all the way out to little Glockenshire-on-the-Vale to interview Liam for a "Whatever Happened To?" piece.

7) Surprising absolutely no one who has seen a romantic comedy, the two fell in love and moved to Florida for a fresh start. Luckily for Liam, "Harbor Me"—or an instrumental version of it at least—got picked up for a car commercial, and since Liam was the sole songwriter on that track (a fact that fills his family with equal parts pride and mortification!) he became, as they say, "well off!"

8) It was this stroke of luck that allowed the Winterses to send their oldest daughter, Eleanor, off to the UK for university, and it was there that the blond girl with the shiny hair and teeth met the heir to the Scottish throne!

9) Ellie—as she's known to friends and family—and Prince Alexander have been dating for nearly two years now, making her the most famous person in her family, which is saying something since her dad was on the cover of *NME*, and her mom once made out with someone in Oasis!

10) Ellie's younger sister, Daisy, works at a grocery store and just got a killer dye job, clearly making her the *real* baller of the Winters family.

There. Now you're caught up.

"Are you staying long?" I ask. The last time they were here together was Christmas, and it had kind of been a disaster. Alexander had needed to sleep on our pullout sofa, which must have been a step down from whatever dynasty-making bed he had back in Scotland (even though he'd spent the entire time insisting that he was fine, and that the sofa bed was "surprisingly comfortable" and "such an interesting innovation"), and then my dad had given Ellie a plastic tiara as a joke, which embarrassed her so much that she spent most of that evening in her room.

Mom had been flustered about everything from setting the table to whether Alexander would be offended if we ordered pizza—our Christmas Eve tradition—and then more or less bullied Alexander's bodyguards into coming in to drink eggnog with us on Christmas Day, which made everyone so uncomfortable that in the end, we all sat there in total silence, Malcolm and David in their black suits, El and Alexander dressed like they were going to church, and me, Mom, and Dad all in our pajamas, Dad with a stray bit of tinsel tucked into his ponytail.

To be honest, after all that, I wasn't surprised Ellie and Alexander had decided on a "surprise" visit. The less time my parents had to stress and think up new ways to be weird, respectively, the better.

"Just through the weekend," Alexander answers, putting his hand on El's knee and squeezing briefly. They're usually so formal that a squeeze feels like the equivalent of them making out in front of me, and that is *so* not okay.

"We have to get back to Edinburgh by Tuesday," Ellie says, "but we wanted to talk to you first."

And then she smiles, covering Alexander's hand with her own, and for the first time, I notice the emerald-and-diamond ring on her hand.

Her *left* hand.

Mom gasps, but it's Dad's reaction that sums up what I'm thinking.

"Bugger me, Ellie's going to be a princess."

Chapter 4

"A DUCHESS, ACTUALLY," ELLIE SAYS, AND I SWEAR
she looks a little bit embarrassed, using one perfectly manicured
finger to push her bangs back to the side.

"Well, still a princess, technically," Alexander counters, putting his hand over hers on her knee. "But yes, Eleanor's title
will be Duchess of Rothesay. Although, more importantly, she's
going to be my *wife*."

El smiles at that, a real smile, the kind we don't see much
anymore. Once she started dating Alex, her smiles got a little
frozen, a little fake.

From his spot in the doorway, Dad says, "Does this mean
you'll be able to have us beheaded? Because if so, I'd like to
remind you that it was your mother who grounded you for
sneaking out when you were fifteen. Granted," he adds to Alex,
"she was sneaking out to get more study time at the library, but
it was still quite the scandal."

"*Dad*," El says, but Alex just laughs, and Mom waves her
hands at Dad.

"Stop it, Liam," she says. "No teasing today."

Mom is wearing an old sundress, and there's ink on her fingers, which means she was probably writing when Ellie and Alex showed up—Mom is old-school and does her first drafts on yellow legal pads—but she's practically glowing. "This is all so *exciting*. Surely the most exciting thing that's happened in our family."

"I beg your pardon," Dad says, folding his thin arms over his chest. "I was once shot out of a cannon filled with glitter at Wembley."

"Liam," Mom says again, but Alex just raises his eyebrows and says, "I think that beats a wedding, sir, I have to say."

Dad holds out one hand, tilting it back and forth. "Equal at least."

"We wanted to come here and tell you in person first, of course," Alex says. Even though he's Scottish, he sounds as English as my parents, if a lot more posh. El has a similar accent but starts sounding more like me when she's home.

"Of course, there will be a formal announcement at Holyrood next week," Alex continues, "and I'm sure there will be a fair amount of press attention, so let's hope my southern cousins get into some kind of scandal, take a bit of the heat off."

He smiles at that, glancing around at all of us, and I'm impressed how he manages to make all that sound super casual and normal. "Holyrood," like it's just a place and not a freaking palace. His "southern cousins" are the royal family of England, and holy crap, those will be El's cousins, too.

El is going to be *royalty*.

"Are you sure about this?" I ask, and everyone's head turns

toward me. I look at Ellie, and . . . oh wow, I never understood the "glaring daggers" thing, but those are some sharp eyeballs.

Maybe that wasn't *exactly* the best thing to say when your sister tells you she's engaged, but I can't help it.

"Oh, Daisy," Mom murmurs, and Alex clears his throat as Ellie's leg begins to jiggle. I know that tremor. I used to see it in the back seat of the car right before she'd elbow me or tell Mom I was being a jerk. Before Ellie left for Scotland, she could actually be a real person sometimes, complete with a temper, and every once in a while, bits of that person reappear.

"I'm sorry," I say, looking around. "And, I mean, I guess we all knew this was coming, but it's just . . ." I wave my hands around. "You've spent all this time keeping us separated from Alex's family, and Alex's family separate from *us*, and now you want to, like"—I move my hands again—"squash everyone together."

Ellie's face goes red, but whether it's from embarrassment or rage, I'm not sure.

"It's a wedding, not a *squashing*," she finally says, but then Dad scratches his scruffy beard and says, "When you think about it, weddings *are* just very formal and expensive squashings."

"*Liam*," Mom chides, but she's laughing and then adds, "Can you imagine the invitations? 'We request the honor of your presence as our daughter squashes herself to this man.'"

Dad guffaws and Alex's lips twitch a bit while Ellie's nails dig into her thighs.

I widen my eyes, pointing at Mom and Dad. "See? This is what you'd be inflicting on Scotland. These people as the future king or queen's grandparents."

Mom laughs again, wiping her eyes. "Lord, I hadn't even thought of that," she says. "My grandbaby, a king!"

"Or a queen, don't be sexist, Bessie," Dad says, then wonders, "Do we get titles for that? Royal Grandad?"

It's hard to know if he's serious or joking, because such is Dad, and by now Ellie has gone so stiff and still that I think she might actually shatter into a billion shiny pieces in front of us.

Alex pats her knee again, then gives us the same game smile he probably has to give to crazy people who run up to him and insist *they're* the real prince of Scotland. "We'll see what we can do about that, sir," he tells Dad, then looks to me.

"I realize this is going to be quite a change for you, Daisy." Now I'm getting the Sick Kids in the Hospital Look—chin tilted down, brows drawn together, compassionate blue eyes. He does this a lot, relying on the combination of handsomeness and royal authority to convince us everything is going to be okay. "But possibly not as much as you're thinking. We all do try to live fairly unremarkable lives, really, and we're going to do everything we can to mitigate any . . . unpleasantness for you."

Leaning back in my chair, I fold my arms over my chest. I like Alex—I do. He's a genuinely nice guy, but he comes with a lot of baggage, and I can never escape the feeling that it's more than a little unfair that I'm going to have to carry some of the weight, just so that Ellie can be a princess.

Which, I mean, I get the appeal, and lord knows she has looked like a princess since she was about three, but it just seems . . . I don't know. So pointless. Waving at crowds, cutting ribbons, being this *ornament* all because of an accident of birth.

Or, in Ellie's case, of marriage, I guess.

"And I assure you," Alex goes on, "this will, at the end of the day, be a fairly normal wedding."

"It's going to be on TV," I remind him. "That's not normal."

The corners of Ellie's mouth turn down, and in that second, she once again looks like my regular older sister, the one who once stole all my colored pencils because I'd used her favorite lipstick in one of my drawings (in my defense, that shade of pink made a *killer* sunset, and that picture is still hanging up in Mom's office).

It's Alex who steps in again. "We understand this is going to be a lot for all of you," he says. "The attention, the travel, all of that. And we're already putting things in place to ensure this whole process goes as smoothly as possible. Like Ellie said, we want this to feel like the family event it is rather than a . . . spectacle."

From her spot in the corner, Mom leans forward and says, "And we appreciate that, Alexander, we truly do."

"I don't," Dad says, still leaning in the doorway. "Love a bit of spectacle, me."

We all ignore him, and Ellie flexes her fingers where they interlock with Alex's. "The wedding is going to be in the winter," she tells us. "Christmas."

Now Mom blinks, her hands coming up to fiddle with her long necklace, the one I bought her on a school trip to Boston two years ago. It's a pewter tricorn hat, and she's worn it pretty much every day since I gave it to her. "December?" she repeats. "That's only seven months from now. Ellie, surely you'll need more time to plan—"

"There's already protocol in place for a royal wedding," Alex interjects. "And our dates are rather limited due to my mother's calendar as well as the twins' school schedule."

Right. The twins.

At the thought of Prince Sebastian and Princess Flora, my stomach drops all over again. Like I said, we've gotten used to Alexander, but we've had nothing to do with any other part of El's fancy life, and that includes meeting Alexander's siblings. They're my age or just a little bit older, and even though he's only seventeen, Prince Sebastian is basically one of the most eligible bachelors in the world. And Princess Flora? If Ellie seems glamorous now, that's nothing compared to Flora, who had a *Vogue* cover when she was *eight*.

And they're going to be part of my *family* now. What is that even going to mean, really? Will we go on vacations with them? Will we exchange Christmas gifts? What do you even *get* for a freaking princess?

All of a sudden, I feel dizzy and a little sick, and I find myself lurching to my feet. "You okay, kiddo?" Dad asks, and I nod, pushing my sweaty hair back from my face.

"Yeah, just . . . I think I need some air."

When I walk out onto the porch, it's even hotter, but being out of the living room, even for just a little bit, helps. It smells like rain is coming, and I take deep breaths, closing my eyes, listening to the sound of Mom's wind chimes.

After a while, the door behind me opens, and I expect Mom to be there, her hands fluttering like they do when she's nervous. But when I turn, it's Ellie.

"Can you maybe not do this?" she asks, frowning a little.

I raise my eyebrows. "Not do what? Freak out because things are about to get deeply weird for me?"

Her frown deepens, and I suddenly feel like a total garbage person. "El, no," I say, propping a hip against the porch railing and pushing my hair out of my eyes. Even El is looking a little shiny.

"I'm happy for you," I tell her, but she just shakes her head, looking up at the porch ceiling for a second.

"Maybe practice saying that so you *don't* sound like you're dying," she says, and I shift my weight from one foot to the other, arms crossed. The wind is picking up a little bit now, but strands of hair still stick to my face and neck.

"Maybe if two weeks ago, my boyfriend hadn't decided to use my connection to *you* to score a little extra cash, I'd be happier, but he did, so I'm not."

"How is it *my* fault that you have terrible taste in boys?"

"Michael was not terrible," I say, even though half an hour ago, I for sure thought he was pretty terrible.

"I know it's really hard for you to comprehend that not everything is about you, Daisy," Ellie goes on, "but—"

"It's not!" I interrupt, and here we go again. Maybe the seven years between our ages is too much, maybe we're just too different, but put me and Ellie in a room together for more than ten minutes, and we always end up here somehow. "I get it," I go on, "but you're not thinking about *us*. Like, I know it's going to be super sweet to be a princess and all, but none of us signed up for that. For tabloids and pictures and"—I wave one hand at the car of bodyguards—"*that*."

Huffing out a breath, Ellie shoves her hands into her back pockets. She's definitely sweaty now, and it's honestly a relief to see some of her princess coating cracking.

"Well, life isn't always fair," she says, "and I'm *dreadfully* sorry my falling in love with a wonderful man is an inconvenience to you."

I snort. "Oh, right, because you'd've fallen for Alex even if *he* worked at the Sur-N-Sav, I'm so sure."

Ellie's eyebrows nearly shoot up into her hairline. "What is *that* supposed to mean?"

But before I can answer her, I glance up and catch a glimpse of what's happening through the front window, and—

"Oh god, Mom," I say, and Ellie whips around, giving me a face-full of blond hair.

"No!" she gasps, and we both scramble for the front door, united for once.

Mom is sitting on the couch next to the future king of Scotland, one arm wrapped around his shoulders, the other holding her phone out.

She may be old-fashioned about her writing, but when it comes to phones, Mom is very up on her technology, which means in the past year or so, she has become Queen of the Selfies. And then some evil person, probably our neighbor, Mrs. Claire, taught her about silly filters, and our lives have been a hell of dog faces and anime eyes and unicorn horns ever since.

God love him, Alex is smiling gamely as Mom lowers her phone, chuckling. "Oh, this is a new one, this is perfect!" she crows before turning her phone to face us.

There are Alex and my mom, both wearing oversize cartoon crowns and heavy chains around their necks, a bubble coming out of Alex's mouth that reads, "It's good to be king."

"*Mom*," Ellie says, like Mom just stabbed Alex in the face as opposed to taking a goofy selfie with him, but she waves Ellie off, still chuckling as she types. "Oh, relax, Eleanor, he's family now! And it's not as though I'm going to put it on Facebook or some nonsense. It will just be for me."

For her and twenty of the ladies she knows around town would be my guess.

"It's a very good picture of us," Alex says, and Ellie and I both turn to look at him. Maybe he's not a prince so much as a saint.

Then Dad sticks his head out of the kitchen, a bottle of champagne in one hand. "Shall I open this, then? Granted, I can't drink any. Last time I had champagne was 1996, and I ended up snogging Ewan McGregor in the lobby of the Mandarin Hotel." He shrugs. "Very pretty bloke, must say, didn't mind a bit. But anyway, since then, off the sauce for me. Well, not just because of the kiss, because of all the other stuff as well, you know." Dad waves his hand. "Addictions, car accidents, life ruination, and such."

Peeling the gold foil from the champagne, he gestures toward Alex with the bottle. "Now, there's a story for you. That last big hurrah, before I gave it all up for good, happened in Scotland, actually, and involved one of those shaggy cows you have up there. I don't know if you know many of those cows by name, but this one was called Eliza. No, Elspeth."

Dad wanders back into the kitchen, still expounding on Scotland and cows and a stolen train, and I look over at Alex, sitting on the couch, his hands locked together between his knees as my sister goes to sit next to him, a hand on his shoulder.

"Welcome to the family," I mutter.

THE BRIDE WORE PLAID

Or she *will*? Maybe a sash at least? WE CAN HOPE. So Prince Alexander of Scotland announced his engagement to Actual Human Barbie Doll Ellie Winters (ugh, that naaaame! Shouldn't she be the plucky lead on some kind of lawyer show set in the Deep South? Oh, wait, I bet we'll have to call her Eleanor now because ROYAL). Anyway, Eleanor-Not-Ellie has been dating the utter snooze that is Prince Alexander for like ages now, so no one is really surprised, although it's been a long time since Scotland had a royal wedding, and given this *particular* family, I'm expecting things will be balls OUT.

The wedding will be in December in Edinburgh—blah blah, WEDDING STUFF—let some other blog handle that. Let's get to the REAL questions:

1) Is Seb going to bring a date? If so, can it be me?

2) Are the "Royal Wreckers" going to throw a bachelor party—sorry, "STAG NIGHT"? How many people will be arrested/deported/killed if they do?

3) Does Eleanor-Not-Ellie even HAVE a family to come to this thing, or is she a fembot? (You know MY vote.)

4) No, seriously, how come we never hear about her family? People cannot shut UP about a Certain Sister of a Certain Royal down in London, so how come we haven't heard anything about Eleanor-Not-Ellie's peeps? Hmmmmm . . .

("The Bride Wore Plaid," from *Crown Town*)

Chapter 5

"YOUR NEW BROTHER-IN-LAW REALLY IS SUPER HOT," Isabel says, and I frown at her over the top of our laptops. We're sitting at a small table in the corner of the Bean Grinder, Perdido's one and only coffee shop, and while we're supposed to be taking a practice SAT test, it's clear Isabel is using the internet for something very different.

"A," I tell her, "he is not my brother-in-law yet, and B, what happened to helping me ignore all things Ellie?"

Isabel doesn't even bother to look guilty as she sucks the straw of her iced white chocolate mocha. "That was back when Ellie was just dating a prince, not when she was *marrying* one," she reminds me, "and since you're so determined to ignore everything, I figure someone needs to keep an eye on you."

"By reading trashy royal gossip websites?" I ask, blowing on the surface of my orange blossom tea.

"By reading trashy royal gossip websites," Isabel confirms, eyes still glued to the screen in front of her. "It's a sacrifice, but that's what I'm willing to do for our friendship, Dais."

"You do go above and beyond," I reply, rolling my eyes. I try to go back to the multiple-choice test in front of me, but after a few seconds of staring at the same vocabulary words, I glance back over our screens. "Anything about me?"

Isabel shakes her head, black hair sliding over her shoulders. "Not that I've seen, but I haven't checked *Crown Town.*"

"Please think about the words you just said, then ask yourself how you feel about them coming out of your mouth."

Isabel flips me off, her other hand clicking something on her keyboard. "There are tons of these blogs. Some of them are about all the various royals in the world. There are, like, really serious ones, like *Royal Watch* and *Moments of the Monarchies.*"

She turns her laptop so I can see the page. This is *Royal Watch*, and there's a giant Union Jack across the top. Underneath, I can see a few tasteful pictures of the English royal family.

"Those are mostly run by Americans," Isabel tells me, and tilts her computer so she can click something else.

"Then there's *Prattle*, a magazine about posh people for posh people. You know, 'What Hotel Has the Best Concierge?' and 'Which of Your Family Servants Are You Allowed to Snog?'—that kind of thing."

"Charming," I mutter, taking in the giant type of the title and the picture of a frowning aristocrat holding a cocktail.

"But then there's stuff like *Off with Their Heads* and *Crown Town*, and those are the trashy ones," Isabel finishes, turning her laptop back toward her.

"Which makes them more fun?" I guess, and Isabel shrugs.

"I wish I could say no, but yeah, those are the ones I've book-marked. Guess Ellie was right that with your family being in

Florida and the rest of the royals making *plenty* of headlines in Scotland, no one cares all that much."

She meets my gaze, eyebrows drawn together. "Is that good or bad?"

"It's good," I say, relief turning the words into a sigh. For all that Ellie had claimed that nothing much would change right away, I hadn't actually believed her. But it's been over two weeks since the engagement announcement, and while that was a big deal, the spotlight is still firmly on Ellie and Alexander.

"People love Ellie, by the way," Isabel tells me, moving her straw up and down in her cup to poke at the ice. "Like, apparently, some of the ultraposh people are stuck up about Alex marrying an American, but the commoners are allllll about it."

"You just said 'the commoners,' so we're not friends anymore. We had a good run, but—"

Isa pulls the straw out of her drink, flicking me with drops of iced mocha. "I'm trying to give you the lay of the land here, Dais. I am being your *wing woman*."

I wipe my cheek with a napkin, then toss it at her. "No, you're just reading gossip, and besides, none of that really has anything to do with me."

Narrowing her dark eyes, Isabel props her elbows on the table. "You really think that?" she asks, and I shrug, uncomfortable.

Okay, so yes, this will have *something* to do with me, but maybe I can just take a crash course in royal etiquette before the wedding, then go back to living a life where I never have to know how deeply to curtsy to anyone.

"So what is my super hot *not* brother-in-law up to on those sites?" I ask, more to distract myself than anything else. Over at another table across the shop, I can see Hannah Contreras and Maddy Payne glancing over at Isabel and me, and I have a feeling we're the subject of their whispered conversation. I like Hannah and Maddy fine (when you live in a town as small as Perdido, you've basically known the same people all your life), but I've never been the subject of gossip before and have to say, it's not a fave.

"Well, he broke up with his girlfriend, so sayeth *Off with Their Heads*," Isabel informs me. "Some *also* super hot Argentinean girl whose brother is a famous polo player. So to get over that, he and his buddies went to Monaco, but then . . ." She leans closer to the screen, squinting a little. "One of Seb's friends noticed a dude taking pictures and decided to fight him. Threw the guy in a fountain. Then Seb pulled the photographer out and sent him a *very* large check the next day to cover the cost of his camera."

"So basically, the same as one of our typical weekends," I say, turning back to my test. "Got it."

Giggling, Isabel takes another sip of her iced mocha. "Easy icebreaker at the wedding, at least." Picking up her laptop, she turns it to face me. There's a huge picture of Sebastian in a gorgeous suit, flashing a big grin, one hand up in a wave. His hair darker than Alex's, but the camera's flash still picks up hints of red. His eyes are just as blue as Alex's, though, and I swear to god, even in a crappy paparazzi picture, they seem to sparkle. There is a guy on either side of him, one a good head shorter than Seb with dark curls and a scowl, the other sandy-haired and actually smiling at the cameras.

Isabel taps each guy in turn with one pink fingernail. "These guys are, like, *always* with Sebastian. Tabloids call them 'the Royal Wreckers.' Guys from crazy-posh families who went to school with Seb or something."

"'Seb'?" I echo, raising an eyebrow, and this time, Isabel has the grace to blush a little bit.

"I've been reading tons of this stuff!" she insists. "And all the papers and websites call him Seb. That's the kind of thing you need to know, Dais. I mean, we haven't even gotten to Princess Flora yet, and that's where the *real* scandal is."

I shake my head and click through to the next page of my test. "The less I know, the better," I say. "I'm just going to get through the wedding, come home, and then the rest of . . . that" —I wave my hand at the screen, taking in the website, drunk Sebastian, his debauched, rich friends, all of it— "can be Ellie's thing."

Isabel makes a face at me, setting the computer back on the table and studying it again. "It's a shame that proximity to boys like these is wasted on you."

"It would be wasted on you, too," I remind her, "what with Ben and all."

At the mention of her boyfriend, Isabel just shrugs. "Ben would want me to fulfill my dreams, Daisy, and if one of those dreams is making out with a prince—"

"Ugh, stop!" I toss a balled-up napkin at her, and she laughs again.

But then, after a second, she rests her elbows on the table. "I'm serious, you know. Not about making out with Seb—well, I mean, I'm serious about that, too, but you really do need to look into all of this. Know what you're getting yourself into."

I look back to the page in front of me, chewing my lower lip. "I didn't get myself into anything. El got us all into this, and she and Alex say nothing is going to change."

Isabel goes quiet, and I look up from my test. She's leaned back in her chair, her dark eyes slightly narrowed, and that means I'm about to get some serious Isabel Alonso Truthiness in my life.

"Dais," she says, and yup, here it comes. "Why are you so resistant?"

Scooting closer to the table, she takes my wrist, shaking my arm. "A *prince*, Daisy. *Castles*. It's a whole new world opening up to you, and you should be, like . . ." She lets go of my wrist to clench both fists in the air, opening her mouth to give a sort of silent shriek of excitement, eyes squeezed shut.

I laugh, flicking her with my pencil. "I'm not all"—I mimic her gesture, then drop my hands back to the table—"because this isn't *my* thing. It's Ellie's. And now it's . . ." I don't want to get into that, not even with my best friend, but Isa is merciless.

"Oh no," she says. "Not the wistful 'if only . . .' look. Spill."

Shooting her a glare, I shrug my shoulders, wondering how even to explain it. Finally, I settle on an example.

"Okay, remember when I was in fourth grade, and my parents lost their minds and decided to do that road trip out west?"

"The Grand Canyon Incident," Isabel says, nodding sagely, and I point my pencil at her.

"That's the one. So on that trip, we ended in California for the last day, and I wanted to go see the Winchester Mystery House because *obviously*."

"*Obviously*," Isa echoes.

"But that same time we were there, this college Ellie wanted to check out in San Francisco was doing an open house, and she wanted to go to *that*. So my parents said we'd add an extra day—do Ellie's college thing first, then, on that extra day, go see *my* thing."

Isabel tilts her head to one side. "Fair," she decides, and I nod.

"Problem is, we all ate these little shrimp thingies during the open house, and then got food poisoning, so there was no second day. No Winchester Mystery House. And I get that it was an Act of God—"

"An act of bacteria, but continue."

"But the point is that it's always been like that. Ellie's thing, then my thing if we have time. And I can't even be mad about it because Ellie's thing is always, like, going to see a college, or volunteering at Habitat for Humanity, or taking a summer trip to Guatemala to teach English."

I hold up my hand, turning it to one side, keeping my palm straight. "She's always been laser-focused on stuff that matters."

Dropping my hand, I shrug again. "And I just want to see weird houses or exhibits or whatever, so I get why her stuff has to come first. It's just . . . marrying Alex means her stuff is *always* going to come first. We're going to spend the rest of our lives planning Christmas around *her* schedule. And like I said, I can't be mad about it. I *get* it. I just . . ."

This time when I trail off, Isabel doesn't call me on it, and I shake my head.

"Less focus on Ellie and royals, and more focus on Key West," I say, tapping the end of my pencil on the top of her laptop screen. "We are now at *two* weeks, and we still haven't coordinated wardrobes."

If there's one thing that can distract Isabel from talk of "Seb," it's our Key Con visit, and she nods, giving me an exaggerated wink.

"You're right," she agrees. "Eyes on the prize."

We're talking about the trip—namely, what we're going to wear and what panels we want to hit up—when Hannah and Maddy enter my peripheral vision.

I've known both of them since third grade, but they're both approaching so hesitantly, you'd think we were total strangers. I can actually feel my heart sinking.

"Heeeey, Daisy," Maddy drawls, playing with the ends of her hair. It's about the same dark blond mine used to be before the big dye job.

"Um. Hi?"

"So. Your sister." That's it. Literally all she says, like that explains it all, and I just nod at her. Across the table, Isabel is slumped down in her chair a little, watching them both as she taps her nails on her plastic cup.

"You're going to be in the wedding, right?" Hannah asks. She has the same black hair as Isabel, although hers is cut in a long bob, the points brushing her shoulders as she leans closer. "And, like, on TV?"

Maddy shifts her weight from one foot to the other, moving a little closer. "And are you gonna move there? To Scotland?"

Hannah shakes her head at that, eyes wide. "I mean, you're basically going to be a princess, right?"

Sighing, I take a sip of my tea before saying, "I'm not really allowed to talk about it." Then I drop my voice to a whisper and add, "For security reasons."

Maddy and Hannah both widen their eyes, stepping back a little, and Isabel grins at me before schooling her face into a serious expression and adding, "Yeah, she had to sign papers and shit. If she talks about any of it, she'll get in trouble. I mean, *big* trouble."

"Isa!" I say sharply, and then glance around, like people might be watching us. "You know what happens if they hear us!"

I give Isabel my best solemn look, then draw my finger across my throat. Isabel swallows hard, looking properly scared.

"Jesus," Hannah breathes, and Maddy looks at me with her jaw hanging open.

"Just . . . don't ask me about it, okay?" I say, and both Hannah and Maddy nod so hard I'm surprised their necks don't snap.

They go back to their table, whispering again and genuinely looking a little pale.

"We're evil," Isabel says, rattling the ice in her cup, and I shrug.

"Proactive."

Going back to my test, I let Isabel go back to her gossip surfing, thinking I might grab some kind of fried seafood on my way home this afternoon. High-stress days require high calories, so . . .

"Oh holy god!" Isabel yelps, and my head shoots up. For a second, I think maybe she saw a bug or, even worse, a snake—Isabel is deathly afraid of all things slithery—but then I see her eyes still glued to the screen, her face going kind of gray underneath her tan, and I know it's much worse.

EXCLUSIVE: "DAISY WINTERS DUMPED ME FOR A ROYAL UPGRADE!"

Seems like Eleanor Winters is not the only member of her family with royal ambitions. According to our exclusive interview with Michael Dorset, Daisy's most recent boyfriend, now that Daisy's sister, Eleanor, is not *just* Prince Alexander's girlfriend, but his fiancée, Daisy has seen her own prospects skyrocket.

"Daisy has always been a really chill girl," Michael tells us. "You know, laid-back, never gave a [expletive deleted] what other people thought of her. But she's been different since Eleanor started dating Prince Alexander. And once they were engaged? She wouldn't give me the time of day."

When asked if he thought Daisy would be setting her sights on Alexander's brother, Prince Sebastian, Mr. Dorset shrugged. "I wouldn't be surprised. It's obvious everything with her sister has gone to her head."

Mr. Dorset then played for us a sample of a song he'd written for Daisy Winters, a song, he claims, that left the soon-to-be-royal-adjacent high schooler unmoved.

I KNEW IT!!

Ahem, Gentle Readers, was I NOT just wondering wheeeeerrrrre the heck Eleanor-Not-Ellie's family was? And did you not DELIVER, my angels?? YOU DID! SO! So we knew our Miss Eleanor comes from $$$. Maybe not the same kind of F You Money she's about to marry into, but still. Her dad was a rock star—albeit suuuuuper briefly—and her mom writes those mystery books where people get killed in small towns in really cutesy ways. You know, "Oh no, the local pastry chef was stabbed with a cake server!" THAT kind of thing. But we KNEW that stuff, so the BIG FIND is that our Eleanor-Not-Ellie has a HOT YOUNGER SISTER. Don't they all? Attaching a pic someone sent me below, and ommmmggggg, the hair!! Don't you KNOW Miss Eleanor is NOT HERE FOR THAT? I swear I used to have a Little Mermaid doll with hair that color. ANYWAY, her name is Daisy (and her dad once had a song called "Daisy Chain," which adds a nice touch of ICK to everything), she's in high school (this is why we haven't heard much about her before now, according to my "sources"—Alexander's scary family wanted her left alone because she's not eighteen, which seems kind of dumb based on how many Celebrity Rug Rats I've seen in tabloids, but whatevs). TMZ has an exclusive interview with her wastrel of an ex, who is saying she dumped him because, like her sister, she has PRINCELY AMBITIONS. She works at a GROCERY STORE of all things, aaaaaand I'm giving you a link to her Facebook because hey, not like we don't already know I'm going to hell, so let's add RIBBONS TO THE HANDBAS-KET, SHALL WE? It's pretty boring, NGL, but come on. She HAS to be the slutty one, right?

("I KNEW IT!!," from *Crown Town*)

Chapter 6

"CAN I JUST STATE FOR THE RECORD THAT BEING called 'the slutty one' when I had exactly one boyfriend for less than a year is *deeply* unfair?"

Even through the computer screen, I can feel El tighten her shoulders as she shoots a glare toward the tiny camera. "Daisy, this is not funny."

We're all in the dining room, me, Mom, and Dad, crowded around my laptop. Ellie is in Edinburgh in the flat she shares with another girl who works at her publishing company, and since it's about 2 a.m. there, she's speaking in a whisper for the most part throughout our emergency family Skype session. She's still dressed from work, too, which, weirdly, makes me feel kind of sorry for her. "Jammies by 5 p.m. or die" is practically my motto.

So maybe that's why I keep my own voice soft when I reply, "Trust me, I know it's not, El. *I'm* the one who had to delete her Facebook. Which, by the way, was so totally not boring. I had all those pictures from last year's trip to Colonial Williamsburg!"

"I feel the lack of a book of faces is truly the least of our concerns at the moment," Dad says. He's sitting next to me, drinking cranberry juice out of a wineglass.

Mom is currently indulging in a cigarette. She quit about ten years ago but still gets three smokes a year to be used in either celebration or crisis.

There is no doubt what kind of cigarette this is.

"It's just one blog post," Mom says, stubbing out her cigarette in the lumpy clay ashtray I made for her two years ago when I went through a pottery phase. It's supposed to be shaped like a hand, but it looks a lot more like a claw if I'm being honest. The fact that I painted it green doesn't help. "It isn't as though this is in the papers, or on the telly. Who reads those blogs anyway?"

"More people than you'd think. Even the lower-level blogs like *Crown Town* get around a million unique visitors per month," a voice says off camera from Ellie's side, and I see my sister glance off to her right before she turns her laptop slightly, sharing the frame with a woman in a cream jacket and tartan scarf, a gold pin winking at her throat. Her hair is dark and sleek, tucked behind her ears, and honestly, she could be twenty-five or fifty. It's impossible to tell.

"Mom, Dad, Daisy, this is Glynnis," Ellie says. We can only see half her face now, Glynnis's taking up most of the screen. "She works for Alex's family as a sort of . . ."

When Ellie just trails off, Glynnis's scarlet lips spread in a wider smile. "Let's say a *liaison*," she supplies, giving the word the full French treatment. "I'm here to smooth anything that needs smoothing."

Another flash of teeth, and Dad grumbles, setting his

wineglass down so hard a bit of juice sloshes over the side. "Oh, I know you people," he tells Glynnis, nodding at her. "The ones who keep things out of the papers, you are. The ones who made up 'exhaustion,' as though that's a thing people actually have."

Glynnis's smile doesn't falter even a little bit, which impresses me. For the most part, my dad is the mellowest dude in the world these days, but when he uses that piercing stare, it's easy to remember that once upon a time, he could hold the attention of entire arenas.

"Even so," she says, her voice brisk. Unlike my sister and Alex, Glynnis actually sounds Scottish, especially when she adds, "So it's clear that we're in a right fix now, isn't it, Winters family?"

I can feel cold sweat breaking out between my shoulder blades at that. I kept thinking that if I just pretended this blog post was no big deal, it actually *wouldn't* be a big deal. Kind of like how I thought I could just keep out of the wedding stuff except for actually showing up at the wedding. Isabel would have called that naive, but I was calling it "self-preservation."

"The problem with these sorts of sites," Glynnis continues, pulling out her smartphone and tapping at the screen, "is that new information triggers a game of one-upmanship. *Crown Town* posts your Facebook, so *Off with Their Heads* will want yearbook photos, interviews with friends or old boyfriends, anything they can find. And then, of course, some of the more legitimate press will follow, and before we know it, the entire thing is out of our hands."

My sweat situation gets worse as thoughts of me on the covers of magazines with stupid headlines over my face start filling my brain. Why would they want me when they have El, who is way better at this kind of thing anyway?

Glynnis is still talking as I fight off my panic attack, and it takes me a minute to realize what she's saying. Only when I hear "So I can arrange Daisy's flight" do I look at the screen.

"Wait, what?"

Mom is sitting back in her chair, arms crossed, looking over the top of her glasses at Glynnis. "The entire summer?" she says, and I look over at her, my eyes wide.

"Hold up, what's going on? Sorry, I was having an existential crisis, so I wasn't really paying attention."

Ellie's face appears on the screen again as she leans over Glynnis to give me a Maximum Big Sister Look. "Maybe try to focus on things that are explicitly about you?"

"Maybe don't give me a hard time when this whole thing is happening because of *you*?" I snap back, and Mom touches my arm, shaking her head slightly.

"Not now, girls," she says, and flashes El a look through the screen, too. "You too, young lady."

Ellie scowls, and I see her look over at Glynnis, who is very diplomatically focusing on her phone and not our sisterly sniping.

"The plan is," Glynnis says, still not looking up, "for you to come here for the summer. To Scotland, rather. It will be far easier for us to control access to you if you're in Eleanor and Alexander's circle."

"I don't want to be in a circle," I reply, "and besides, I *can't* go to Scotland. Isabel and I are going to Key Con in Key West in a couple of weeks."

Mom hums, nodding. "That's true, you've been planning that for ages. Maybe after——"

Glynnis leans a little closer, her smile becoming a grimace. "I'm so sorry," she says, "but the family is rather insistent we get this sorted as soon as possible, and the summer schedule is already locked. It would really be *so* much easier to slide Daisy in *now*."

"Easier for who?" I ask, but that's stupid, because of course she means the royal family and Ellie.

"Daisy, we're trying to help," Ellie pleads, pulling her hair away from her face. When she does, I notice how sharp her jaw is. El definitely looked skinnier when she was here, but for the first time, I see that she's *really* skinny now, and that there are faint violet shadows beneath her eyes. I had one stupid blog post about me, and it was making me feel like my skin didn't fit right. What is it like to have *thousands* of those types of posts?

But then I remember that she's trying to make me give up this trip, this thing Isabel and I have been excited about for a year. How am I supposed to tell Isa that, sorry, my sister pulled rank and now I can't go?

And then, ugh, it's so stupid, but I feel my throat tightening up. "No," I say. "I'm not canceling on Isabel just because of one stupid gossip website, and one stupid boy. We *planned* this. Ash Bentley is going to be there, and she's our favorite author, and——"

Sighing, Ellie throws up her hands. "Oh my god, Isabel can just come here for a few days or something."

Glynnis nods and starts tapping on her phone. "Ash Bentley,

you said?" A few more taps, then she flashes a grin. "She's actually on a UK book tour next month. I can make some calls to her publisher, have them add a stop in Edinburgh. We'll fly your friend over to see her, too."

"Great," Ellie says, then looks back at the screen. "See?" she says. "Fixed."

I just sit there, gaping at her. "No, *not* fixed. I don't want your 'people' pulling weird strings, I want to see her in two weeks in Key West with Isabel *like we planned*. And it's not just seeing Ash Bentley. It was the entire con. It was . . ." I trail off because I have no idea how to make them see that this was something I was looking forward to. To Ellie, it's probably just another one of my weird hobbies, but Key Con was going to be the highlight of my summer.

Glynnis leans back, clearly so Ellie can handle it from here, and my sister cuts her eyes to the side before lowering her voice and saying, "Mom, talk to her."

I jerk my head to look at Mom, who is now raking her hands through her hair. She's blond like Ellie (and me, before the dye job), but it's a little grayer and ashier, cut in a shag haircut that frames her face. It's my face, pretty much, just older, and when she looks at me, I already know what she's going to say.

"You're going to take her side in this," I say, and Mom reaches out, laying a hand on my arm.

"Darling. This does seem like a fair compromise. More than fair, really."

And the thing is, I know that. I know that going to a smaller signing rather than a massive convention where we'll just be faces in the crowd is better, but it's just . . . that was *ours*. Our idea, our plan, our *choice*. Nothing about this is my choice.

When I don't say anything, Ellie picks up the laptop, holding it closer to her face. "This story isn't just some random gossip thing, Daisy," she says. "What Glynnis is being too nice to tell you is that it made the papers *here*, and I'd really like my future in-laws to meet you—all of you—and see for themselves what lovely, totally normal people you are."

"Are we normal?" Dad asks, tugging at his ponytail. "That's so disappointing."

Glynnis takes the laptop again, giving us that bright smile. I wonder if it would be too forward to tell her she needs to tone it down about a thousand notches because that grin makes her look like she's about to eat us.

"We were already planning a get-together closer to the wedding," she says, "but with it being summer, this really does seem like the perfect time, I hope you'll all agree."

"No," I say again, "because I have a . . . god, what would y'all say? A 'prior commitment.' Besides, I haven't learned the protocol or anything yet," I argue. "I might say the wrong thing to the wrong person and cause an international incident. What if I screw up so badly that Scotland declares war on Florida? What then, El?"

My sister is still holding her hair in a ponytail over one shoulder, her head tilted slightly to one side, and her eyes narrow. "Why are you like this?"

I shrug. "Dad, probably."

At my side, Dad mimics my shrug. "Probably," he agrees,

and I think if Glynnis weren't sitting right next to her, Ellie would've slammed her computer shut.

As always, Mom is the peacemaker. "All right, all right, enough. I'm your mother, so I get the final say in this. Glynnis, you think having Daisy over there during all this engagement . . . kerfuffle will make things easier on her?"

"Mom!" I squawk, but she just holds up her hand, still looking at the laptop.

Glynnis looks up from her phone and gives that man-eating grin again. "I do. The more control we have over this situation, the better. I know it just looks like one measly blog post now, but trust me, these things spiral." Her accent turns that word into an actual spiral, vowels stretching, the *r* twisting.

Before any of us can say anything, Glynnis goes on. "Of course we can start small. Most of the bigger, potentially more stressful functions won't start up until we get closer to the wedding. There's no need to throw Daisy into the deep end of the pool with Their Majesties."

Their Majesties. The Queen and Prince Consort of Scotland, who I'd now be hanging out with.

Now it's my stomach spiraling.

"Isabel—" I start.

"Can come visit you here," Glynnis finishes smoothly. "We'll arrange everything."

"I need to at least talk to her," I say, but Glynnis is already talking again.

"Next week, the Marquis of Sherbourne is throwing a little house party for Eleanor and Alexander. That will be close family and intimate friends only, and just the younger set. It would be a good place to start, don't you think?"

Glynnis turns to Ellie on that, and I can tell my sister isn't so sure. Her long fingers are still twisting her ponytail, making her massive engagement ring wink. "If . . . if you think that's best," she says, and Glynnis pats her arm. Her nails are the same bright red as her lipstick.

"Seriously, am I invisible? Are you just planning this like I haven't said no a thousand times?" I cut in, looking between my parents, and Dad heaves a sigh, thin shoulders moving beneath his Hawaiian-print shirt.

"The train is rolling, my Daisy-Daze," he says in a low voice. "Best to get on board before you're crushed on the tracks."

"I know you've been looking forward to Key West, love," Mom says on my other side, "but I really do think Glynnis here and Ellie have come up with a fine solution. And think how thrilled Isabel will be to come to Scotland to see you! Key West isn't going anywhere, either, and you can always go when you get home."

"Exactly," Glynnis says, gesturing with one hand like she's showing me the fabulous prize I just won. "And of course, Mr. and Mrs. Winters," she adds, "we'd love to have the two of you as well. As I said, the party is mostly for the younger set—"

"And for drinking and debauchery," Dad says, sitting up in his chair with a sigh. "Yes, yes, I've had my fill of that, so we can pass on the party. Get right to meeting Berry's new family, shall we?"

"Dad!" El says, her cheeks turning pink, eyes shooting again to Glynnis.

"Sorry, sorry," Dad says with a wave of his hand. "Meeting Eleanor's new family."

Ellie's hands go round and round her hair, and had I just not had my own summer trampled on, I'd feel kind of sorry for her. She's worked so hard for the past few years to keep things in their separate boxes, and now, thanks to one stupid blog, those boxes are about to be dumped out on her head.

"So it's set, then?" Glynnis asks, leaning in so that her face almost completely blocks Ellie's. "The Winters family is coming to Scotland?"

Mom, Dad, and I share a three-way glance, and after a pause, Dad lifts his wineglass in a salute.

"Aye," he says, putting on a broad Scottish accent that has El's eyes widening. "We are indeed, lassie."

Chapter 7

SITTING IN THE BACK OF A TOWN CAR, WATCHING the gentle hills of the Scottish Lowlands roll by, I wonder if jet lag is making me hallucinate.

Last week, I was working at a grocery store, studying to retake the SAT, and hanging out with Isabel. Today, I'm on my way to a castle.

We got in yesterday after flying first class into Heathrow in London, then taking a smaller plane to Edinburgh. While I might object to a lot about my sister's new lifestyle, first class was something I could appreciate. We didn't just have seats, we had these little pod things, complete with actual beds. I'd spent the first few hours of the flight just scrolling through all the movies and TV shows available, then listened to fifteen minutes of the spa channel just because I could. There had also been *great* food, free champagne (not that I'd gotten much more than a sip before Mom had taken my glass away), and, best of all, *free pajamas*. Really comfy white cotton ones, too. Dad had said they made us all look like cult members, but I'd noticed him stroking his own arm once he'd changed into them.

Once we'd landed, we'd been hustled off to a hotel, but that was a blur of suitcases and cars and Glynnis's very red smile. She had looked even more terrifying in person, and I'd snapped a surreptitious pic to email to Isabel once we were at the hotel. ("That lady is totally getting you ready for the Hunger Games" had been Isabel's reply.)

Staying at the hotel—an enormous place called the Balmoral—had been a nice surprise since I'd been afraid we'd be ushered straight into royal living, no matter what Glynnis had said about "easing into things." But nope, Alexander's parents were in Canada at the moment, and so Glynnis had decided we might want a night at the hotel to "adjust."

We'd mostly just slept, and then this afternoon, Ellie and the car had come to get me to drive me a few hours south to Sherbourne Castle, where the engagement party was being held this weekend.

There had been a fair amount of cloak-and-dagger with getting Ellie to the hotel and me out, but there were no photographers or gawkers, and I had to admit that Glynnis clearly knew her stuff about being "in the circle." I had no idea how they'd arranged it all, if there had been decoys or other cars or what, but when we drove out of the city without one single flash, I breathed a sigh of relief and told myself that maybe this summer wouldn't be so bad.

It's even easier to think that now, watching the scenery go past. I've been to Scotland before. We'd visited Ellie a few times back before she started dating Alex, and the whole family had gone when I was around eleven, but I've never been to this part of the country before. It's all green fields and rolling hills and shifting light.

I like it.

Next to me, Ellie fidgets in her seat, adjusting the slim leather belt around her waist and picking imaginary bits of lint off the leather seats. "Did you read the stuff Glynnis put together for you?" she asks, and I think of that massive manila folder shoved in my bag in the trunk—sorry, the *boot*—of the car.

"Kind of?" I offer, which is the truth. I opened it, saw there were things in it, and was like, "I will read this later when my eyeballs don't feel like they're filled with sand."

But now, El does that thing where she clamps her lips together and flares her nostrils, turning to look out the window. "I know it's important," I tell her. "And I really appreciate Glynnis doing it for me, and I don't think she's even a little bit scary." I flash my sister a smile. "How's that?"

El turns back to look at me, the corner of her mouth twitching, and finally, she gives me a smile. It's half-hearted, but at least it's not blinding and fake.

"Glynnis is a bit scary, I'll give you that," Ellie says, crossing one ankle over the other, "but she's also efficient and smart. I couldn't get through all of this without her."

The words shouldn't sting, but they do. It's a reminder that Ellie didn't really want us here for this, the biggest thing that's ever happened to her, that she's depending on Alex and his family and his family's *employees* during all of this. I get it, but that doesn't mean I like it.

"I obviously read the part about my appearance," I tell

Ellie, gesturing to my newly dyed strawberry-blond hair. I wasn't getting rid of the red altogether, but I'd toned it down after Glynnis had made a "gentle suggestion." I'd also gone and bought a couple of completely boring dresses for the trip. I smooth a hand over my skirt. "Polka dots, El. I'm wearing *polka dots.*"

But that doesn't seem to cheer her up. She just sighs and says, "All the polka dots in the world aren't going to save you if you call an earl 'my dude' or make jokes about kilts."

I roll my eyes. "You know I do have, like, basic manners, right? Wasn't raised by wolves? Although I guess Dad's not far off from—"

"I just need you to be on your absolute best behavior," she interrupts, and I fight the urge to make a smart-ass comment that would basically prove her point.

Instead, I shift to face her, sliding one knee up on the seat as I do, only to have her quickly pat my leg and shoot a glance up at the driver. I sigh—my dress hadn't ridden up all that much—and put my foot back on the floor, smoothing out my skirt and sitting like the sister of a soon-to-be princess should.

"So what are we going to do at this party?" I ask, trying to make peace. "Shoot small animals? Play inappropriate drinking games? Uncover hidden treasure?"

I'm joking, but the little smile that was on Ellie's face falls, and I sit up straighter in my seat. "Wait, we're not really shooting things, are we?"

Ellie leans closer, looking over at the driver before she whispers, "Daisy, the people at this party . . . they're more Sebastian's friends than mine or Alex's."

Her blue eyes keep darting toward the driver, but he's staring straight ahead, no sign that he's overhearing us at all. I guess if you have a job driving royal types around, you get pretty good at tuning things out.

"The Royal Wreckers," I whisper back with a nod, and El jerks like I've slapped her. And then she's leaning in so close that her long blond hair nearly touches my arm.

"Oh my god, you won't read the stuff Glynnis prepared for you, but you *will* read internet gossip?"

"I didn't read the internet gossip, Isabel did," I fire back. Whisper-fighting is hard to do without spitting, but Ellie and I have practice with these hissed arguments in back seats. Years of family road trips will do that. "And to be honest, that's the kind of thing I might need to know more than how to address an earl in 'formal written correspondence.' See? I did look at the file."

Ellie's only reply to that is a very eloquent eye roll, but at least she sits back a little and stops clenching her fingers in her lap. "The point is, I want you to know that—"

Looking out the windshield, her eyes go wide, and I turn to follow her glance, only to find my own jaw dropping.

We're coming up a narrow dirt road, and at the end, there isn't a castle but a low stone farmhouse, pretty and perfect with a slate roof and green hills rolling in the background. It's like something out of a fairy tale, but that's not what has me and Ellie staring.

It's the line of pipers in kilts outside the house.

There are at least twenty guys standing there, bagpipes at the ready, and as the car approaches, there's this . . . *blast* of sound. Even with the windows up, it's loud enough to make my teeth

59

rattle, and that first wheezing note as they all fire up at once makes me cover my ears even as I grin and look over at Ellie.

"Oh my god," I say, but she ignores me, leaning forward to say to the driver, "This isn't Sherbourne!"

She has to shout, that's how loud the bagpiping is, and the driver raises his voice to reply, "This was the location I was given, ma'am!"

"I mean, obviously, El," I say, elbowing her in the side. "Isn't this the welcome you get *everywhere*?"

I honestly think she'd tell me to shut up, but that's not very princess-y, so she settles for shooting me a look as the car pulls to a stop in front of the line of pipers.

Then we both just sit there for a second.

The music is still going, and now that they're really into it—I realize now they're not playing some traditional Scottish tune but a version of "Get Lucky," which is . . . something—it's really not bad. It's kind of cool, actually, and I suddenly wonder if maybe I should pick up the bagpipes while I'm here. Now *that* would be a hobby to bring back to Florida.

"Shall I get the door, ma'am?" the driver asks, and I look over at El.

"If we open the door, it might actually be loud enough to kill us," I say, and my sister grimaces, her hand flexing on the seat next to us.

"Picture it, El," I tell her. "'FUTURE QUEEN OF SCOTLAND AND FAR SUPERIOR YOUNGER SISTER KILLED IN TRAGIC MUTUAL HEAD EXPLOSION— PIPERS HELD IN CUSTODY.'"

She doesn't laugh, but she does relax a little. "You are so

60

weird," she mutters, but then she opens the door and steps out.

I do the same, and I was right—the sound nearly rocks me back on my heels. There are twenty pipers exactly, ten flanking each side of the low, shallow steps leading up into the farmhouse. They're all beautifully dressed in bright red kilts, sashes over their chests, and thick wool socks covering muscular calves.

I don't want to be impressed, especially since these guys just nearly deafened me, but I kind of can't help it. It's just . . . we're standing in front of this gorgeous stone house, behind which is this perfect valley full of soft, buttery light, and now we've been greeted by twenty—*twenty!*—literal pied pipers, and I can't help but laugh, shaking my head.

"I get the princess thing now," I tell Ellie. "For real. I might try to marry a prince, too, just so these guys can announce me showing up to, like, the mall."

Ellie cuts her eyes at me before flicking her hair over her shoulders. "I'm still not sure why we're here and not at Sherbourne," she says in a low voice.

"Have we been kidnapped?" I ask in a near whisper, but before Ellie can tell me to get bent or whatever the new, Fancy Ellie version of that is, there's another screech of bagpipes.

This time it definitely doesn't come from the gentlemen in front of us, and unlike the song earlier, it doesn't suddenly resolve itself into a recognizable melody. This is an actual assault on eardrums, and I look around, trying to figure out where it's coming from.

The pipes get louder, and suddenly there are two guys basically skipping out the front door and down the steps.

They're in kilts like the professional pipers, but their socks are pooling around their ankles and one of them is wearing an insane hat that sort of looks like a beret but has a sharp purple feather jutting out of it. He's about my height, with shaggy dark hair, and then I glance over at the other guy and realize he looks nearly identical.

There are two cute boys in kilts murdering bagpipes and dancing toward us.

"Did we take drugs in the car?" I ask Ellie, but then the boys are there, and one of them spins in front of me before dipping into a low bow.

"Ladies!" he says as his twin gives Ellie the same treatment, his twirl so intense that for a second, I'm afraid I'm going to learn exactly what boys wear underneath their kilts.

Ellie gives a startled laugh. "Stephen?" she asks the boy in front of her before glancing at the one still bowing to me. "Donald? What—"

"Ellie!"

Oh, thank god. It's Alex coming out the door now, and he's wearing pants.

I never thought I'd be so relieved to see pants.

Alex is the closest thing to chagrined I've ever seen him as he rushes down the steps toward my sister, and when he gets to her and literally takes her in his arms, I wait for the bagpipes to start up again.

He gives her a hug, then, one arm still wrapped around her, opens his other arm to me.

Aren't royals supposed to be all closed off and dead inside? Isn't emotion embarrassingly common? Why do I now have to join a three-way hug with my sister and her fiancé?

But I do, letting Alex briefly press me against his Ralph Lauren and my sister's Chanel, and then he pulls back, looking at us both before smiling hesitantly.

"It was a surprise," he says, and Ellie, her hand still on his arm, looks past him to the pipers and the twin boys who are now no longer bowing but using their bagpipes in some kind of vaguely phallic swordfight.

"You planned this?" El asks, eyebrows raised, and Alex swallows so hard I can see his Adam's apple move.

"Actually—" he starts, but then a voice interrupts him.

"I'm afraid it was all me."

WHO ARE THE ROYAL WRECKERS?

Prince Sebastian of Scotland may only be seventeen, but he's already on every girl's Dream Date List. And while not many of us can hope to land a prince, there are other options in Seb's circle! Ever since his primary school days, he's had a cadre of similarly well-heeled boys following him around. But who are these fellows, and are they interesting past their involvement with Prince Sebastian? Let's find out!

1) Andrew McGillivray, "Gilly" to friends, second son of the Duke of Argyll. Of all the Wreckers, Gilly is the richest, his family's net worth said to rival the royal family's. Only eighteen, Gilly has an appetite for expensive horses, good wine, and an assortment of "Instagram models," whatever that means. I guess all that money helps them overlook his weak chin.

2) Thomas Leighton, Marquis of Sherbourne, son of the Duke of Galloway. He's the most highly titled of the Royal Wreckers, "Sherbet," and also probably the best looking. We actually think he gives Prince Sebastian a run for his money in the Handsome Department. Those eyes! The cheekbones! Sadly, ladies, it's well known that the marquis does not, shall we say, play for our team. He's said to be dating Galen Konstantinov, son of shipping magnate Stavros Konstantinov.

3) The Fortescue brothers, Stephen and Donald. If they have nicknames, we haven't heard them, but these two brothers are

always paired together, seems like, so I suppose they're just grateful if no one calls them Tweedledee and Tweedledum. Both are the sons of the Earl of Douglas, and while they're not twins, they're only thirteen months apart in age. Recent additions to the Royal Wreckers, the Fortescue brothers are the only ones who didn't attend Gregorstoun with the prince. They're Eton boys and proud of it.

4) Miles Montgomery. Interestingly enough, Miles is the lowest on our list in terms of title and wealth. He's the son of a baronet, Sir Peregrine Montgomery, and rumor has it that the family has fallen on hard times. Not a manor home to be found in this family's portfolio these days. But in spite of that (or maybe because of it), Miles is Prince Sebastian's closest friend, and frequently found at the ne'er-do-well prince's side. Most intriguingly, there were rumors he was briefly involved with Sebastian's twin sister, Flora. Was that weird for the Gregorstoun chums? We'd have to think it's just the slightest bit awkward.

(*Prattle*, "The Royal Wreckers," *September Issue*)

Chapter 8

ONE THING I'VE LEARNED FROM BEING AROUND
Ellie these past couple of years is that no one is actually as pretty
or handsome as they look in magazines. Even El, who is awfully
pretty in real life, is like ten times more glamorous in the pages
of magazines.

The boy stepping out of the farmhouse now?

I've seen him in magazines and on websites and acknowl-
edged that he was good-looking, sure. I like boys, I have eyes,
there's no doubt he's an attractive example of his sex.

But that does not prepare me in *any way at all* for seeing
Prince Sebastian in the flesh.

He's tall, his entire upper body is so perfectly v-shaped that
I think geese probably study him to get their flight formation
just right, and he's wearing a gray long-sleeved shirt and jeans
that were clearly crafted just for him, possibly by nuns who've
devoted themselves to the cause of making boys look as sinful
as possible so the rest of us will know just how dangerous they
are, and he's . . .

Just a dude, oh my actual god, get ahold of yourself.

Ellie glances over at me, her eyebrows drawn together, and to my horror, I realize I just whispered that last sentence out loud to myself.

Luckily, Prince Sebastian didn't overhear me because the pipers have started up again, the real ones this time. Just a handful, so it's not as overwhelming as it was when we drove up, and this time they're playing "Isn't She Lovely?"

Seb comes to a stop in front of us, clasping his hands together, and as the last note dies away, I swear to god, the clouds part and a sunbeam shines down on his head, making the red glints in his dark hair shimmer.

"Ellie," he says, stepping forward to give my sister a quick hug.

And then he turns his blue eyes to me. "And you must be Daisy."

I get a handshake instead of a hug, which is probably for the best as I think a hug with this boy might count as sexual contact. Still, his hand is warm and strong, and yeah, this is the same as third base with a regular boy.

"Surprise!" he says to all of us once he's dropped my hand and stepped back. He spreads his arms wide, grinning at us, and Alex gives him a tight smile.

"Still not really sure what this is, mate," he says, and Seb reaches out, punching his brother on the shoulder.

"An engagement present, you prat," he says. "And since it was on the way to Sherbourne, I wanted to show it off to you first!"

Ellie and Alex look at each other, Alex's arms going around

my sister's waist as Seb begins to walk back to the house. "An engagement present?" Alex calls after him, and Seb jogs up the stairs, turning to glance over his shoulder.

"Your very own farmhouse in the Scottish lowlands," he says proudly. "Wait until you see the view."

"You bought us a *house?*" Ellie asks, breaking away from Alex to trail after Seb, and I pick up the rear, the two boys in kilts—Stephen and Donald—suddenly coming around to flank me.

"That is the reddest hair I've ever seen," says Stephen. Wait, maybe Donald? I didn't get it straight earlier.

"Thank you?" I say, even though I'm not sure it's a compliment.

"Oi, you two! Don't monopolize her!" someone cries from the doorway, and I look up to see yet *another* ridiculously handsome boy. This one is dressed in jeans, a plaid button-down, and a sweater vest that should really take his hot points down by at least a hundred, but he's also got particularly swoopy brown hair, lovely eyes, and a charming smile, so not even a sweater vest can compete against that.

"Sherbourne," he says, coming down to shake my hand, and I blink for a second.

Isn't that the name of the castle we're going to? So why is he—

Oh, right. Sherbourne is not his first name—it's his title. The Marquis of Sherbourne. The castle we're supposed to be going to later is *his*.

Crap, how do you greet a marquis? Your Grace? No, that's for dukes. God, I really should've read Glynnis's stupid folder.

I promise myself that I'll study it religiously once we actually get to the castle.

But before I have to say anything in reply, another guy appears in the farmhouse doorway, a bottle in his hand, his golden hair tousled in a way that seems too perfect not to be on purpose. "We call him Sherbet," this new blond boy says, winking at me in a way that immediately has my face feeling hot. Seriously, what sort of pheromones do these guys exude?

Sherbourne—Sherbet, I guess—elbows the blond guy, then inclines his head toward me. "Forgive Gilly here, he was raised in a barn and therefore has no manners."

"Gilly?" I repeat, and the blond guy shakes my hand as well.

"Andrew McGillivray," he says, and then he gestures for us to all go inside.

The farmhouse has stone floors and truly massive furniture, plus a fireplace so big that I can only assume people once roasted elephants in it. There's a fire crackling happily there now, and the back of the room is basically one giant window looking out into the valley.

I go to the window now, staring down at all those green rolling hills, shadows moving, the light constantly shifting. There are sheep down there in the valley, little white puffballs milling around. As far as wedding presents go, this one is pretty nice, I have to admit, and I'm smiling when I turn away from the window.

Aaaand nearly smack right into *another* guy. Seriously, how many cute boys can one farmhouse hold?

This one puts out his hands to steady me. He's got dark blond hair, almost brown, and the best set of cheekbones I've ever seen on anyone who wasn't a statue. Like all these dudes, he looks kind of like a romantic poet who decided to join a boy band, his eyes very green as they look down at me.

With . . . dislike?

Seriously, his upper lip is nearly curling, which is such a weird reaction that I step back.

He's taller than Sherbet and Gilly, but not that much taller than me. Not that that's stopping him from looking down his nose at me as he drops his hands from my arms. "All right, then?" he asks, his voice lower than the other boys', but every bit as posh. Those syllables are clipped and crisp as he looks past me toward the window.

And then, suddenly, I realize why he looks familiar.

"Monaco!" I blurt out, and he blinks in confusion.

"No, *Monters*," Gilly says, coming up to us and smacking a hand on the other guy's shoulder. "Miles Montgomery, professional prat," he says, but he's grinning, and Miles doesn't seem all that offended.

"She means that incident with Sebastian," he says, and I am so embarrassed I feel like I have to be the same color as my hair.

"I did some research," I say, which really only makes the whole thing worse, and Gilly snorts with amusement.

"God, if you were reading up on Seb's foibles, I'm surprised you came here at all."

But Monters is watching me with this unreadable expression. All the guys here are handsome, but this guy is particularly . . . interesting. All handsome face and good posture, his eyes a really pretty shade of green. Sherbet may be the marquis, but this guy seems more aristocratic than any of them.

Or maybe he's just stuck up.

"Wasn't aware tabloids counted as 'research,'" Miles says, folding his arms over his chest, and okay, yeah, definitely stuck up.

I cross my own arms, mimicking his pose. "They're actually all we're given to read in America," I say. "Tabloids for books, sad slices of cheese in plastic for lunch . . . It's truly a godforsaken place."

Gilly hoots at that, elbowing Miles in the ribs. "Blimey, she's got your number, mate."

Miles only gives me this look somewhere between a smirk and a grimace, and I'm tempted to ask what his problem is.

But before I can, Seb strides to the middle of the room, lifting a glass of champagne. "A toast!" he calls, and Sherbet approaches carrying several flutes of bubbly. I take a glass and thank him.

Ellie comes to stand right next to me, while Alex hangs back, still watching his brother with this wary expression, his head tilted down slightly.

"To Alex and Ellie," Seb says, and the rest of us lift our glasses with him.

"To Alex and Ellie," we repeat, and I take the tiniest sip of champagne. The bubbles tickle my nose, and I wrinkle it as I look for somewhere inconspicuous to stash the glass.

I've just turned toward a little table near the sofa when the front door opens with a crash.

"What in the hell is going on here?"

Or at least I *think* that's what the man in the doorway says. His face is red, white hair jutting out from underneath a cap and a matching white beard reaching nearly to his sternum, and his accent is so thick that the words are mostly a series of rolls and grunts and a kind of spitting sound.

Still, there's no mistaking the fact that he's *really* pissed.

In the middle of the room, Seb just grins and wags a finger. "McDougal," he says, his own Scottish accent musical but comprehensible. "You weren't supposed to be here today."

"What?" Ellie asks, looking between Seb and the man, and Alex steps forward, his shoulders tight. "Sebastian—" he starts.

The man—McDougal—is still talking, the words coming fast and furious, his cheeks scarlet above his white beard, and there's a lot of pointing and possibly cursing, and while I have no idea what's being said, it doesn't seem all that friendly.

"Calm down, mate," Stephen—Spiffy—says, throwing back his champagne. "It's not like he's not gonna pay for the place."

Ellie's head swings to the side to look at Seb. "Wait, what? I thought you said you bought this house."

Sighing, Seb shoves his hands in his pockets and rocks back on his heels. "Well, I'm certainly *going* to," he says. "If this gentleman will just be reasonable."

"Um . . . are we . . . *trespassing*? Is that what's happening right now?" I ask, glancing around the farmhouse.

Seb shoots a look at me and gives me an easy smile. "Of course not, love," he says, and even though I might be an unwitting accomplice to a crime, I still feel my stomach flutter at that endearment.

"Ye damn sure are!" the man bellows, and okay, maybe I'm actually getting better at the accent because I understood him perfectly.

Sebastian is still all charm as he approaches McDougal, who is now incandescent with rage. I'm not sure how this went from "super-charming welcome party" to "property theft" in just a few minutes, but here we are, and I look up at that rude guy, Miles.

He's still standing by the window, champagne undrunk, his expression somewhere between irritated and bored. Or maybe his face just always looks like that, hard to say.

"If you had accepted my offer last week, we wouldn't be in this mess," Seb says to Mr. McDougal. Then he turns to look over his shoulder at Ellie and Alex.

"I found this place last time I went to Sherbourne, and the view was too good to pass up. But Mr. McDougal here wouldn't sell, so . . ." He shrugs, and I glance over at Ellie, my eyebrows somewhere in my hairline, probably.

"Holy crap," I say in a low voice, but she just hisses, "*Not now, Daisy.*"

"I'm not selling my house to ye, ye smug bastard," McDougal says, poking Seb in the chest, "just because ye like the look a'tha land. Ye canna steal things just because ye take a fancy to 'em!"

"It's like we're in *Outlander*," I whisper to El. "This is really a lot more than I bargained for."

"Daisy!" El says again, giving me a glare before walking forward with her best princess smile, Alex coming to stand next to her.

"Mr. McDougal, we are *terribly* sorry for this misunderstanding," she says, her voice so soothing it's like an auditory head pat. "You do have a lovely home, and—"

"This is breaking and entering!" Mr. McDougal continues, and Seb sighs, rolling his shoulders.

"I did not break, although I *did* enter."

"And who let ye in?" Mr. McDougal is practically panting now, his barrel chest heaving, and I glance over my shoulder to see Spiffy and Dons edging close to the wall, choking back giggles. What are they—

"Bloody hell," Miles mutters next to me, and I look up to see he's watching Spiffy and Dons, too.

My eyes land on the crossed swords affixed to the wall just as Seb grins at Mr. McDougal and drawls, "Lovely lass who lives here gave me a key." Making an exaggeratedly innocent expression, he adds, "I believe she said she was your granddaughter?"

If I'd thought that Mr. McDougal seemed rage-y before, it's nothing to how he looks now. Face purple, he gives this huge shout and lunges for Seb just as Spiffy and Dons pull the swords from the wall, metal scraping along stone as the points of the swords drag on the floor.

"Duel!" Spiffy shouts, and for the first time, I realize just how drunk he and his brother are. Like, *crazy* drunk.

And now they're armed with swords that look like they were last used about three hundred years ago.

"Stephen!" Alex says, stepping forward to snatch the sword away from him, but before he can, Dons rushes forward with his own sword.

Straight at the farmer and Seb.

Chapter 9

SOME GOOD THINGS THAT HAPPENED THIS AFTERNOON:

1) Mr. McDougal did not press charges and accepted both Alex's sincere apologies and his offer to meet the queen upon her return from Canada.

2) We managed to get to Sherbourne Castle just as a huge rainstorm swept in, literally walking up the front steps as the bottom seemed to fall out of the sky, drenching everything.

3) No one actually got stabbed. Dons had been trying to toss the sword to Seb in some sort of cool maneuver, but it ended up just clattering to the floor before it could do any damage.

4) . . .

No, that's it. Those were the good things that happened today, and the rest was a complete disaster.

The castle, however, is gorgeous. Well, parts of it are. The entire back end of it appears to be a ruin, but the main building is exactly what I would've dreamed of as a kid had I been into the whole princess-and-castle thing. There's even a turret with a flag flapping in the wind, and it's easy to imagine standing there, watching, like, Braveheart come riding in from battle, all blue-faced and yelling about freedom.

As Ellie and I step through the big double doors of the castle, I scoot closer to her and whisper, "So is there a reason you failed to mention that Alex's brother and all his friends are basically human dumpster fires?"

"Shhhh!" Ellie hisses, looking around her, but Alex is talking to Miles, and the rest of the Royal Wreckers are heading back to the parlor, laughing, punching each other, basically a walking advertisement for bad decisions.

"I thought Flora was the only one who was a mess," I add, still whispering. "Is she here?"

Turning back to me, she smooths her hair with her hands, probably drawing power from its mystical shininess. "We'll see her once her school term is over," Ellie says, "and as for Seb and his friends, I know they can get a little out of hand, but—"

"Out of hand?" I whisper back. "Ellie, that was full-scale insane. There was nearly a duel! Seb, like, tried to steal some dude's house! And you're worried about *our* family being embarrassing?"

"No one is worried our family will embarrass me, first of all," she says, and I scoff.

"Okay, sure."

Ignoring that, she goes on. "And those are Seb's friends, not Alex's."

"Are you sure about that?" I ask.

I glance over to see Alex thumping Miles's shoulder in that way boys do, and Miles shoots a quick look at me before heading off in the same direction as the other Wreckers. Only Ellie,

Alex, Sherbet, and I are left in the main foyer, and while I want to ask Ellie more about Seb, Alex is already walking toward her, one hand out.

"Drink, darling?" he asks, like we're in a *Masterpiece Theatre* show about murder in the 1930s or something.

Ellie sighs and places her hand in his. "Yes, please," she says, and off they go, violins probably swelling on the soundtracks inside their heads.

As I watch them go, I wonder: Is *this* why Ellie kept things so separate? Was it less to keep us from embarrassing her new fancy-pants family and more to make sure we never knew how *not* perfect her new life was?

That's . . . interesting to think about.

Sherbet moves closer to me, hands in his pockets. "Shall I show you up to your room?" he asks, and I nod. I wouldn't mind holing up somewhere private for a little bit.

"Follow me," Sherbet says, jerking his head toward the main staircase.

As we walk along, our footsteps muffled by the thick carpet on the steps, I glance around again at all the stuff. Paintings fill up all the wall space, and little tables covered in clocks and porcelain eggs and miniature portraits are scattered everywhere.

"How would you know if anything went missing?" I ask, and Sherbet turns, looking at me and then around again as though he's just now noticing that his house is full of *things*.

"Huh," he says, gripping the banister with a long-fingered hand. "I'm not sure we *would* know, really." He laughs then, some of his dark hair flopping over his forehead. "Most houses like this are stuffed to the gills," he says, continuing up the stairs.

"I guess owning a place for like a thousand years will do that," I reply, and he laughs again, stepping onto the landing.

"Yes, that, but also, families like ours would always make sure to have extra trinkets lying about in case anything caught the monarch's eye when they visited."

I stop just behind him, looking at an end table littered with all sorts of bits and bobs: a magnifying glass with a jeweled handle, a thumb-sized naughty shepherdess figurine, a leather-bound journal so old the spine is flaking. "What do you mean?" I ask, and he looks back at me, eyebrows raised.

"Oh, just that if the king or queen were visiting your house, they might see something they wanted, and they'd take it. So it behooved hosts to fill their house with extra knickknacks or objets d'art, so they could give away something less valuable or sentimental."

I try to imagine someone visiting my house and just . . . taking whatever they wanted.

"But what if you didn't want them to have it? What if they didn't fall for the extra junk and wanted, like, a book your dead grandmother gave you?"

Sherbet shrugs. "Then you gave it to them," he says. "They're royal."

Like that explains everything. And heck, for these types of people, maybe it does. Seb did just try to commandeer someone's farm, after all.

"I hope you enjoy your stay here, Daisy," Sherbet goes on. "I know today was a bit mad, but tomorrow is the race, and that should be a good deal calmer."

Oh, right. The race, aka An Reis, a fancy, Ascot-like thing

we'll be attending that's *probably* in that folder Glynnis prepared for me. I know nothing about horses or races, but how hard can it be?

We make our way farther down the hall until Sherbet stops at a door and opens it with a flourish, giving a little bow. "If anything is not to your satisfaction, please let me know," he says, and then he's off down the hall, back toward the stairs and, I'm sure, more drinks.

The room is smaller than I'd expected, but maybe that's just because the bed is so massive, it takes up most of the space. It's covered in a floral bedspread, and there's a tiny canopy that I like, but other than that, it mostly feels . . . weird. Other than my bag—resting on an ancient-looking luggage rack at the foot of the bed—it's all deeply unfamiliar and even a little unwelcoming. The walls are stone, and while there are two windows looking out toward the stream that cuts across the property, the glass is so warped and distorted that it makes it seem like I'm looking outside through water.

It's also *cold* in the room, and while there's a radiator under the window, no matter how I twist and pull at the knobs, nothing seems to happen.

Defeated, I flop down on the bed, pull the musty-smelling bedspread up around me, and am asleep in minutes.

When I wake, it's dark outside, which means it's late. Really late. Past ten, at least, and I sit up, groggy. I'd fallen asleep in my dress and cardigan, both of which are now hopelessly wrinkled, *and* hopelessly ineffective against the chill in the room.

I've probably missed dinner, but even the rumbling in my

stomach doesn't make me want to face what's downstairs, so instead, I open my bag and start pulling out clothes. I settle on a pair of pajama pants (plaid, very fitting), a tank top, an old long-sleeved T-shirt on top of that, a sweater, and, for extra measure, a scarf wrapped around my head. Even in all those layers, though, I'm still not warm.

Shivering, I rub my upper arms. How the heck is this place so cold in *June?* Back home, we were running the air conditioner nonstop by this point. It's not like I'd expected Scotland to be balmy or anything, but when we'd been here before, it was in the fall and winter. I expected cold then, but this was ridiculous.

I go back to the radiator lurking under the nearest window, but twisting the knob on the bottom only results in a bunch of loud thumps and a rushing-water sound that is, to be honest, pretty freaking alarming.

I twist the knob again and the noises stop, but the room is still freezing, and with a sigh, I get back in the bed, being sure to pull out the folder Glynnis put together for me as I do.

Settling against the lumpy mattress, I decide that if I'm not going to go downstairs tonight, at least I can get prepared for tomorrow.

I page through the folder, and despite the fact that I'm about to die from frostbite, I can't help but grin and shake my head. No wonder El likes this Glynnis lady so much. This packet of material with its fancy font and little clip art of crowns is definitely Ellie's style. No one has ever excelled at organization quite like my sister.

Glynnis has broken her guide down into sections, and while

I'm tempted to skip to the part marked "Royal Residences," I figure the bit I need most is "Aristocracy: Titles and Honorifics."

Sherbet—sorry, Sherbourne—is the son of a duke, the first son, which means that if I'm talking to him, I need to say, "Lord Sherbourne" or "my lord," but if I was writing to him, I'd say, "My Lord Marquis." Also, I learn that a marquis is pretty high up on the list of fancy people, and that dukes are the fanciest people besides actual royalty, although some dukes are *also* royalty, like how Alexander is Prince of the Scots while also being the Duke of Rothesay, which, if you ask me, is a little greedy. No need to go snatching up all the—

There's a knock on my door, and I look up, startled. Then I remember about the heating and wonder if someone heard me banging on the radiator. Or even better, maybe someone is bringing me food.

Scrambling off the bed, I don't even bother throwing anything on over my pajamas since I'm wearing two layers and have a scarf wrapped around my head.

I fling open the door, hoping it'll be Ellie with a tray, being all sisterly and good-hearted.

It is very much not Ellie.

Standing in my doorway, dressed in dark pants and a white button-down, jacket thrown over his shoulder like he's about to walk down a runway, is Prince Sebastian.

Seb.

And he's smiling at me.

Chapter 10

"KNOCK, KNOCK," HE SAYS WITH A SMILE, RAPPING his knuckles on my door, and I stand there, frozen.

I thought I'd gotten used to how good-looking he was early this afternoon, but apparently this kind of handsome just smacks you in the face every time you see it.

And then I remember I am currently standing in my doorway staring at him wearing pretty much everything in my suitcase.

"Hi," I say too loudly, stepping back and trying to gesture for him to come in while also yanking at the scarf around my head, hopefully not looking like I'm strangling myself. I kind of *want* to strangle myself, but that's not the point.

"We didn't get much of a chance to talk. Thought I'd come say hello, apologize for that mess earlier, see how your first night here in the madhouse was going," Seb says lightly, his hands in his pockets as he ambles into my room. The way he walks . . . look, I know this sounds stupid, but I have never in my life seen a boy move like that. Most of the guys at my school slouch forward like they're carrying invisible turtle shells on their backs.

But here's Seb, with his shoulders back, all this easy grace, smooth motions, and when he leans against the high footboard of my bed to grin at me, I think I might actually swoon.

"This place doesn't seem that bad," I say. "It's a little cold," I acknowledge, gesturing at my layers, and Seb chuckles.

"Let's see what I can do," he murmurs, walking over to the radiator.

"I tried that," I tell him as he crouches down and my face flames red even though I'm still freezing. I have never ogled a guy, but Seb is oddly ogle-able, and in that position, his pants are really tight across—

Okay, no, no, this is not happening, and I am getting ahold of myself starting *now*.

I half expect Seb to do some macho dude thing like slam a fist on the radiator, after which it will magically work, having been subdued by the force of his overwhelming masculinity.

Instead, he fiddles with some knobs at the bottom, and then there's a soft hissing sound that I guess is heat actually coming back into the room.

"Sorted," Seb says, standing up and turning back around.

His eyes slide down to the monkey socks I'm wearing, then make a leisurely journey back up to my face.

"You don't look much like your sister," he finally says, and I have no idea if that's meant to be a criticism or a compliment. His handsome face isn't giving anything away, and I fight the urge to fidget. Being around Seb this afternoon had been one thing; there were lots of other people around, plus pipers, plus the incomprehensible farmer and the kilts and the champagne and the swords . . . even a very hot prince couldn't compete with all that excitement. But now he's here in my room, and it's nighttime, and the soft golden light from the lamp makes everything cozy and romantic, and I feel roughly 9,000 leagues out of my depth.

"You don't look much like your brother," I finally manage, and Seb winks at me.

"Thank god for small favors, eh?"

Then he turns and walks to the fancy desk in the corner of the room, the one with the cabinet over the top, and slides the cabinet open. "Ah, there you are, my beauty," he says, his Scottish accent rolling.

I curl my toes into the thick carpet, holding on to the bedpost as he cradles a bottle of amber liquid. "You hid booze in your friend's house?"

Seb yanks out the cork in the top of the bottle, lifting it to me in a little salute. "I did not actually hide this bottle, I'll have you know," he says. "That was Sherbet's father's doing."

"So instead of hiding booze, you're stealing it," I say.

He walks closer, then stops to lean against the opposite bedpost as he lifts the bottle to his lips, taking a truly massive gulp of whatever is in there. My stomach rolls in sympathy.

"I cannot *steal*," Seb informs me, "because, *technically*, anything in this house belongs to me, as I am a prince of the land."

I'm just about to roll my eyes when that boyish grin flashes again. "Kidding, of course," he assures me. "I am indeed stealing Sherbet's father's fine whiskey."

I give a kind of breathless laugh that doesn't sound anything like me, and honestly, I kind of want to punch myself in the face for how ridiculous I'm being, but this is some next-level swoony material happening here.

Then Seb tilts the bottle up, taking another one of those massive gulps, and I shudder. Drinking straight alcohol like that would probably result in me projectile vomiting. Is he . . . used to this kind of thing? Earlier today, he'd been all charm and decorum while his friends were the ones totally out of their minds. Well, most of his friends. The tall guy had seemed sober enough.

"So you're to be my new sister-in-law," Seb says once he's done damaging his liver. "What do you think of the family so far?"

I can't tell if he's genuinely curious or just making small talk, but in either case, I kind of wish he'd leave already. I'm getting tired again, and I feel like talking with Seb might require more brainpower than I can currently access. There's a light blanket on the end of the bed, and I pick it up, wrapping it around my shoulders.

"It's great," I say. "Alex is . . . great."

Seb sucks in a deep breath through his nose. "Great," he echoes. "He is indeed that."

Silence falls between us then, and it is most definitely the awkward kind, but only on my end, I think. Seb appears to mostly be studying the patterns in the carpet.

Then up goes the bottle again, and I have the strangest urge to call Isabel, or at least take a quick phone video of Seb for her. *This guy is not nearly as dreamy as you thought,* I'd tell her, but then I look again at Seb, and okay, so he's getting drunk and maybe not quite as polished as I'd imagined he'd be, but I'm not sure the visual would get that across. He actually looks pretty good right now with his loose collar and perfect pants.

And then I realize I've been staring at him for several beats, and when I lift my gaze back to his face, he's watching me, and I realize that he may not have understood that I was mentally composing a text message to my best friend about how disappointing he is.

In fact, he might think—

I can't even finish the thought before Seb is letting go of the bedpost and moving toward me with the same grace I'd admired earlier. There's no time to admire now, however, as he immediately swoops down on me, his lips meeting mine.

Chapter 11

HE MUST TAKE MY GASP OF SURPRISE FOR AN invitation because he is full-on kissing me immediately. No lead-up, no questioning, just a royal tongue in my mouth, and *oh my god.*

I place both hands on his chest and shove hard.

Seb lets me go immediately, stumbling back a few steps, his brow furrowed. "What?" he asks, and I stand there, gaping, the taste of whiskey—which, turns out, I really don't like—still stinging in my mouth.

"You kissed me," I tell him, and he nods, even as he keeps looking at me like I'm speaking another language.

"I did . . . yeah," he says slowly. "Because you were looking at me in such a way that seemed to indicate you'd be amenable to such a thing."

I am shocked and still a little jet-lagged, so it takes me a second to work out that sentence, and when I do, my face heats up.

"I was *not* amenable," I assure him, wrapping my little

blanket cape more tightly around myself. "I was looking at you and thinking you weren't really what I expected."

That seems to take some of the wind out of his sails. Backing up a few more steps, he sits heavily on the edge of the bed, the whiskey bottle still dangling from one hand. He hadn't even put it down to kiss me.

"Not. What you. Expected," he says, shoulders slumping, and for a second, I feel kind of bad. I didn't mean to hurt his feelings.

"You're still really good-looking if it's any consolation," I offer up, and he raises his head, smiling a little.

"It is, thanks." Then he sighs again before bringing the bottle back to his lips.

"Sorry," he says once he's finished, and wow, that bottle is a lot emptier than it was a few minutes ago. His eyes are starting to look hazy, too, not quite as bright as they struggle to focus on my face. "I only . . . that interview. With your sodding boyfriend."

I stare at him. "Michael?" I squeak. Somehow, it never occurred to me that someone like Seb would actually *read* that. I understood people who worked for the royal family, people whose *job* it was to keep an eye on that kind of thing, knowing about it, but the actual prince?

"He said you dumped him to shag me," Seb goes on, and I would throw my hands up if I wasn't clutching the blanket so tightly.

"He was lying," I said, but Seb isn't really listening.

"Besides," he adds, "it's what everyone expects."

He gestures between the two of us, the bottle wobbling in his hand. "You and me. Alex's brother, Ellie's sister. And people bloody love Ellie, so now they bloody love Alex."

His blue eyes move up and down my body again, and I'm pulling the blanket so tightly around me, it's a wonder I still have circulation in my arms.

"So maybe people will love you, and if I loved you—well, not loved, exactly, but you get the idea—that would mean they love *me*."

He frowns, a trio of creases appearing between his auburn brows. "I said love too many times, I think."

"People totally love you," I say. "Maybe not random farmers your friends try to duel, but back home, you're pretty freaking popular, dude."

He just shakes his head. "You clearly didn't do your research, Ellie's Sister."

"It's Daisy," I remind him, but he just shrugs.

"In any case, I thought we might as well get it over with." He jerks his head toward the bed then, and this time, it's not fancy sentence structure or flowery words that have me struggling to process what he just said. It's shock.

"You came here to . . ." I can't even finish the sentence because it's too mortifying, so I just jerk *my* head toward the bed. "With me? A girl who's known you for five minutes?"

He blinks at me, and I remember that he's famous, rich, extremely attractive, and a royal to boot.

"Okay, so the five-minutes thing is probably the norm for you," I allow, "but for me—wow, you do *not* have to roll your eyes at me."

But Seb is not rolling his eyes at me. His eyes are rolling back into his head because he's passing out.

I watch as Scotland's most eligible bachelor slides off the edge of my mattress and crumples to the floor.

My very own Sleeping Beauty.

"You have got to be *kidding me*," I mutter as I look at the unconscious body slumped on the carpet. He's over six feet tall and definitely outweighs me, so it's not like I can help him up. Is there someone I should ring for?

I look around the room, either for a phone or for some kind of old-fashioned bellpull. They have to have someone who deals with this kind of thing, right? Was Glynnis around? Because I do *not* want to explain to Ellie why Seb was in my bedroom at night.

I'm just about to panic when there's another knock at the door, this one softer than Seb's, and for a second, I hover between my bed and the door, not sure what to do.

Then the knock comes again, and I dash to the door, opening it just a crack.

The douche guy from the farm, Miles, is standing in the doorway. He's changed clothes since I saw him earlier and is wearing jeans and a gray T-shirt now. But he's standing up so straight and looking at me so coldly that he might as well be wrapped in nine sweaters and maybe some tweed.

"I'm looking for Seb," he says, lips quirking with irritation. "He's not in his room, and my inner best friend alarm sensed he *might* be here, making bad choices."

I open the door wider, letting Miles take in the fact that the man who's second in line for the Scottish throne is currently out cold on my floor.

"Ah," Miles says. "Alarm still functioning, then."

I have to say, for a guy who just came to a strange girl's room to find his bestie passed out, Miles is pretty chill about the whole situation. It takes both of us, but we manage to maneuver Seb up off the floor, draping his arms over our shoulders.

"Luckily," Miles says once Seb is more or less on his feet, "his room isn't far."

Patting Seb's face—okay, patting is a nice way of putting it, it's basically gentle slapping—Miles says, "Gonna need you to wake up a bit, Seb. Use your feet. One, two, one, two, one in front of the other."

Miraculously, Seb does as he's told, and the three of us shuffle out the door.

It's dim in the corridor, and between the crazy-patterned carpet, the paintings and paneling on the walls, and the doors all being identical, I get a weird sense of vertigo, like I'm in a funhouse. How does anyone find their way around this place?

Also, Miles's definition of "not far" does not line up with mine. We half carry, half drag Seb down this corridor, then turn into another. At one point, we go through an arched doorway, and the hall we step into looks exactly like the one we just walked down.

"Where are we going?" Seb asks blearily. He slurs it, really, so it's more "Whuurwegoooin'?" but Miles clearly speaks Drunk Seb.

"Bed, my good man," he replies. "Your own this time."

Seb nods slowly. "Solid plan, Monters."

Just when I think my upper body strength might desert me completely, Miles pauses and opens a door that leads into a

chamber a lot bigger than mine, but still a little drabber than I'd
expect to see in a castle. The colors are muted burgundies and
golds, and I feel like we just stepped back in time or something.

"I could have you thrown into the dungeon for this," Seb
slurs out, but Miles just laughs, patting Seb's cheek.

"Keep threatening, mate. Maybe one day it'll actually
happen."

Seb swings his head toward me, his blue eyes hazy. "Would
never," he tells me in what I think he thinks is a whisper. "Can't
do without Monters."

"Clearly," I reply, watching as Miles lowers Seb to sit on the
edge of the mattress. I wonder how many times he's done this
over the years because even though Seb is just as tall as Miles
and probably a fair amount heavier, he pulls off the maneuver
smoothly, like he's very used to it.

Seb flops back onto the bed, feet still on the floor, and heaves
a sigh. "I did it again, didn't I?" he asks the canopy, and Miles
pats his leg.

"Not as bad as usual. No one got punched, no arrests, not
even a camera phone picture."

"Oh, I took one as we were walking down the hall. Was I not
supposed to?" I say, widening my eyes, and Miles shoots me a
dirty look. Honestly, how does he do that thing with his mouth
where it's like his face eats his lips in sheer disdain? Is there a
course in that at whatever fancy boarding school they go to?

"That was a joke," I tell him. "We colonists do that
sometimes."

I'm clearly not worth Miles's time because he turns away,
looking back at Seb.

"Sleep it off," he says, and Seb nods as though that's a sensible idea.

"Bed," he mutters, sinking back down. "Bedfordshire."

"Even so," Miles says, and after a second, Seb's eyes drift closed.

I'm just about to back up from the bed and start heading for the door when Seb suddenly sits up slightly, eyes popping open. "Ellie's Sister!" he calls, and I sigh, waving one hand.

"Daisy," I remind him, but he just fixes his bleary blue eyes on me. "Ellie's Sister," he says. "I'm sorry. About the part where I kissed you and suggested we shag. It was ungallant and . . ." He struggles, lifting one hand in the air and pointing, like the word he's looking for is right in front of him.

"Inappropriate," I supply, my face flaming. Miles isn't looking at me, but I'm pretty sure I can actually hear him creaking, he stiffens up so much. "Also gross and kind of sexist."

"All those things," Seb admits on a sigh. Then his eyes slide closed again, and Scotland's most eligible bachelor is soon snoring on his fancy bedspread.

Miles backs up from the bed slowly, jerking his head to indicate I should follow. Once we've exited the room, Miles carefully and quietly shuts the door behind us, and then we're standing there in the dim hallway. It's quiet in the castle, the only light coming from the sconces lining the walls.

"Well, that was fun," I start to say, but Miles is looking somewhere above my head, a muscle ticking in his jaw.

Then his eyes meet mine. "So," he says. "Did that go as you'd hoped?"

Chapter 12

I STARE AT HIM, SO SHOCKED I ACTUALLY MAKE A noise, this sort of *huhngh?* sound that's way too loud in the quiet hallway. When I can actually find my voice again, it's to squawk out, "Did you miss the part where he was in *my* room? Like, he came there himself. He just showed up like a posh vampire I accidentally invited in, then couldn't make leave."

Miles frowns, and I roll my eyes.

"Look at me." I spread my arms out to both sides, letting Miles take in the insanity of what I'm wearing. "Is this what girls usually wear to seduce princes in Scotland? I mean, I know it's cold here, and maybe after years of an all-boys school those of you who are straight aren't all that picky, so I guess it's *possible* forty-seven layers of pajamas are a real turn-on."

By now, Miles has pulled himself up so straight and tall that I think he might actually be creaking. His arms are down at his sides, chin lifted, and I don't know if they teach this type of arrogance at whatever fancy school he goes to with Seb, but if they do, he's clearly aced his How to Be a Total Dick class.

"Honestly, I was giving you points for originality," he says, one corner of his mouth quirking in a near smirk. He nods at my plaid pants. "And for staying on theme."

I snort. "Are you this paranoid about every girl who comes into Seb's orbit?" I ask. And then something occurs to me.

Dropping my arms and my attitude, I lean closer to him. "Wait . . . are you into Seb?"

That actually seems to surprise some of the permafrost right off him, because Miles blinks and takes a step back, looking—for just a second—like an actual teenage boy and not someone about to order a beheading.

"Into . . . no." He shakes his head, and ah, there it is, the crusty layer reforming itself.

"No," he repeats, pushing his shoulders back a little. "I'm not *jealous*. I just don't want to see Seb dragged into your particular scheme."

Parting my lips, I shake my head, totally confused. "I have no idea—" I start, and then I remember what Seb said in my room.

About Michael.

About that stupid interview.

"Ohhhhh my god," I say, putting my hands on either side of my head. "You give *me* crap for knowing gossip, but you guys are, like, drooling over TMZ?"

He has the grace to look just a little bit chagrined, but he lifts his chin and goes for haughty again.

"You're hardly the first girl to throw over one boy and set her cap for Seb," he says, and I would absolutely mock him for saying something like "set her cap," but he's still going. "And that's the last thing he needs right now."

"Why?" I ask. "I mean, trust me, I'm not interested in Seb no matter what the internet told you, but why would me and Seb be such a disastrous thing?"

When he doesn't answer, I press a hand to my chest, gasping with faux shock. "Is it because I'm . . . American?"

Miles scowls.

"Or wait, it's because I don't have a nickname, isn't it?" I give an exaggerated frown. "Maybe one day, I, too, can have a bevy of stupid things people call me instead of my own name, *Monters*, but alas, I am nickname deficient." Sighing, I let my shoulders rise and fall, and now Miles rolls his eyes at *me*.

"Just stay away from him," he says, and honestly, I'd take Spiffy and Dons and their stupid kilts and dancing over this jerk any day.

"Maybe tell *him* to stay away from *me*. And I'll find my way back to my room on my own," I reply before marching down the hallway in what I think is the general direction of my room.

He doesn't follow, thank goodness, and as I stomp past hall tables and portraits and one truly enormous clock, I try to get my temper under control. But seriously, who does that guy think he is? He doesn't even *know* me, but one stupid interview with my stupid ex-boyfriend has him convinced I'm scheming to land a prince for myself. Which . . . no thank you. Ellie can do all the ribbon cutting she wants, I'm gonna take a hard pass on the royal life.

And seriously, if he's been Seb's friend for so long, doesn't he *know* his friend is a disaster of a human? Why not talk to *him*?

Unless that's treason?

Maybe that's treason.

My feet touch a stone floor, cold even through my socks, and I stop, suddenly looking around me. I'm in another hallway, this one lined with . . . I don't remember seeing this part of the castle before.

I turn around, looking behind me, trying to remember if I'd made a turn anywhere while I'd been busy arguing with Miles Montgomery in my mind, but no, apparently I was too angry to notice my surroundings.

Aaaaand I'm lost.

Like. Really lost.

Which is stupid because this is a house, not the freaking Amazon rain forest, but it's a really *big* house, and it's filled with more hallways and rooms than I'd accounted for.

Okay. We didn't take any stairs going from my room to Seb's, so maybe I'm at least on the right floor? Unless the hallways slope and I didn't notice.

Ugh.

I tuck the blanket a little more tightly around me and start heading back the way I came. I'm not someone who's easily spooked, but this is all just a liiiiiitttttle too Gothic for me, swanning around the dark halls of a castle at night. Plus, I'd also dealt with having a charming scoundrel in my room, *and* a fight with a stuck-up snob.

Not even a full two days into my trip, and I was already going full Jane Austen.

There's a lamp on one of the nearby hall tables, and I walk over to it, deciding that some light might help me get my bearings. As I flip it on, something behind the painting hanging above the lamp catches my eye.

It's . . . the hilt of a knife?

Maybe you can resist pulling out what appears to be a dagger from a little leather holster hidden behind a painting, but I'm not that strong.

The metal is cold when I draw out the knife, and sure enough, it's a short, sharp dagger, just . . . strapped to the wall. Are castles more dangerous than I thought? Gotta arm yourself just to walk down a corridor?

"It's for the painting."

I whirl around, the little knife still in my hand. It's Miles, of course, standing in the doorway with his hands clasped behind his back.

I look back at the blade. "The painting needs a dagger?" I ask. "Why? In case it gets in street fights with the other art?"

To my surprise, Miles actually cracks a smile. Okay, it's not so much a smile as a tiny lifting of one corner of his mouth, but given that I've barely seen anything from him other than contempt and disdain, it's close enough.

"In case there's a fire," he says, walking a little farther into the room, "someone can slash the painting out of the frame quickly and carry it to safety."

I get that, but it also strikes me as really stupid. If there's a fire, who cares about art? Even really fancy art.

"Rich people are weird," I say, and that little baby smile Miles was working on dies immediately.

"It's priceless art," he tells me, and I put the knife back into its holster. It makes a little *schick* noise in the quiet corridor.

"I happen to think my life is kind of priceless, but whatever."

We face each other, and after a moment, Miles takes a deep breath.

"I'm sorry," he says, even though the words come out like someone is holding a gun—or a tiny dagger—to his head. "I shouldn't have implied anything about you and Seb. He's . . . it's just been a long night."

I notice he doesn't apologize for his general jerkitude before that, but then he tilts his head to the left and says, "I'll show you back to your room."

I don't want to spend any more time with him, but I'm glad he doesn't bother to mention how obviously lost I got in the five minutes I was away from him, so I just nod and follow him.

It doesn't take nearly as long to get back as I'd thought it would, which means I definitely took a wrong turn or twelve, and as we walk down my hallway, I say, "Okay, seriously, how does anyone find their way around this place?"

Miles shrugs. "A lot of people don't. Sherbet says that in the thirties, his great-grandparents used to give every guest a silver bowl full of a different color of confetti. That way, you could leave a trail back to your room."

I stop in the hallway, scuffing my foot over the carpet. "You're making that up."

But Miles shakes his head. "God's truth," he swears. "'Course Sherbet says it was more so that people could find their way to each other's rooms."

"Aren't you afraid you're just giving me hints?" I ask him, then wiggle my fingers. "Might spend all night cutting special confetti to lure Seb into my womanly clutches."

His lips thin, a thing I've already seen him do a couple of times when he's annoyed. Maybe if I annoy him enough, he'll do it so much that he won't even have a mouth. That would probably improve his general personality.

I go to open the door, and as I do, Miles leans in a little. "I really am sorry for thinking the worst earlier, but . . . it occurs to me that you might need a guide," he says. "Someone to show you the ropes. Make sure you don't get in over your head."

Staring at him, I tilt my head to one side, pretending to think it over. "Hmmmm," I hum. "Hard pass."

And when he glowers at me, I take great pleasure in shutting the door in his face.

AN REIS

The official start of the Scottish season, An Reis is the annual horse race held along the southern border. The words mean simply "the Race," and it's said the tradition began during the "rough wooing," when Henry VIII harried the lowland Scots in the hopes of taking young Mary, Queen of Scots, for his son's bride. What was once a test of horsemanship is now, like Ascot farther south, more a social event these days, and attendants of An Reis are just as serious about their headgear as their southern neighbors. A favorite of the younger set of Stuarts, this year's An Reis should also prove an excellent opportunity for Royal Watchers to observe Prince Alexander with his new fiancée, the American Eleanor Winters. Rumour also has it that Eleanor's younger sister, Daisy, will be accompanying them this year, providing the Florida high schooler with her first taste of the life her sister is stepping into this winter.

(*Prattle*, "Och Aye, We've Got the Scoop on the Best Events of the Scottish Social Season!" *April Issue*)

Chapter 13

"I AM NOT WEARING THAT."

I'm in Ellie's room at Sherbourne Castle, the early morning sunlight spilling in through lace curtains. It had surprised me that Ellie and Alex weren't sharing a room, but I didn't like to think about that part of their relationship, so I hadn't said anything. There are certain things about her sister a girl should maybe not know.

Ellie looks like summer come to life, standing in a pale pink dress and cream-and-rose heels, her blond hair shiny and smooth underneath a hat that matches her shoes, a little pink netting covering her eyes, a riot of flowers at the crown. It's a silly hat, don't get me wrong, but it looks right on her. She's doing that Ellie Thing where everything that touches her manages to get an extra sheen of class.

I don't possess that particular talent, which is why the green monstrosity currently spreading its tentacles on the bed is not going to look nearly as fetching on my head.

Ellie places her hands on her slim hips, that massive emerald-and-diamond ring nearly blinding me as it catches the light. *This is not your big sister,* that ring seems to remind me, *this is a future queen, which means she's going to make you wear that ugly hat.*

Sure enough, the corners of Ellie's mouth turn down. "It's tradition," she says. "The big silly hats. Haven't you seen *My Fair Lady?*"

"I have," I tell her, moving over to the bed to poke at the thing she calls a "hat" but I think might actually be a papier-mâché rendering of the Loch Ness monster. "She wore a pretty hat," I remind Ellie. "Much like *you* are wearing a pretty hat. This"—I flick the furled brim of the hat—"is not a pretty hat. In fact, it's not a hat at all. I think someone just threw some velvet and tulle together, and dyed everything lake-monster green."

"That hat is a one-of-a-kind piece," Ellie informs me. "Made especially for you by Lady Alice Crenshaw, who is not only my friend but whose family has been making chapeaux for the royal family for *centuries*, Daisy."

"Okay, I was going to listen to you about this, but then you said 'chapeaux,' and my brain shut down with how pretentious that was."

Ellie closes her eyes for a second. In another life, she would have already started yelling. The lake monster comment would've done it. But that was a different Ellie, one who didn't feel watched every second of her life.

That thought makes me feel a little ashamed of the fit I'm throwing over something as silly as a hat, a feeling that only gets stronger when Ellie walks over to the bed, picking up the hat and studying it with critical eyes. "I told Alice you had reddish hair now, so she picked out this color especially for you."

With that, she crosses over to plop the hat on my head. For something that appears to mostly be made of fluff and feathers, it's surprisingly heavy. Ellie tugs at the netting, trying to perk up some of the feathers, frowning. "It would look better if you weren't scowling, Daisy," she finally says, and I step away from her, making shooing motions with my hands.

"It's hard not to make a face when you're wearing something like this," I remind her, but when I go to look in the mirror, I can admit that hat isn't *too* . . . all right—it's still really, really bad—but it does look a little like the stuff those girls wear in the blogs Isabel showed me. At least I fit in. And it matches my dress.

That had been waiting for me in a garment bag when I'd gotten up this morning, and I'd cringed as I'd pulled down the zipper, sure I was going to see something completely boring with a high neck and long sleeves and no personality at all.

But the dress is actually really pretty. It's green, like my hat, with cap sleeves, a nipped-in waist, and a fuller skirt, almost like something out of the fifties. The little white gloves that go with it just add to the effect, and it's just different enough not to be boring.

Maybe Glynnis has better taste than I thought.

The cars are coming to get all of us in less than an hour now, taking us the thirty minutes or so south to the racing grounds. Apparently, this particular horse race is super fancy and, according to Glynnis, "a vital part of the social calendar for the summer."

The most vital thing I'd had on *my* social calendar this

summer had been Key West, finishing up my summer reading for school, and maybe visiting the new pool they'd built at the Hibiscus Club, the sort of cut-rate country club we belonged to in Perdido.

Instead, I'm wearing a Disney Villain hat and about to go watch a bunch of horses.

With a bunch of cute guys.

I'd seen a few of the "Royal Wreckers" this morning at breakfast. Sherbet, of course, then the two guys whose actual names I couldn't remember. Spiffy and Dons were their nicknames, but I dare you to say the name "Spiffy" out loud with a straight face. So I hadn't talked much to any of them, and I hadn't seen Miles or Seb, either.

Remembering last night makes my stomach give a little nervous twist, and I glance over at Ellie. She's staring in the mirror, fidgeting with her own hat, and while I really don't want to get into the whole Seb thing, it suddenly occurs to me that he might mention it today, and that it would be way worse if El hears it from him first.

"Soooo," I start, and Ellie immediately spins away from the mirror, blue eyes wide.

"Oh god, what happened?" she asks, and I hold up both hands.

"How did you know I was going to tell you that something happened? Maybe I was just about to lead into how pretty that shade of pink looks on you. Because it does, by the way, look really nice with your skin tone, and—"

Now it's Ellie's turn to hold up her hands. "Daisy . . ." she says. "No. I have been your sister for your entire life, and whenever you start with the 'soooo' thing, it's usually followed by 'I did something catastrophic.'"

Okay, that's just offensive, both that she knows my tells while hers are getting harder and harder to read, and that she thinks I do catastrophic things. Catastrophic things *happen* to me, but it's not like I'm the cause. Last night was totally a case in point.

"Technically, the catastrophe was Seb's," I say now, and that pretty pink blush Ellie had been rocking thanks to her outfit drains right out of her face.

"Seb," she repeats flatly, and I launch into the sordid tale of "Seb Drunk in My Bedroom," hoping if I tell it quickly enough and with enough of a blasé attitude, she won't freak out.

"Anyway," I sum up, "then that Henry Higgins guy showed up and got him, and my brush with debauched royalty was over."

Ellie's perfect brow creases. "Henry Higgins?"

Sighing, I lean against the bedpost, crossing one foot in front of the other. "Honestly, El, we were *just* talking about *My Fair Lady*. That snooty dude. Miles."

I don't get into the part where he implied I was trying to trap Seb with my wily American girly parts and how I called him a snob before getting lost and learning about knife paintings. Or painting knives? And the whole confetti bowl thing. Does El know about confetti bowls? I'm just about to ask her when she shakes her head, sighing.

"Talk about baptism by fire," she says, and I nod.

"I can see the tabloids now. Pics of Seb on my floor, me in all my pajamas, headlines like 'Sleeping Beauty' . . ."

El makes a noise that would be a snort if soon-to-be princesses did that sort of thing. Then she frowns, tilting her head at me. "*All* of your pajamas?"

Laughing, I shake my head. "You don't want to know."

There's a discreet knock at the door—Glynnis, letting us know it's time to head downstairs—and after giving myself a last look in the mirror, I tug at my tentacles and start following Ellie out of the room.

But before we open the door, she turns to me, one gloved hand resting on my arm. "You're going to be fine," she tells me, and then she delivers it: the patented Ellie Winters, soon to be Her Royal Highness, the Duchess of Rothesay Smile.

In other words, the fakest smile known to man.

And suddenly, I'm thinking that wearing a monster on my head might not be my biggest problem today.

Chapter 14

THE RACETRACK ISN'T FAR FROM SHERBOURNE CASTLE, so I haven't managed to get over my severe case of tummy butterflies by the time we arrive.

"You know," I say to El as we get out of the car, "I don't even like horses that much. What if they sense that and feel disrespected?"

Ellie stops, turning to look at me. There are two men in dark suits on either side of us, not David and Malcolm, the bodyguards I'm used to, but they have that same air of being more statues than people. They're certainly working hard at both staying close to me and Ellie and ignoring everything we're saying.

Impressive.

"It's just a race," she says, and I can see the reflection of my stupid hat in her expensive sunglasses. "And there are enough people here that we shouldn't steal the focus."

"From the horses or the other people here?" I ask, and Ellie grimaces.

"Daisy—"

"Is this the part where you tell me just to relax and be myself?"

Turning to me, Ellie fidgets with the lace on her hat. "Relax, yes," she says. "Definitely don't be yourself, though. Just . . ." She steps closer, laying one gloved hand on my arm. "I'm serious, Daisy. I know you come by that ability to say whatever comes into your head naturally, but remember you're *not* Dad."

I want to scoff at that, but she has a point.

A point she's going to keep making, apparently. "Just smile, be polite, and don't try to make jokes, okay?"

She gives my arm a squeeze, and as she turns to walk away, I fight the urge to call after her, "Thanks for the pep talk!"

Instead, I just follow, my knees shaky and my face kind of numb. This is the first time I'll really be *out* among these people, and it's like I'm seeing every tabloid cover, every headline that's featured Ellie over the past year, and suddenly imagining *my* face, *my* name in them. The few brushes with that life I've had have been *more* than enough.

But Ellie is right—as we make our way from the car to the actual track, there's no deluge of photographers or people shouting Ellie's name. There's just . . . a lot of posh people.

And I mean *a lot.*

This may still be the most horrible hat in all of creation, but at least I blend in. I've never seen such an assortment of headgear. There's one girl wearing a concoction of blue, red, and green feathers on her head that makes me wonder if a parrot crash-landed in her hair. I turn and see another girl with long dark hair and a truly gorgeous black-and-white suit rocking a pink hat with so many frills and furls that it looks like something out of an anatomy textbook.

The hats are honestly so ridiculous and over the top that I wonder if this is just another part of the fancy life. Do they wear stuff like this just to prove they can get away with it? Is this hazing via hats?

The girl in black and white with the slightly obscene hat approaches us, her shoulders stiff. Next to her is a redhead all in light purple, her hat small and actually hat-like. "Ellie!" the redhead says. There's a glass of champagne in her hand, and some of it sloshes out as she hugs my sister.

The dark-haired girl is a little more reserved, her smile tight as she looks at me and my sister.

"Daisy," Ellie says, pulling back from the hug, "I'd like you to meet Fliss and Poppy."

I refrain from saying "Fliss" doesn't seem like a real name and smile at both the girls, wondering if I'm supposed to shake their hands or curtsy. In the end, I just give a little wave. "Hi."

"Are you enjoying your stay?" the redhead—Fliss—asks, and I give my best Ellie Smile.

"I am. It's really lovely here."

That part is sincere, at least. Everything I've seen of Scotland has been gorgeous, and this place is no exception. Rolling hills, green grass, blue sky . . . it's a postcard of a day, made even prettier by all the ladies wandering around in bright colors.

"I'm sure Ellie is thrilled to have you," Fliss replies, smiling. Poppy, the brunette, is watching me with a weird, almost-hostile look on her face, and I wonder what *that's* all about.

Once the girls have drifted off, Ellie tugs me toward the

stands and leans in to say in a low voice, "Lady Felicity and Lady Poppy Haddon-Smythe. Sisters. Fliss is wonderful, Poppy is . . . less so. She dated Seb last year, and it was all a bit messy."

Ah, that explains it. If Seb assumed he and I were meant to be (or at least meant to bone), maybe Poppy did, too.

We make our way toward the royal box, flanked by the guards, and while most heads turn our way, there's not the crush I was expecting. But maybe that's because everyone here is fancy, so that would be tacky.

We've just reached the steps that will take us up to where we're supposed to sit when I hear someone call my name.

Glynnis is approaching, dressed in bright red except for her hat, which is stark white. It's a pretty contrast that weirdly doesn't make her look like a candy cane, so extra points to Glynnis. That can't be easy to pull off.

I wave, and then see Miles just behind her wearing the saddest gray suit I have ever seen in my life. I mean, I get that I'm wearing an actual sea creature on my head, and therefore have zero leg to stand on, but his jacket has *tails*, and there's a cream-and-violet-striped tie at his throat, and it's all just so . . . tragic. I'd feel sorry for him if he hadn't been such a jackass last night.

"Your first big event!" Glynnis says happily, her teeth practically winking in the sun. "Are you excited?"

"Super pumped," I reply, giving her a thumbs-up, and behind her back, Miles rolls his eyes, muttering something to himself.

What a fun outing this is going to be.

"Excellent," Glynnis says, then steps back, sweeping an arm out. "In that case, I'm going to steal Ellie away, and I leave you in Miles's capable hands."

I really don't want to be in Miles's anything, much less his hands. "Wait, what?" I ask, but Ellie doesn't even look, and Glynnis is already striding off. I watch the bobbing of the ribbon on her hat before turning back to Miles.

"Why am I in your hands?" I ask, and he looks just as horrified by that image as I feel.

"You're not," he tells me. "Glynnis just wanted to make sure you had someone around to prevent you from embarrassing yourself, and somehow, I was blessed enough to be chosen."

"So I'm *not* going to be able to get up on the fence and sing 'Yankee Doodle Dandy' while waving six American flags and twirling a baton?" I snap my fingers. "Well, there's today's plans ruined."

Miles looks at me like he's wondering what sins he committed in a past life that have led him to this moment, and I decide today might actually be kind of fun after all.

"Would you like something to drink?" he finally asks, his tone frosty.

I brush a green tentacle from my face before responding. "Are you seriously going to hang out with me all day?" I ask. "And, like, teach me about horses and fetch me punch? Because you really don't need to do that."

"Sadly, I really do," he replies, turning to look at me. He's holding a top hat in his hands, and I nod at it.

"Why aren't you wearing that? Is a silly hat just a bridge too far with that outfit?"

His green eyes go from my face to the top of my head, and he raises his eyebrows.

Sighing, I touch the monstrosity currently masquerading as

a hat. "Touché, fair point, all that," I concede, and Miles does that thing again where it looks like he might smile, but then he thinks better of it. He might actually be physically incapable of smiling.

I look around me, shading my eyes with my hand. There still aren't any horses on the track, but I think this event is about showing off fancy hats and drinking champagne more than it's about horse racing. I'm about to ask Miles about the horses—mostly which ones have the silliest names—when I catch sight of that girl glaring at me again. Poppy.

Dropping my hand, I scooch a little closer to Miles, and he follows my gaze.

"Ah. I see you've met Poppy."

"Oh yeah," I reply, picking a piece of lint off my skirt. "She is _not_ a fan."

"She's not a fan of anyone save Seb and the words 'Princess Poppy,'" Miles retorts, and I look up at him again. See, _this_ is the kind of info I need.

"Remember how you thought I was an evil seductress out to ensnare your innocent friend?"

"I literally used none of those words," he says, and I wave him off.

"Gist is right, though. And my point is, do other people think that, too? That I'm after Seb?"

Miles looks down at me. He's not that much taller than I am, especially since I'm in heels, but he's mastered looking down his nose at people, I think. "Most girls are," he says at last, and I wrinkle my nose.

"He's going to be my brother-in-law," I say. "I get that you people are into marrying your cousins and stuff, but that doesn't really work for me."

"I'd hoped to wait until at least week three of our acquaintance to start talking about incest," Miles says in a low voice, still twisting his hat in his hands, and I narrow my eyes at him.

"Are you being funny?" I ask. "Because that was kind of funny, and I don't like it."

Miles snorts, then offers me his elbow. "I can take you up to the box if you want," he says, and I follow his nod to the top of the stands, where my sister is already sitting next to Alex, looking out at the track through little binoculars. Fliss is there, too, but Poppy has vanished back into the sea of hats and champagne flutes, and I can see Seb sitting on Ellie's other side, scanning the crowd through expensive sunglasses. The other Royal Wreckers are up there, too, and Sherbet waves to me and Miles, his handsome face split with a broad grin.

We both wave back, but then Sherbet turns to talk to another man in the box, a man wearing a bright-red-and-green kilt, a sash decorated with all kinds of medals draped across his barrel chest.

"Who's that?" I ask, and Miles glances back toward the box.

"The Duke of Argyll," he says. "The queen's brother, Seb's uncle."

"Oh," I say weakly. So technically a family member. Or a soon-to-be one. And once again, I totally forget how you're supposed to greet a duke. *Your Grace*, I think? Or is that for the queen?

"Shall we go up?" Miles asks again, and I watch as Ellie bobs a quick curtsy to a blond woman in pale blue. Who is that?

114

Clearly someone important, but no one I recognize. I *really* should've read that stupid folder.

"I don't know if I'm ready for that," I say to Miles, looking at the royal box, all draped with bunting and filled with the fanciest of the fancy people here. I'd really rejected the idea of needing a guide through this world, but suddenly milling around with Miles—a guy I don't even like—is preferable to taking my chances up there.

"You mentioned drinks," I say to him now, tilting my hat back as it starts to slide, and when Miles offers me his elbow again, I place a hand there.

Better the devil you know, I guess.

Chapter 15

WE MAKE OUR WAY THROUGH THE SEA OF HATS,
and while I want to drop my hand from Miles's elbow, I actually
kind of need him for balance. My heels keep sinking into the
grass, and I have horrifying visions of me on the front page of
the paper, sprawled on the grass, skirt up over my head.

Holding on to Not-Hot Mr. Darcy isn't as bad as *that*.

"So," Miles says as we make our way past a grouping of high
tables littered with crystal champagne flutes, "this is An Reis.
That's Gaelic for 'the Race,' which is not exactly the most orig-
inal of names, but—"

I stop, looking up at him from underneath the tentacles.
"Dude."

He glances down at me and pulls his arm back. "What?"

Some kind of trumpet-y fanfare is starting up in the distance,
and I glance toward the royal box to see my sister and Alex waving as the crowd claps politely. At the high tables, I see a few
women smirking behind gloved hands, their eyes darting up at
Ellie, and I frown.

"I don't need to know about the race," I tell Miles now. "I'm sure it's fascinating and historically thrilling, but that kind of information is not exactly useful. However . . ." I nod at the women who are now moving away from the table, taking some satisfaction in the way they wobble on their heels in the damp grass, too. "Knowing why people are smirking at my sister? That would be helpful."

Miles sighs and, to my surprise, reaches up to loosen his tie. "Let's go get something to drink," he says.

He leads me to a yellow-and-white-striped tent and with a "wait here" ducks inside, leaving me to stand awkwardly beside the entrance. I should've brought my phone so that I could at least pretend to text someone, but instead I'm stuck with a fake smile on my face, trying not to notice that people are looking at me.

One woman in particular is *really* looking at me. Glaring, almost. She's older, probably in her fifties, but she's definitely been nipped and tucked here and there, her face seeming just a little tighter than faces should. She's thin and reedy, dressed all in black except for a massive burst of yellow feathers on her head, and to my shock, she comes to stand right in front of me.

"So," she says, her mouth curling around the word, "you're the latest American invader? How unfortunate."

I'd thought Miles was snobby, but this woman is next level. She looks at me like I'm something unpleasant she just stepped in, and I know that I should let it go, that I should smile politely and murmur something bland.

But I'm not Liam Winters's daughter for nothing.

"Yup!" I say brightly. "Here to throw your tea in the harbor and marry up all your princes."

Her lips purse even tighter, and I think she'd narrow her eyes at me if her face could actually move from the nose up. "Charming," she says in a way that lets me know she finds me anything but. "And here I thought your sister was the worst embarrassment to happen to the Baird family in quite some time."

My temper flames higher. I can admit that I'm not cut out for this thing, but Ellie? Ellie has been nothing but perfect as far as I can tell, and I'm not letting this slide.

"Your hat is lovely," I tell the woman, giving her my sweetest smile. "I'm sure Big Bird's sacrifice was worth it."

I hear the soft murmuring of voices around us. A couple of gasps, some smothered chuckles, and a bunch of whispering. For the first time, I remember there are a lot of people around, and I mentally kick myself. This is clearly why I can't be trusted around fancy types, because I have never been able to hold my tongue.

Just like Ellie said.

The woman just lifts her chin a fraction of an inch higher and swans off, practically leaving a trail of ice crystals in her wake.

"Here you go."

Miles has returned, a drink in each hand. They're filled to the brim with iced tea, pieces of fruit, and, I think, even cucumber jumbled up with the ice. He's scanning the crowd, a little crease between his brows. "Did something happen while I was gone?"

"Someone was rude to me, so I caused an international incident," I reply before taking the sweating glass from him gratefully.

And then I promptly choke.

Whatever is in the glass, it is *not* iced tea. It's sweet and bitter all at once with some kind of medicinal flavor happening. It's not that strong, whatever it is, but for someone who's only ever had half a lukewarm beer, it's way too much, and my eyes water as Miles looks at me, his eyes wide.

"What," I manage to gasp out, thrusting the glass back at him, "is *that?*"

He takes the glass, nearly dropping both drinks in his haste, and now people are definitely watching us, probably because I look like I'm dying.

"Pimm's Cup," he tells me, and I wave my hands, indicating that he needs to keep going with that explanation.

When he just continues to stare at me blankly, I roll my eyes and say, "I have no idea what that is."

You would think I just told him I'd never seen a dog or the color red or something. He seems *that* incredulous. "It's a drink. Popular here in the summer, always at the races or regattas."

I can breathe again now, and I dab at my watery eyes with one gloved finger, hoping I haven't smeared my mascara beyond repair. "And what's in it?"

"A lot of things."

I look up at Miles, waiting, and he clears his throat. "Mostly gin."

"Lovely."

We stand there for a moment, and then Miles takes both glasses back into the tent. When he comes out again, this time he's holding a goblet filled with ice and sparkling water. "Better?" he asks, handing it to me, and I nod.

"Thanks."

For a second, there's an awkward silence, and finally I clear my throat, turning the sweaty glass of water in my hands. "Now that we've gotten my attempted poisoning out of the way, spill the tea."

Miles is still watching me with a slight frown, hair curling over his forehead, hands shoved in his pockets. "Spill . . . tea . . . ," he says slowly, and I roll my eyes.

"Tell me why everyone is all sneery. I thought people here loved El."

Understanding dawns on Miles's face, and he rocks back on his heels a little. "Ah. Well." He glances around us, and I notice the top hat he was holding seems to have disappeared. I hope it's gone for good, because honestly, no one should be forced to wear that thing. "Let's walk a bit, shall we?" he says, offering me his elbow again. I take it, and he leads me away from all the people, nearly to the fences lining the racetrack.

A cloud moves over the sun briefly, the light shifting, and Miles puts one shiny shoe up on the lower rail of the fence. "I'm trying to think of a way of saying this without sounding like a ponce," he finally says, and I cut him a look from the corner of my eye.

"Point taken, too late for that," he mutters, then looks up at the sky for a second before saying, "Regular people love your sister. Think she's down-to-earth, kind, smart . . ."

"She *is* all those things," I say, folding my arms on top of the fence, glass dangling from one hand, and Miles nods. "Right. But these people"—he tilts his head, gesturing to the crowd behind us—"would rather see one of their own as the future queen."

"Would you?" I ask, lifting my drink to take another sip, and he turns his head, surprised. When he's not looking down his nose at everything, it's easier to remember he's kind of cute, or at least aesthetically appealing, what with the good bone structure and pretty eyes.

"I *like* Ellie," he says, which I notice isn't really an answer, but I let it go for now, turning my attention back to the track in front of us.

"So how did you end up a Royal Wrecker?" I ask. "Because, honestly, you don't seem all that wreckish."

"Is that a compliment?" he asks, and I shrug.

Taking a deep breath, Miles rests his arms on the top fence rail as well. "I met Seb at school. Gregorstoun."

"That scary boarding school up north where Alex went. Ellie's mentioned it. Isn't it all up at six a.m. and freezing showers and gruel?"

Miles grimaces just a little, reaching up to push his hair back. "That's the place. Scottish princes have gone there since the 1800s. And," he adds, giving the lower fence rail a kick with the tip of his shoe, "the Montgomery sons as well."

When I just raise my eyebrows, waiting for Miles to go on, he says, "We're like Sherbet. Courtiers, really. Titled, usually a big house or three somewhere in the family, some of us rich, some of us skint. And we all have families that have been tangled up with the royal family for generations. Sherbet's dad? Nearly married Alex and Seb's mum. Her parents ended up sending her off to Paris to get her away from him, in the hopes that she'd fall for someone more suitable to be a prince consort. Which she did. Not sure Sherbet's dad's ever gotten over it. He was looking forward to that crown."

I wrinkle my nose. "So what, he was more upset about not getting to be a prince than he was about not marrying the woman he loved?"

It's Mile's turn to snort. "Not sure if he did love her, to be honest. Love is never a big part of royal matches."

The silence that falls between us is definitely of the awkward variety, and Miles frowns, puzzled, until he suddenly remembers who he's talking to, I guess.

"Not anymore, though, of course. Alex is absolutely mad about Eleanor; anyone can see that."

They can, actually, so I don't think he's just trying to kiss up, but still, it's another reminder that this world Ellie is stepping into is completely different from anything we know. What kind of family doesn't have their first real marriage for love until the twenty-first century?

Clearing his throat, Miles moves back from the fence. "So," he says, "was that the sort of 'tea' you were hoping for?"

"It was lukewarm at best, but better than learning about the history of horse racing," I reply, and there it is again, that little moment when I think Miles might actually smile.

But he doesn't. Instead, he nods toward the royal box. "The race is about to start. We should head up."

I know I can't put it off any longer, so I nod, too, but I don't take his arm this time, just trail behind him as we reach the stands. I can feel eyes on me the whole way, but I try to pretend I'm Ellie, sailing through it all without a care.

There are only a few steps up to the box, and I use them to take deep breaths, preparing myself to be the picture of respectability.

And come face-to-face with Big Bird Head herself, standing right by Alex and Ellie, both of whom are wearing the expressions I've only seen in pictures where they're visiting hospitals and cemeteries.

Oh no.

Oh *nononononono*.

Ellie turns. "Daisy," she says, giving me a tight smile. "May I present you to the Duchess of Argyll?" Her smile hardens. "Alex's aunt."

Chapter 16

"TO BE FAIR, HER HAT DID LOOK LIKE BIG BIRD'S ARSE."

I snatch the paper back from Dad, swatting it with him as I do. We're all in a parlor at Holyroodhouse, the Baird family palace in Edinburgh. We've been given our own suite of rooms, complete with two other parlors and three bedrooms, although we're only using two of them. Ellie is still staying in her apartment in the city, but no more hotel for us. We're being officially wedged into royal life.

Or we will be if all the headlines don't lead to my banishment.

I know yesterday was a disaster, and while I apologized profusely to the Duchess of Argyll, there was no doubt that I'd been a major screwup. I'd spent last night reading the file Glynnis had made me, hoping that in the future, if I decided to run my mouth, I wouldn't end up insulting one of Ellie's future relatives.

Dad picks up another paper and turns it to face me. There, on the front page, is a huge picture from the race, blurry but brightly colored, my green hat and red hair especially standing out, as does the duchess's yellow feathered hat. "FOR THE

BIRDS!" the headline blares, then right under that, "ELLIE'S LITTLE SIS GIVES THE DISDAINFUL DUCHESS WHAT FOR!"

I glance over at Ellie, who leans forward from her spot next to me on the sofa, blond hair falling over her shoulders. I haven't mentioned to El that I only said what I said defending *her*, mostly because I don't want her to know that Alex's aunt doesn't like her. I mean, she probably already knows, but if she doesn't, I don't want to be the one to tell her.

"Glynnis is going to die," she mutters, and I feel my face heat up as I study the photograph. You can't really read the expression on my face due to the low-quality shot, but I'm standing there with my hand on my hip, something I don't even remember doing, and the duchess is so ramrod straight, she looks like she might snap in half.

Dad turns the paper back to face him, snapping the pages. "Glynnis should be thrilled," he tells Ellie. "This article is practically fawning all over Daisy."

"What?" Ellie and I ask at the same time.

"No one's ever liked Argie," Seb says from his spot near the window. He'd been the one to show us to our rooms when we came into the palace today, which had surprised me. I was even more surprised that he was just . . . hanging out here, drinking tea, but he hadn't shown any signs of leaving.

"Argie?" I repeat, then work out that that's a nickname for the duchess. Probably not one anyone uses to her face.

"She's the worst kind of snob," Seb continues, stirring his tea. "Daisy giving her a right bollocking probably did her some good."

"I didn't . . . I don't even know what that means," I say, leaning back against the sofa. Everything in this room is done in shades of rose and gold, and I think every pillow, every lampshade, every drape has been weighted down with tassels. Outside the windows, the afternoon has gone dark and rainy.

Seb looks up from his tea and grins at me, a dimple flashing in his cheek. "It means you told her off. And there's nothing the Scots love more than a mouthy lass."

I wrinkle my nose, looking at the stack of papers in my dad's lap.

How does Ellie stand it, that constant itch at the back of her brain that tells her people are talking about her, people are *always* talking about her, and that both the best and worst things she could ever hear about herself are just a few clicks away? How does that not make anyone insane?

There's a brisk knock at the door to the sitting room, but before any of us can say anything, Glynnis is striding in. I've begun to realize she doesn't ever walk anywhere. It's all striding, marching, trooping . . . she was probably a heck of a general in a past life.

"Just the girl I was looking for!" she says brightly, but her eyes are laser-focused on me, and I swallow hard.

"Hi, Glynnis," I say, waggling my fingers.

Her smile doesn't drop as she addresses the entire room. "So, bit of a rocky start, but we're here now, and I think course correction should be easy enough."

Course correction doesn't exactly sound great, but I guess it's better than what I'd been expecting, which was something like, "Some time in the dungeons will do *wonders* for Daisy's attitude!"

"If I could just steal Daisy for a wee bit . . ." Glynnis continues, holding her thumb and forefinger apart.

"Sure," I say, but it comes out like a squeak, and to my surprise, El gets to her feet, too.

"Mind if I come with?" she asks, and I shoot her a look of gratitude. I don't *really* think Glynnis is going to imprison and/or eat me, but having Ellie along for whatever is about to happen seems nice.

"Bring them back in one piece!" Dad calls cheerfully, opening another paper with my face on the front. Then he frowns, thinking. "Well, two pieces. Their two separate bodies, that is." He waves a hand. "You know what I mean."

"Of course," Glynnis says through a tight smile, and I have to roll my lips inward not to giggle.

Ellie doesn't look nearly as amused, sighing a bit as she steps closer to me, and the two of us follow Glynnis out of the room.

"Are we going to the—" I whisper, but Ellie cuts me off with one lifted hand.

"Hush."

"You don't even know what I was going ask."

We're going down some stairs now, big, wide stone ones with shallow grooves in the center from hundreds of years' worth of feet.

"You were going to make a joke about dungeons or drawing and quartering. Something weird. Something Dad would say."

"Both offensive and also kind of true," I concede.

We pass under several portraits of Alex's ancestors and finally come to a set of double doors carved with unicorns.

One of my favorite things about Scotland so far is that the unicorn is their national animal. You really can't hate a country where that's the case.

The doors open up into a well-lit room that's a lot more spartan than the other rooms I've seen in the castle so far. There aren't little knickknacks resting on every available surface, and there's only one sofa and two chairs as opposed to a whole showroom floor's worth of furniture.

One wall is completely lined with mirrors, and I catch a glimpse of myself, my hair very bright in this room that's mostly gray and white.

And then I see the table against the window, clothes draped across it.

Skirts, sweaters, slacks, a few dresses that come kind of close to 1950s housewife . . .

"Oh my god," I murmur. "Makeover montage."

"What?" Ellie asks, walking over to the table.

But it's Glynnis I turn to. "Makeover montage, right? This is the part where you give me a bunch of conservative clothes, maybe fix my hair, some upbeat song plays, and at the end, I'm gonna look at myself in this mirror"—I walk to the back of the room, reaching out to touch the glass and widening my eyes, lips parting—"and I say something like, 'Is that . . . me?' And then everyone claps and tells me I look great, and I *do* look great, but deep inside, I'm afraid something within me has irrevocably changed."

I turn, and Glynnis and Ellie both stare at me.

"Have neither of you ever seen movies?" I ask, putting a hand on one hip.

"It's just new clothes, Daisy," Ellie finally says, and I roll my eyes, going to stand next to her.

"You're exactly zero fun," I tell her, my eyes scanning over the clothes lined up for me.

They're all . . . fine, really. Boring colors, mostly, definitely Ellie Wear, but nothing too terrible.

Ellie is flipping through a catalog Glynnis has left lying on the table, and she pauses on a page with several ballgowns on it. "Oooh," I say, pointing at one that seems to be a mix of tartan patterns, all purple and green and black. The skirt is wide and floofy, and a narrow green ribbon belt separates it from the purple strapless top, and I tap the page. "Can I get one of these?"

Glynnis looks over Ellie's shoulder and makes a tutting sound. "You may have an occasion to wear a ballgown, but that one is a bit . . . out there."

"I like out there," I say, but Ellie is already closing the book and handing me a gray cardigan.

"Go try this on," she says, nodding toward a screen set up in the corner, and I frown, taking the sweater from her.

"You're less than zero fun," I tell her.

"Something that *should* be fun is your friend Isabel's visit," Glynnis calls out as I step behind the screen and I poke my head out the side.

"Is that all set up? Isa coming, the Ash Bentley signing . . ."

Gathering up more clothes from the table, Glynnis nods. "She'll be here the day after tomorrow, just in time for the signing." Then she flashes that predatory smile at me.

"Won't it be nice to surprise her with your new look?"

Ah. I get it. This is the payment for getting an Isa visit—I princess up.

Well, sister-of-the-princess up.

As I slip the cardigan over my shoulders, scowling at the little pearl buttons, I wonder if even Isa is worth looking like my own grandmother.

Chapter 17

THE PALACE PUTS ISABEL UP AT THE BALMORAL, the same fancy hotel we'd stayed at when we came to Edinburgh. I was finally getting used to saying, "the palace" did this, "the palace" thinks that. Ellie said it so naturally, and so did Glynnis, that I could almost forget that "the palace" meant some weird cabal of people who made all the decisions for anyone even a little bit related to the royal family.

In any case, this was one time when I was really happy with the palace. The Balmoral was gorgeous, and I knew Isabel would love it, especially after I told her that J. K. Rowling finished the last Harry Potter book in one of the suites. That would send Isa into geek heaven.

I didn't get to see her when she'd gotten in the night before, but the next morning, I hop in the back of a black town car (another thing to get used to) and head straight for the hotel.

No one takes a second glance at me when I walk through the front doors, which is a relief. I'd thought after the race, my face might be getting a little more familiar, but then I remind myself that famous people stay at this hotel all the time.

I take the elevator—sorry, the *lift*—up to the sixth floor and walk down the hall to Isabel's room, my head already full of plans. It's not a huge walk from the hotel to the National Museum of Scotland, so we can do that first, see some art, look at weird Scottish knickknacks, maybe say hi to an ancestor or two of Alex's. From there, it's a short walk to Greyfriars Kirkyard, which is both beautiful and *super* creepy. Very much Isabel's bag. Lunch at Nando's, tea and some cake, and then we get to go see Ash Bentley speak and sign books at this amazing little bookshop on Victoria Street. The perfect Isa and Daisy day.

Stopping in front of room 634, I knock a funny little knock, three quick taps, two louder ones with my fist, and after a minute, the door opens just a little bit, Isabel's face appearing in the crack.

Her red, teary, kinda snotty face.

"What happened?" I cry.

Isa opens the door wider to let me in. The second I slip into the room, the door shuts behind me and Isabel's face crumples. "It's *Ben*," she says, spitting out her boyfriend's name like it's a bad word, and uh-oh.

Isabel and Ben have always been the nicest, most stable couple I know. I'd be lying if I said there weren't times I wished Ben wasn't in the picture, but that was only in moments when I was feeling a little lonely, and maybe a little envious. On the whole, he was a good guy, and it definitely wasn't like Isabel to cry over him.

"What about Ben?" I ask, taking her arms and steering her

toward the little sofa in the suite. She's wearing one of the white hotel bathrobes, her black hair still wet from the shower. A room service tray is untouched on the table, so I pick up the silver pot of coffee and pour her a cup, putting in plenty of sugar the way she likes. She takes it from me but doesn't drink, her gaze focused somewhere around her bright orange toenails.

"He sent me this email," she sniffles. "While I was flying across the freaking ocean, my *boyfriend* was typing me out his thesis on why we should maybe take some time apart this summer."

I sit down heavily on the sofa. "What?"

"That's what I said!" Isa takes a sip of the coffee, shuddering a little. "Look at this."

She fishes her phone out of her robe pocket and hands it to me. The email is already open.

"I just saw it," Isabel says. Her voice is still wavering, but she's not crying anymore. "Literally got out of the shower, sent him a text to say I was here safe, and he asked if I'd checked my email yet. That's all he said. Three years of dating, he *knows* he's breaking up with me in an email, and not 'glad you're safe, but we need to talk when you get a chance,' just 'have you checked your email?'" She takes another sip of coffee, her hair dripping water onto her robe. "Are you done reading it?"

"Um, almost," I say, but the truth is, Isabel wasn't lying about this being a thesis. It's like two thousand words of Ben's feelings and concerns, and while I like Ben, I really don't need this much of him.

But I skim it enough to see his general point—because Isabel is going to be gone for nearly a month, and Ben is going up to see his grandparents in Maine, he thinks they should use this time as a sort of "test run" for college, to see what it's like being apart . . . before they're apart? I don't know, I'm not following Ben's logic, and I suspect this is more about wanting to make out with girls in Maine than any sort of journey of the soul he and Isa should take as a couple.

"It's total bullshit," she says flatly, echoing my own thoughts. "He's probably got a thing for some girl in Bar Harbor."

"At least he's not planning on cheating?" I say, but it's the wrong thing to say, and we both know it. Isabel takes a deep, shaky breath.

"But what if he already *has*?" she asks in a small voice, and then she's crying again, and there's this entire story coming out about how Ben was weird after his trip to his grandparents' last year, that there was this girl, Carlie, on his Facebook that he'd only added after that trip, that she didn't have a location listed, but all her pictures sure *looked* like Maine, and as all this spills out, I sit there, stunned.

Finally, when the saga of Ben and Carlie has come to an end, I blink at Isabel. "Why didn't you tell me any of this?"

Isabel gets up from the sofa, sighing as she makes her way to the massive desk and a box of tissues concealed in a marble-and-gilt box. She picks up the whole thing, shaking her head slightly at the over-the-top packaging, then sits down again, tucking one leg under the other.

"You had so much going on this year," she says, pausing to blow her nose. "With Ellie and all the weirdness . . ." She gestures around the room, at the giant bed, the expensive furnishings, the fancy tissue box, too, probably. "This. And I wasn't sure, and I felt so *dumb*, you know? Ben and I have been together forever, and I thought I was being paranoid, and I hated that. Also——"

"Saying it out loud would've made it feel true," I finish, and Isa looks up, her dark eyes wide. "Exactly," she breathes, and I nudge her leg with my knee.

"See? That's why you should've told me. I get this kind of thing."

I lean back into the sofa, nearly swallowed up by the striped cushions. "You're important to me, Isa, and things that are important to you are important to me. No matter what's going on with my sister."

My sister.

Who's the reason I'm here this summer.

Which, in turn, makes her the reason *Isa* is here this summer. Would Ben still have sent that email if we'd gone to Key West like we planned?

I almost say that out loud, the words right there on the tip of my tongue, but then Isa gives a shuddery sigh and tilts her head to the side.

"What are you wearing?" she asks, and I tug at the hem of my cardigan. I'm wearing the green one, not the gray one, at least, but it's over a white sleeveless blouse and my jeans have creases down the legs. I'm even wearing little pearl studs in my ears.

"Nothing interesting," I assure her, and she nods, but then her lips start wobbling again.

Okay, so scrapping the museum and bookstore idea. That

stuff is fun, don't get me wrong, but this is an emergency situation, and hey, I now have some pretty cool stuff at my disposal, stuff I know Isabel has been excited about. Why not use just a little bit of it?

I lean forward. "You wanna go to the palace?"

Chapter 18

THE TOUR I GIVE ISA OF HOLYROOD IS DEFINITELY not as thorough as the one the tourists get, and most of the impressive parts are on display for the public, but Isabel, dedicated reader of royal blogs, is thrilled with this behind-the-scenes look. We stop in one of the parlors, and she touches a sofa covered in tartan pillows. "So, like, the queen sits here?" she asks, and I lean against a doorway. "Yup," I reply. "Puts the royal bum right on it. When she's here, which she's not right now."

Alex's parents still aren't back from Canada, which, to be honest, is quite the relief. Next week, though . . .

No, not even contemplating that.

We leave the parlor and head down one of the long hallways. It's not as cluttered as Sherbourne Castle was—fewer paintings and knickknacks, but then again everything that belongs to the Bairds technically belongs to the country, so maybe most of their stuff is in museums—but it's . . . grand. High stone ceilings arch overhead, and there's this heavy feeling in the air, like all that history is seeping into the rock.

We stop near a thick window that looks down on one of the inner courtyards, watching a line of visitors snaking past. The glass is old and wobbly, same as the windows at Sherbourne, making everything outside blurry.

"It's a palace," Isabel says, turning to me.

"Well, yeah," I joke, "that's why it's right there in the name. Kind of gives it away."

Isabel's bag slides from her shoulder to the crook of her arm. It's so weird seeing something so familiar—Isabel, her black hair caught in a messy braid, her jeans frayed at the knee, that stupid bag she loves so much, made up of different squares of tweed—in this completely foreign place. A good kind of weird, don't get me wrong. I'm so happy to see someone who isn't a Fliss or a Poppy that I could cry. Suddenly, I wonder if this is what Ellie felt like when I'd showed up earlier in the summer. Worlds colliding and all that.

"Your sister is going to be a princess," Isabel says, as if she was just now realizing that.

"Yup," I say with a shrug. "And then she'll be a queen, and one day she'll have a kid who'll be king or queen, which is actually the weirdest part of all this."

Isabel thinks that over, blinking. "Holy crap, yeah," she says, widening her eyes. "Will you have to bow to your own niece or nephew? Do you think Ellie and Alex will let you hold them?"

I roll my eyes, grabbing her hand and tugging her toward the side staircase that leads to our private apartments. "Yes, believe it or not, they let commoners touch the king baby."

That makes her laugh, and as we head to another part of the palace, she doesn't even mention all the paintings on the wall, the bizarrely lush carpets, or how everything that *could* be gilded has been, the gold dull under the surprisingly dim lights. Ellie said that Alex's dad used the lowest-wattage light bulbs he could to save money, something that made no sense to me, seeing as how these were people who lived in multiple castles and had a literal fleet of fancy cars.

Then Isabel turns, grabbing my arm. "Okay, so yay palace, castle, very cool, hurray for fancy. Spill on Seb."

I almost snort at that until I remember that Isabel probably shouldn't know what a tool that guy really is. Hopefully, she won't even have to see him since, as far as I know, he's still gallivanting around in Derbyshire, doing whatever debauched royal types do. Probably having some weird orgy involving costumes and claret or something. Burning twenty-pound notes for fun.

No thanks.

"I've barely seen him," I tell Isa now, which is mostly true. We'd only shared that one conversation in my room, and that hardly counted. I hadn't even spoken to him at the race, and he'd left Edinburgh not long after we got back.

"Okay, but you have to tell me *everything*," Isabel says. "How he looks, if he's as handsome as he is in pictures, how he smells . . ."

I raise my eyebrows at her. "How he *smells?*"

Isa fixes me with a look. "Girl, I am heartbroken and vulnerable. Throw me a bone and tell me a hot prince smells like manly books and leather, okay?"

Seb usually smells of expensive cologne and whatever alcohol he's currently pouring down his throat, but no need to crush

Isabel's dream. "All those things and more," I tell her, and she closes her eyes, tipping her head back.

"Yes. Thank you."

Giggling, I bump shoulders with her. "Come on."

We walk down another hallway, this one less furnished than the rest and colder, our footsteps loud against the stone floor. "So," Isa asks, crossing her arms over her chest, "how are things? Blending in with the royals and all?"

I shoot her a look. "Haven't you been keeping up with the blogs?"

Shaking her head, Isa gives me an elbow to the ribs. "No, I've been *loyal*," she says. "And honestly, reading about what your best friend is doing felt too . . . bleurghy."

"Imagine reading it about your sister," I reply, and Isa stops, her sneakers squeaking a little.

"I get it now," she says, then gestures around us. "Why you were so weirded out by all this." And then she flashes me a classic Isabel Smile, all dimples and shiny teeth.

"It's still kind of cool, though."

And the thing is, she's not wrong. It *is* kind of cool. I don't mind the fancy cars and the nice clothes. I'm never going to like a Pimm's Cup, but the rest of it? It's . . . not that bad.

I don't know how to tell Isabel all that, though, so I just shrug. "It has its moments."

Skipping slightly, she takes my wrist and gives me a little shake. "Like us getting to see and possibly meet and, in my case, marry Declan Shield this fall."

Laughing, I shake her off. "Wait, I thought you were all about Seb."

Isabel gives a shrug and flips her hair over her shoulder. "I can handle both," she says, lifting her nose in the air, and we're still laughing as we turn the corner out of the hallway.

We're just coming back down the stairs when I hear the sound of someone coming up. Taking Isabel's wrist, I pull us to one side, expecting to see a butler or one of the 9,000 secretaries the royal family seems to have wandering around. But instead, I catch sight of a glint of auburn hair, and before I know it, Seb is rounding the curve of the stairwell.

Crap.

He's not as well dressed as he was the first time I saw him—it's jeans and a henley today—but that doesn't stop Isabel from freezing in place, her free hand coming up to grab the fingers I have locked around her wrist.

Seb comes to a sudden stop, looking at us standing there and clearly noticing—and liking—the look on Isabel's face.

Great.

"Ah, Daisy," he says, but his eyes are still on Isabel. "I didn't know you were staying at the palace."

"I'm not," I tell him, inching down a step, pulling Isabel behind me. "I was just showing my friend around. Isabel, this is—"

"*Iknowwhoheis,*" Isa says, all in a rush, and I fight the urge to groan. Of course. Of course we'd run into Seb the day Isabel has just gotten her heart splattered by her boyfriend, and of course Seb would be looking both extremely handsome and not as intimidatingly princely as usual, and oh, this is bad. This is really bad.

Especially because Seb begins to bloom under her obvious smitten-ness.

"Isabel," he repeats, and then he reaches out and takes her hand. Doesn't shake it (doesn't kiss it, either, thank god), but just holds it, his blue eyes bright, his smile a winning combination of charm and mischief. I've seen it on him before. It's a look that says, "Yes, whatever happens with us will probably be a bad idea, but won't it be fun?"

And I am not here for it.

"So we were just leaving," I tell him, fighting the urge to pull Isa's hand from his.

But Seb isn't letting go, and he's also not looking at me. "Where were you headed?" he asks her.

She's still glamoured, pretty much, smiling down at him there on the lower step, so I sigh, roll my eyes, and say, "Museums. Bookstores. Other respectable establishments."

Seb's grin deepens. "Well, that's no fun at all," he all but purrs, and oh my goooodddddddd, how is Isa not seeing this for the line it is?

Because her boyfriend has broken her heart, you idiot, I remind myself, *and now the most eligible teenage boy in the world is talking to her and holding her hand and giving her the full court press.*

"We're actually going to a book signing in a little bit," I say, already preparing to pull Isa away, but he leans against the banister, his eyes still on Isabel.

"Who's the author?" he asks, and Isa answers, "Ash Bentley."

To my surprise, Seb straightens up, lifting his eyebrows. "Seriously?"

"Do not tell me you know who that is," I say, but Seb shoots me a look.

"I read *Finnigan's Falcon* five times the year it came out. I actually went as Finnigan to a fancy dress party just a few months ago. Ask any of the lads, they'll tell you."

It's very hard to imagine Prince Sebastian, royal rogue, reading about the adventures of space mage Finnigan Sparks, but he does look genuinely . . . excited? His eyes are bright, he's grinning, and this is actually *worse* than his usual prince schtick. Cute, royal, *and* into a nerdy book series?

No girl could resist.

"I'll come with," he says, and I lift a hand, palm out.

"Okay, no, because, A, no boys allowed, and, B, you're going to cause a total scene if you just roll up to a bookstore. No one will pay any attention to the author if you're there."

Seb's brow wrinkles as he thinks that over. Then his face clears and he snaps, pointing at me.

"No worries, ladies," he says, but I have *all* the worries as he adds, "I've got a plan."

Chapter 19

"THIS IS," I SAY AS I WALK DOWN THE STREET BETWEEN Isabel and Seb, "by *far* the stupidest thing I have ever done."

We're headed to the Ash Bentley signing—I insisted we walk rather than take cars because the cars would be too conspicuous—and I feel like at any moment, someone is going to notice that the tall dude next to us in the cloak and space helmet is Prince Sebastian.

"Given that you participated in the Cinnamon Challenge not once, not twice, but *three times*, that's really saying something," Isabel replies, moving her bag up higher on her shoulder as she keeps looking at Seb out of the corner of her eye.

There's basically no part of his face visible, and the cloak covers him from neck to ankle, but I'm convinced someone is going to figure it out. How can they not? Even completely hidden, he seems to stand out. Too tall, too swaggery . . .

And too into Isabel.

"Does the cloak accentuate my eyes?" he asks her, and honestly, how is he capable of flirting while wearing a *space helmet*, I ask you?

Giggling, Isa looks up at him, squinting slightly. "I can't actually see your eyes," she reminds him, and he ducks his head closer to her.

"You're not trying hard enough," he says, and I am going to vomit right here on this perfectly charming street.

"Less talking, more walking," I say to Seb. "Your face might not be recognizable, but your voice is."

He scoffs inside the helmet. "I sound like every other bloke on the street. And here, watch this."

Stepping just a little ahead of us, Seb lifts his arms wide, black cloak billowing, tilts his head back, and yells through the helmet, "GOOD PEOPLE OF EDINBURGH! 'TIS I! YOUR PRINCE!"

A guy in a jean jacket gives him the side-eye and mutters some variation of the f-word, while a group of girls in school uniforms nudge each other and roll their eyes as they walk past.

Seb drops his arms, and even with that helmet (which, gotta admit, is a pretty perfect replica of what Finnigan Sparks wears on the cover of *Finnigan's Moon*), I swear I can feel him grinning.

"See? No one gives a toss."

"No one gives a toss, Dais," Isa repeats with a shrug, then breaks into giggles again, jogging a little to catch up with Seb, and I watch them, fighting the urge to stamp my foot.

It's silly, really, feeling jealous or upstaged or whatever it is currently twisting my stomach. It's just that I'd looked forward to this day with Isa, and now it's becoming a Seb day.

But then I remind myself that, hey, Isabel is having fun, and after the whole thing with Ben she deserves that. Besides, it *is* kind of nice to know that Seb is a genuine Finnigan Freak. On the way here, he made a pretty good case for Team Jezza, complete with examples from the book, and now, as we make our way to the bookstore, I hear him telling Isabel, "Miranda was ace in *Finnigan and the Starhold*. Most I've ever liked her."

"That's because she spent the entire book under an accidental love spell," Isabel says, "so she was actually into Finnigan for once."

"Aww, come off it," Seb says, elbowing her. "She's liked him the whole time."

While it's definitely next-level surreal to watch my best friend nerd out with a costumed prince, we're close to the bookstore now, so I scoot in between them, ignoring the look Isa cuts me.

"Okay, so here's the deal," I say. "Glynnis basically strong-armed Ash Bentley's publisher here in the UK to do this signing since me and Isa missed out on Key Con thanks to all . . . this." I wave my hand, taking in Seb, Scotland, all of it. "Which means best behavior from all of us, and by *all of us*, I mean *Seb*."

He pushes his shoulders back, looking down at me, but the helmet kills any intimidation factor he may have been going for.

It strikes me suddenly that I sound a lot like Ellie the day of the race, reminding people how to act, but this book signing is important to me, and the race was . . .

Important to El.

Okay, so maybe a few more apologies are in order once we get back to the palace.

For now, I stop just outside the bookshop. It has a bright blue door with a bell over it, and next door, the window frame is painted hot pink, the colors especially cheerful against all the dark stone and the gray sky. It hasn't rained yet, but it's been threatening it all day, and I wish I'd thought to bring an umbrella.

"So," I say, tugging my jacket tighter around me. "This is the Ash Bentley Show, not the You Know Who Show." I nod at Seb. "We're letting you tag along because . . . well, I'm not sure, really. I mean, if you're this big of a fan, couldn't you have seen her at a signing like a hundred times by now?"

Seb nods. "Oh yeah, I have signed first editions of the whole series." Then he spreads his arms out, palms up. "But this is fun."

I don't mention that it's not a huge amount of fun for *me* because Isabel is smiling up at him again and is clearly living her own royal dream date today, which is something she deserves, frankly.

So I open the door to the shop and hope for the best.

The store is already pretty crowded, but because the date was announced so late, it's not quite the packed house it could've been. Still, all the chairs are filled, and I immediately see that Seb is not the only one in costume. There are a lot of purple Miranda wigs, plenty of helmets that match Seb's, and more mage robes than I can count.

Seeing them, I feel a smile start to spread across my face. Okay, this? This is much more my scene than a race or a party at a castle or whatever other crazy stuff I might have to do in Scotland. *Here*, I actually feel like I've got a pretty good handle on things, and I'm still smiling as I make my way to the table of Finnigan Sparks books near the middle of the room.

Which is when I hear the first squeal.

It's a high-pitched whistling sound that immediately makes me wince, and I'm already whirling around, expecting to find

Seb with his stupid helmet off smiling his stupid smile like a stupid person.

But Seb is still near the door, still behelmeted, Isabel at his side, and, confused, I look around.

And realize the squealer is looking at *me*.

"Oh my god, oh my god, oh my god," she burbles, coming up to stand in front of me, practically shivering. She's not in any kind of cosplay, just a T-shirt and jean shorts over black tights, and she flaps her hands, beaming at me.

"Daisy!" she goes on. "You're Daisy Winters! Oh my *gooooodddddddd*!"

Her accent is pretty and rolling, but her voice is *loud*, and suddenly a lot of heads are turning in my direction, and then there's this . . . Look, "stampede" is way too strong a word, but there are definitely a lot of people heading toward me, and a lot of voices suddenly talking at once.

"You changed your hair!" I hear one girl wail, while another scoots closer, her Miranda wig slightly crooked. "When you told off that duchess at An Reis, I nearly died. I mean, I didn't see it, but I read about it, and—"

"Is it true you're dating Prince Sebastian?" another person asks, and in that weird moment of panic, I do the absolute worst thing I could possibly do.

I turn to look at Seb.

And maybe if there had only been a couple of girls standing there instead of about thirty, they wouldn't have put it together, but one lone voice cries, "*Is that him?*"

I don't even think, really. I just react, shaking my head and backing away. "Nope, just two friends from the US. Anyway, just came in to look at books, and"—I make a show of turning my head this way and that—"there . . . seem to be lots in here, so good job with that, bookstore!"

Giving the world's most awkward thumbs-up, I turn to go, nearly dragging Isabel and Seb behind me, the bell over the door clanging cheerfully as we spill out onto the street.

Underneath his helmet, Seb is laughing, and to my surprise, even Isabel is smiling.

"So *I* was going to be the problem, was I?" Seb asks, and Isa puts an arm around my shoulders.

"How come you didn't mention you got famous over here?" she asks, and I shake my head, still confused by what just happened. It's not like I don't know that people are interested in me, but they've always been interested because of *Ellie*, not, like, in actual me as a person. But those girls felt like . . . *fans*. Of *mine*. Which is bizarre since I haven't done anything worthy of fandom.

"I just never thought . . ." I start, and then trail off, not sure where to go with the rest of that sentence.

Then I look up at Isabel, frowning. "We can go back in. Or you can. I'm sorry, I just freaked out, I guess, and—"

Clapping a hand over my mouth, Isabel shakes her head, dark eyes shining. "I can see Ash Bentley speak some other time," she says. "Seeing the day my best friend became famous? *That* was worth the trip." Then her gaze moves over my shoulder to Seb. "And the day's had other perks."

Eurgh.

So instead of seeing our favorite author sign books, we spend the rest of the afternoon wandering, Seb still in his costume, which, oddly, doesn't attract nearly as many looks as you'd think. We go up the Royal Mile to Edinburgh Castle, then make our way back down again, toward Holyroodhouse. It's summer, which means touristy season, so the streets are crowded, bagpipes competing with each other, and more guys dressed as Braveheart than should be allowed.

Maybe I'll talk to Alex about that.

By the time we get back to the palace, it's evening, although sunset is still pretty far away, and I'm hoping I can talk Isabel into some takeout food and bad British television tonight, although the way she looks at Seb when he steps into the main hallway of the family entrance and takes off his helmet is . . . not promising.

"I need to find Glynnis, tell her the day didn't exactly go as planned," I say, watching Seb smile at my best friend while she smiles back.

"I'll keep Isabel company," Seb offers, and I grimace, but what can I say? So against my better judgment, I leave them there in the foyer, heading up the narrow stairs to the back hallway where Glynnis's office is.

She's not in there, though, and while I check a couple of other places—a sitting room, the small private kitchen—I don't want to leave Isa and Seb on their own for too long.

But when I get to the foyer, I see that I'm already too late. Seb's helmet and robe are hanging up on the hat stand by the door, and Seb and Isabel?

Are nowhere in sight.

Chapter 20

I TRY ISABEL'S PHONE, BUT THERE'S NO ANSWER.
And then I pull up my Facebook app and start messaging her.

Still nothing.

In fact, I almost think she's purposely ignoring me, which is very much *not* okay and a sacred violation of our friendship, which I plan on informing her of as soon as I freaking *find her*.

Which, I realize, means finding Seb.

The palace is a confusing warren of halls and rooms, smaller than Sherbourne Castle, plus there's the added issue of parts of it being open to tourists and other parts private and for family only.

I know I'm technically "family" now, but I still feel funny creeping the halls of the palace, ducking in rooms, looking for Seb and my best friend. My best friend, whose rights to that title might be stripped if she doesn't turn up soon.

It's actually kind of a relief when I run into Spiffy—or Dons (I still have trouble telling them apart)—on one of the staircases.

"Hey . . . you!" I say, trying to seem normal and not at all freaked out. Spiffy-or-Dons stops, grinning at me, hands in his pockets. He's dressed like a banker in his forties—polo shirt, khakis, shiny shoes—rather than a teenage boy, and I wonder if Miles is the only one of them who ever manages to look semi-normal.

"Lady Daze," Spiffy-or-Dons says, and, great, apparently I have a nickname, too. How does anyone know who people are talking about around here? "Getting the lay of the land?"

"Kind of," I reply, resting my hand on the banister. "You haven't seen Seb, have you? Possibly with a girl?"

It's the strangest thing, but I can actually *see* Spiffy-or-Dons shut down. Like a door closing in his face or something.

"Can't say I have," he replies, and I know he's lying.

I press harder. "It's just my friend Isabel might be with him, and we had plans for tonight. With her parents."

That part is a lie—Isa's parents are still in London, coming up tomorrow afternoon—but I'm hoping that invoking parental authority will rattle him a bit.

Doesn't work.

He shakes his head again and gives me the fakest apologetic look I've ever seen. "Maybe she went back to the hotel," he suggests.

I smile at him. Or grit my teeth, more likely. "Maybe," I say, but I am pretty sure that's not the case. Where could Seb have taken her?

And then I realize who might know.

And who would have a vested interest in preventing any scandal involving Seb.

"Is Miles around?" I ask.

Spiffy-or-Dons grins. "Thought something might be afoot there," he says, then literally nudges me in the ribs with his elbow and winks.

I shake my head. "Ew, no."

Spiffy—it is Spiffy, I'm pretty sure now—rocks back on his heels, face falling. "Ew?" he echoes. "Monters is really the least *ew* of all of us, I feel."

I smile in spite of myself at that but reach out and grab his forearm. "Spiffy. Focus. Where *is* Miles?"

It turns out Miles has a flat—his *own*, which is crazy to me—not far from the palace, and within a few minutes, I'm in the back of one of the palace's fleet of cars, heading for the part of Edinburgh called "New Town." The fact that it was built in the eighteenth century is apparently enough to make it "new" around here.

"Should I wait here, miss?" the driver asks, and I nod, barely thinking about how weird it is to have a driver, to have him waiting for me.

I guess you get used to those things pretty quickly.

Miles's door is painted deep blue, and there's no buzzer, so I just knock, hoping he'll be home and that he might know where Seb has taken Isa.

And sure enough, after just a few seconds, I hear footsteps coming, and then Miles is there, back in his regular uniform of jeans and a T-shirt, clearly puzzled to find me on his doorstep.

"I need a list of every den of iniquity in the city of Edinburgh," I blurt out.

Miles stares at me for a moment before blinking owlishly.

"I . . . don't have a list like that?" He thinks for a second, rubbing his hand over the back of his neck. "Although I really wish I did now."

I roll my eyes, and he ushers me in. It's unsurprisingly adult and stuffy. Heavy leather furniture, lots of wood, books. There are two pairs of shoes lined up just inside the front door, and as I look at them, I realize they both have cedar shoe trees inside them.

Shoe trees. What teenage boy even knows what those *are*, much less uses them?

But then I remember I'm here on a mission, and I don't have time to marvel at how Miles might be a time traveler from 1812. Instead, I follow him into the living room and, as quickly as I can, tell him about what happened back at the bookstore, then the palace. By the time I'm done, Miles has his arms folded over his chest, his brow creased. "Okay, so your friend is visiting from America, and her boyfriend just chucked her."

"If 'chucked' means 'dumped,' then yes, that's what happened," I say, leaning on the arm of his couch, and dear *god*. How did they even make leather that soft? I refrain from stroking the couch while Miles turns to walk back toward the bar separating the living room from the kitchen. "And now your friend is out with Seb—where, by your own admission, she wants to be—and you want us to go . . . rescue her?" He picks up a bottle of water, twisting off the cap and frowning at me. "From what exactly?"

I throw my hands up. "From Seb, obviously. Isn't that your whole deal?"

He's still looking at me, fiddling with the water bottle.

"What?" I ask.

"I'm just not clear on why she needs rescuing if she's with Seb by choice. Look, he can be a complete tosser, I know." He blows out a long breath. "Trust me, I know. But . . . Seb doesn't exactly have to kidnap women. Young ladies who choose to spend an evening with him do so quite willingly."

I stare at him. "Okay, what?"

"What?" he replies, but his eyes slide away from mine.

"Don't what my what," I tell him, crossing one foot in front of the other. "I what-ed first, and you *know* what I was what-ing about."

Miles does that pressed-lips thing again, and when he doesn't answer, I go on. "You freaked the freak out about me with Seb, but now that I tell you my friend is off with him, you're all, 'Oh, no big, that's just Seb'?" I stare him down. "That's what I'm what-ing."

Miles waves his hands, one still wrapped around his bottle of water. "It was different," he says, and I tilt my head.

"Because it was me," I say. "Because . . . of Ellie? Of me personally?"

"Because of a lot of things," he says, but then, before I can get to the bottom of that, he adds, "The point is, I don't understand why your friend needs rescuing unless you think Seb kidnapped her, which would be a bit much, even for him."

Frustrated, I shake my head. "No, she totally went with him willingly, it's not that, it's just . . . she's not making good choices, and as her friend, it's my job to save her from those bad choices if I can." I fix Miles with a look. "Something tells me you of all people can understand that."

Miles heaves a sigh, his chest expanding in . . . interesting ways underneath his black T-shirt. Ugh, why did I have to notice that? I don't like Miles being filed under "boy" in my head, I really don't.

"Oh god, you had to invoke the squire's code," he says, and I frown.

"The what?"

"Squire's code. When our knights go errant, we must go fetch them."

"Is that a real thing, or are you being a jackass?"

"I'm being a jackass," he agrees easily, turning to get his jacket from where it's draped over a nearby barstool. "But I'm a jackass who's going to help you."

Chapter 21

WE TAKE THE CAR I'D USED A LITTLE DEEPER INTO the city, the driver eventually pulling over at a series of tall houses, not unlike where Miles lives. We get out of the car, and the house Miles leads me to doesn't look any different from any of the other houses lining the street. They're all the same, tall, narrow buildings made of white stone, a black wrought iron fence with sharp points standing guard between them and the plebes on the sidewalk.

Miles walks to one of the buildings right in the middle, but instead of walking up the wide marble stairs to the blue front door, he turns, jogging *down* a set of steps I hadn't even noticed.

The little alcove at the bottom is so small that the two of us can barely fit, standing there so close that Miles has to move one arm around my waist just to keep us from squishing in like sardines.

"Can you go back to the part where Seb dressed up like a spaceman, yet *you* were the one who caused a scene?" he asks, and I try to wiggle away from him. I'd filled Miles in on the details of our bookstore visit both at his place and in the car, but he was still struggling with it.

"Shut up," I mutter, and I swear he smirks before lifting his other hand and rapping his knuckles against the door. I'd expected some kind of secret knock, like Morse code or something, but as far as I can tell, it's just your regular knock. Not even "a shave and a haircut."

And there's not some cool slit that slides open in the door, either, revealing just a pair of eyes and a barked order for a password. Instead, the door opens, and it's a tall guy in a dark suit. From his earpiece and the general boringness of his suit, I know this has to be one of Seb's bodyguards.

"He here?" Miles asks, and the guy nods, stepping aside to let us in.

"He's fine tonight," the man tells Miles, his eyes briefly moving over me, a little crease between his brows. I wonder if he knows who I am. He'd have to, right? They must be briefed on that kind of thing.

And then I wonder if he'll tell Ellie I was here.

No time to worry about that, though, and even if he does, I can tell El I was here just to help Isabel and probably prevent a scandal. She'll like that, right?

"That's good to hear," Miles says to the bodyguard, and I think of him coming to my room that first night. Is he always the one who goes in search of Seb? The bodyguard clearly thinks he's here to check up on him.

"Downstairs, then, Simon?" Miles asks, and when the bodyguard nods, Miles gives him one of those quick smiles.

"Excellent," he says, then steers me away from the door and deeper into the room.

"What is this place?" I ask. I'd been prepared for strobe lights, pounding music, a general air of debauchery tinged with just a hint of desperation. But this place is nice. Fancy, too. Paintings covering nearly every bit of wall space, heavy furniture, soft lamplight everywhere. At one end of the room is a massive mahogany bar, a long mirror stretching behind it. The carpet beneath my boots is a pale cream color with some kind of pattern worked into it in red, gold, and blue, and it's so thick underneath my feet that I feel like I might sink into it. This isn't some party place. My grandmother would have tea here.

Then I see one of the Royal Wreckers—Gilly, the blond guy—sitting on a damask sofa, a girl practically draped over him. She seems to be made of about 80% leg, and nearly 100% of those legs are on display in a short and sparkly minidress.

Gilly looks up as we pass, grinning and raising his glass. "Monters, my good man!" he yells, even though there's no reason to be loud—this place is nearly as quiet as a library. "Thought you were staying in tonight."

"I am," Miles replies, stopping in front of Gilly's sofa, his hands shoved deep in his pockets. "Or I was. Just looking for Seb."

The brunette draped over Gilly sits up, pulling the strap of her dress up one narrow shoulder. "Seb is here?" she asks, and Gilly heaves a sigh.

"You had to mention his name."

"It's his club, mate," Miles replies, then, with a nod at Gilly, he nudges my lower back, propelling me farther into the room.

"This was just a regular house," Miles tells me as we come to yet another flight of stairs, this one covered in deep-burgundy carpeting and spiraling down into a dim space. Sconces affixed to the wall light our way as we head down. "Seb bought it two years ago because it's close to this restaurant he likes, La Flamina," Miles continues, "and he wanted a private space where he could hang with his mates."

"And girls," I add, and Miles pauses on the step just below me. His hair is still damp, and it's curling underneath his ears. I fight an urge to touch one of those light brown curls, but that would be both weird and inappropriate, and this night has enough of that already.

"Yes," he concedes. "And girls."

"Upstairs was not *exactly* a den of iniquity," I allow, and Miles stops again, several steps below me now. He's got one hand in his pocket, the other resting lightly on the banister, and for a second, I think he's going to say something.

Then he just shakes his head and continues down the stairs.

I follow, trying to figure out Isa's state of mind. It isn't like her to be reckless, but I have a feeling Seb can override any girl's senses. And suddenly I'm beating myself up for not *saying* something to her about how Seb is less Prince Charming and more Prince Garbage Fire, but then we're walking into an *actual* den of iniquity, and all thoughts in my head that aren't a sort of low-level shriek are promptly silenced.

For just a second, it reminds me of the race day. I see the same shiny hair, the same rail-thin figures and tall shoes and expensive dresses. But it's like the Wonderland version of that day. This time there are no hats, and there is *definitely* no decorum.

There is, however, a lot of booze.

The entire room reeks of the floral, medicinal hit of gin, and the music is thumping so loudly I can feel it in my chest. Even over that, I can make out voices as people shout to be heard, laugh, and, in the case of one guy standing on the bar, a striped tie wrapped around his head, sing a song completely different than the one currently blasting through the speakers.

It's like a nightclub, but instead of the dim blue light I'd imagine in an *actual* club, everything is fairly well lit by the chandeliers overhead.

Somehow that makes it worse.

"Is this, like, some Lord of the Flies thing?" I ask Miles as a blonde in a deep-purple dress throws back her head laughing while also dropping a flaming piece of paper into a highball glass.

I can't hear Miles sigh, but I see his shoulders rise and fall as he takes in the scene around us.

"This is Seb's place," he says, and I nod, moving closer.

"So totally a Lord of the Flies thing, got it. Sucks to your ass-mar!" I call out to the blonde, but she's still laughing and doesn't hear me.

Miles does, though, and I think he might actually laugh a little himself as he pulls me deeper into the room.

There aren't *that* many people in here—it's definitely not as packed as a real club would be—but there are enough that I can't spot Isa or Seb.

"You're sure they're here?" I ask Miles, but before he can reply, a redhead has launched herself off a nearby sofa and directly onto him.

"Monnnnnnnnteeerrrrrrrssss," she drawls, wobbling on very high, very thin heels. She's wearing a pair of jeans that probably cost more than our mortgage and one of those blouses Ellie wears a lot that seems to be made of anywhere between three and forty-seven layers of sheer material. Various ruffles of fabric flutter around her as she hugs Miles, then steps back, both hands on his shoulders, peering up into his face.

"You look hotter," she says, narrowing her eyes slightly. "Did you get hotter?"

I don't want to scoff, but it's hard not to. Miles is traditionally handsome and all that, but hot? No, hot is reserved for boys who *don't* own shoe trees, sorry, but—

"Sitting for my Higher in hotness this year," Miles says to the girl now, one corner of his mouth lifted in something between a smirk and a grin. "Glad to see all the revising I've been doing has paid off."

I stand there, feeling like someone just punched me in the chest. Miles is very much not hot, but that thing he just did? That flirty, witty . . . whatever that was?

That was kind of hot, which means this is clearly not just a secret club but actually a parallel universe where Miles Montgomery is a guy who girls would be into.

"Ooh-er," the girl says, which is either some kind of nonsense word or possibly posh people code. Then she squeezes his shoulders again and looks over at me.

Her eyes widen a little, and I see that, like the girls at the race, she's both beautiful and not all beautiful at the same time. Like money and centuries of power have put a gloss over her ordinary features.

"You're Eleanor's sister," she says, then glances back at Miles before giving him a grin and slapping at his shoulder. "Monters, you prat. Does Flora know?"

Flora? She has to mean Princess Flora, Seb's twin sister, but why would Flora care about Miles?

Glancing over at me, Miles ignores that and says, "Missy, Daisy and I are looking for Seb. Have you seen him?"

She blinks at me, then looks back to Miles, shifting her weight to one foot so quickly that I'm a little worried she'll topple right over.

"Yar," she says, because apparently she can only speak in that posh people code, or maybe she's actually a pirate. "With a girl, natch. Pretty one, too. He's by the bar."

Miles winks at her—Winks! What is even happening?!— with a "Cheers," then gently steers me away and toward the back of the room.

"Lady Melissa Dreyfuss, known as Missy," he says in a low voice as we steer our way around a guy in a pink polo shirt kissing a girl who must be six inches taller than him. "Youngest daughter of the Duke of Drummond. The duke went missing about ten years ago after he tried to murder one of their stable grooms, so that's a bit of a scandal, obviously. Missy has an uncle who's trying to have the duke declared dead so that he can take the title, and—Daisy?"

I glance over at him, still remembering how genuinely cute he'd looked flirting with Missy. How *bizarre* that was.

Then I clue into what he's saying and, more accurately, what he's doing.

"Tea," he tells me very seriously, and I nod at him.

"Absolutely tea. Murder and disappearance? Scorching Earl Grey right there."

Pleased with himself, Miles keeps moving forward, and I keep following, trying to listen to him, process the fact that he *might* be cute, look for Isa, and not get accidentally sucked into an orgy.

It's clearly a tall order.

But then, finally, the crowd parts a little bit, revealing a bar against the back wall, and standing in front of it are—

"Oh my god."

Chapter 22

WHEN YOU'VE BEEN BEST FRIENDS FOR AS LONG AS
Isabel and I have—ten years and counting—you get pretty good
at reading each other's faces. Isabel knows when I'm making my
"I'm embarrassed and about to make it worse with a terrible
joke" face. I know her "I'm maybe not telling the entire truth"
face. And I *definitely* know her "I'm about to hand this stupid
boy his ass" face because I've seen it in class about a hundred
times.

And that is very much the face Isa is wearing now.

I thought we'd find them all cozied up, Isabel's face aglow
with princely attention. Or maybe they'd be kissing, which
would be worse.

What I didn't expect was to see them standing near the bar,
staring each other down, with Isabel yelling over the music,
"You're a complete jackass, you know that?"

Seb is looking as stunned as I feel, and next to me, Miles pulls
up short.

"This is . . . unexpected," he mutters.

"I beg your pardon?" Seb asks. Neither he nor Isabel have noticed us yet, so intent on whatever it is they're arguing about.

"A jackass," Isabel repeats, not even fazed. Her shoulders are back, chin lifted, and ohhhh, this is bad. "Or whatever word you use for that here."

"I'm familiar with the term," Seb replies, some of his shock giving way to the icy disdain thing I've seen El pull. "I'm just not sure why it's directed at me."

Before this can get any worse, I step forward, practically dragging Miles with me. "Hey, you two!" I say, and my voice is so loud and so bright that I actually wince.

"What's going on?"

Seb and Isa both startle a little looking over at us.

"Monters?" Seb asks, confused, and Miles goes to stand next to Seb, slapping one hand on his shoulder. I do the same on Isabel's side—well, minus the show of testosterone—and Miles and I glance at each other, suddenly realizing all we're doing is hemming our feuding besties in closer together.

Which is clearly an issue since not even our presence is going to stop this argument.

"It's not sexist, if that's what you're trying to imply," Seb says to Isabel, obviously just picking up wherever this left off. "I certainly have no problem with women, but Gregorstoun isn't the place for them. It would be . . ." He waves one hand, looking up at the ceiling like the answer might be there. "Distracting," he settles on, and Miles groans, tipping his head back.

"Seb," he says, "we've talked about this."

"I'm right!" Seb insists, turning to look at Miles. "You know

I am. And that place is a bloody nightmare, Monters, do *you* think girls would like it there?"

"Wait, there really aren't any girls at your scary boarding school?" I ask, and Miles meets my gaze again, his expression apologetic.

"There aren't, and it's become a bit of an issue. Some of us live in the twenty-first century and think going coed is not a bad idea. Others of us are—"

"Sensible," Seb finishes, giving Miles a light shove. "Honestly, Monters, this has nothing to do with gender and everything to do with tradition. And . . . and *safety*."

Isabel's eyes are practically blazing. "Why wouldn't girls be 'safe'"—she makes air quotes before tucking her hands back under her elbows—"at your school?"

Seb looks so flummoxed that I almost feel sorry for him, and when Isabel's meaning dawns on him, he seems genuinely horrified. "I don't mean they wouldn't be safe from *us*, Christ, what sort of person do you think I am?"

"I think you're a spoiled, selfish, sexist jackass," Isa says, not even hesitating, and on the other side of Seb, Miles's eyes go big. It's clear no one—and certainly no girl—has ever talked to Seb like this.

"I'm a prince," he finally splutters, and Isa makes a clicking sound with her tongue like that explains it all.

Shaking his head slightly, Seb looks down at the floor. All around us, his friends—or people who'd just like to be his friends—are still dancing and drinking and probably lighting more things on fire, but we're having a conversation about coed schools. "Gregorstoun is isolated and remote. They make us . . . sail boats in awful weather, and climb bloody mountains, and run in the freezing cold. That's all I meant, that it's simply too . . . too physically taxing for women."

With that, he fumbles on the bar to his right, grabbing a glass of whiskey that may or may not be his. He throws it back, then looks to Miles.

Miles just shakes his head. "Not a shovel big enough to dig you out of this one, mate."

Sighing, Seb slams his now-empty glass back onto the bar. "This night is really not going the way I expected," he mutters, and Isabel huffs out a sigh before turning to me.

"The feeling is mutual," she says, and then goes to push her way through the crowd.

But before she's swallowed up, she turns to look over her shoulder at Seb and calls out, "For the record, I've had better kisses from *band geeks*."

That actually gets the attention of some of the people on the dance floor, and one girl with long, stick-straight blond hair actually covers her mouth with her hand, eyes going wide.

With that, Isabel walks off, leaving me standing by Miles and Seb, Seb's face going stormy, Miles looking like he wished he was anywhere else.

I know that feeling.

I hurry after Isabel, dodging Missy, who somehow got even drunker in the past few minutes and calls after me, "Is Monters still here?"

"He's by the bar!" I shout back. "Knock yourself out!"

She wrinkles her nose, but I'm already at the stairs, catching up with Isa.

She's halfway up, and I catch her arm.

"You kissed him?" I ask, breathless from the drunk rich people gauntlet I just ran through, and she sighs, rolling her shoulders.

"Unfortunately, yes."

Pausing, she tilts her head, long black hair sweeping over her shoulders. "And I lied about the band geek part. It was actually pretty awesome, but I'm retroactively taking away points because he's such a toolbox."

We make our way up the stairs. The main part of the club is empty now, Gilly and his leggy lady nowhere to be seen. The bodyguard is still by the door, though, and Isabel stops, moving her bag to her other shoulder.

"I'm sorry," she says, and I look at her, confused.

"For calling Seb a toolbox? You shouldn't be, he kind of is. I was going to tell you that earlier, but I didn't want to ruin your—

"Not that," Isabel says, shaking her head. "For ditching you. I was just . . . everything with Ben, and then there was a *prince* asking me if I wanted to get away for a little bit, and I . . . got dazzled."

She wrinkles her nose. "Which is totally unlike me, but this place is weird."

That's the truest thing I've heard all day, and I nod, throwing my arms out to the side, taking in Seb's club, Seb himself, this entire day. "Welcome to my world."

Shuddering a little, Isa shoves her hands in her back pockets. "Thanks, but no thanks. I'll stick to reading the blogs from now on."

We head for the door, and Isa gives another sigh. "It was all going really well up until I asked about his school, too. I mean, not *well*, maybe the conversation was kind of awkward, but the kiss was promising." Then she screws up her face. "I can't believe I kissed a dude who doesn't think women should go to his precious boarding school."

I wonder if I should bring up my own Seb kiss but then decide that no, this night has been a lot already.

Something Isabel confirms as she says, "I just want to forget the past few hours ever happened."

"Solid plan," I agree as the bodyguard opens the front door for us.

But any thought of forgetting this night happened is erased as about a thousand flashes go off in our faces.

Chapter 23

LATER, I'LL LEARN THAT THERE WERE ONLY FOUR photographers outside the club, but at the time, it feels like there are dozens. Hundreds, even. The flashes are blinding, the clicking incessant. Somehow it's worse than that day on the Mile, maybe because it's dark and the flashes seem so bright, or maybe because then I was with Ellie and the other guys, and a whole bunch of bodyguards. Now it's just me, and I can hear people calling my name.

"Daisy, are you dating Seb?"

"Daisy, does your sister know you're here?"

"Who's your friend, love?"

It's a constant barrage, and I blink against it, frozen until I feel a hand on my elbow and look up to see Miles standing next to me, Seb right behind him.

"All right, gentlemen, that's enough," Miles says calmly, and bizarrely the flashes stop. Well, they pause, at least, and then Seb steps forward.

"Slow night, lads?" he teases. "Can't imagine what the going rate is for me spending time with my future sister-in-law."

Smiling down at me, Seb steps closer, and Isabel is basically hidden behind his back, Miles just off to the right. Weirdly enough, it's Seb's calm that makes *me* calm.

Maybe too calm, because when a photographer calls out, "What did you think of Seb's club, Daisy?" a reply jumps to my lips before I can stop it.

"Disappointing," I reply. "Hardly any naked ladies, and only one chimpanzee."

There's a burst of laughter at that, and the cameras start up again.

Seb laughs, too, putting a friendly hand on my shoulder, but I realize it's less for show and more to start gently but inexorably pushing me toward the waiting car. His bodyguard is out of the club now, making a path for us to the car, and as the four of us pile in, I feel Miles's hand at my back. The shutters are clicking again, but then the door closes with a *thunk*, and the chaos outside is muted.

I flop back against the seat with a sigh, placing a hand on my forehead.

"Chimpanzee?" Miles asks, and I shake my head.

"I panicked."

The corners of his mouth turn down as Seb settles into the back seat, the car gliding away from the curb.

Isabel doesn't seem as freaked out, just looking out the window with a frown. "So that's what it's like," she muses softly, and Seb looks over at her sharply.

"It's usually worse," he tells her, flicking his auburn hair out of his eyes. "That was mild, love."

"Don't call me love," she shoots back, and then she fishes in her bag for her phone.

To say that it's awkward in the car is a bit of an understatement, and I clear my throat. "Sorry your first night wasn't the best," I offer to Isa, but she smiles at me and shrugs.

"It was actually kind of fun. I mean, before this guy." She jerks her thumb at Seb, who gapes at her.

"This guy?" he repeats, but she's still looking at me.

"Tomorrow is bookstores and museums, right?"

"Absolutely," I say, relieved. Okay, so we're back on track. One brief aberration, a quick toe dip into potential scandalousness, but we are okay, and we can all just forget this night ever happened.

We're quiet for the rest of the ride, and when we pull up to the Balmoral, it's fairly empty. No photographers, no one gawking. I start to get out to walk Isabel to her room, but before I can, she lays a hand on my knee and says, "I'm good, promise. Tomorrow, bookstores, yeah?"

"Yeah," I reply, "total nerdery, here we come."

Isa flashes a grin at that, then adds, "Bye, Miles, nice to meet you."

Pointedly ignoring Seb, she climbs out of the back seat and heads for the hotel without a backward glance.

Seb rolls his eyes, but then goes to get out of the car, too, and I grab his arm.

"Okay, you're not following her," I say, but he shakes me off with a sniff.

"Bloody right I'm not. But I need a drink before heading

home, and the Balmoral makes the best martinis. You two go on back."

With that, he slams the door, leaving me and Miles in silence. The car pulls out onto the street just as a misty rain starts falling again, and I sigh, sinking deeper into the leather seat. "So that was a thing that happened."

Miles doesn't say anything, and I glance over at him. He's sitting stiffly there in the back seat, head turned to look out the window.

"I hate having to say this, but thank you," I tell him. "We saved the day, and I couldn't have done it without your help."

He doesn't say anything, and I reach across the back seat to poke him in his arm, which is surprisingly hard under my fingertip. "Hi, I'm trying to be nice? Even though it causes me physical pain?"

Finally, he looks over at me. "You know those pictures are going to be in every paper tomorrow morning."

There's that muscle tic in his jaw again, and I twist in my seat to face him better. "A thing that is very much not *my* fault," I remind him, and he waves one elegant hand, swatting that thought like it's a bug.

"I'm aware of that, but the point is, before you got here, there were never any photographers at Seb's club. *Someone* let them know that you were here."

Now I think my own jaw muscle might be acting up because I am clenching my teeth pretty hard as I stare him down. "Again with this?" I say. "Because I could almost forgive it at Sherbourne, what with me being a total stranger and all, but if you could honestly spend all of that stupid race with me and *still* think I'm interested in Seb or getting my picture in the paper, or whatever it is you think I want——"

"I know you're not out to get Seb," Miles interrupts, "but for someone who claims not to want to be in the tabloids, you've certainly been there enough over the past week." He pauses, his eyes on my face, and I remember earlier when I thought he was kind of cute and want to go back in time and punch myself in the head.

"Again, maybe you should have this talk with Seb," I tell him. "Because Seb was the problem tonight, not me."

Miles looks away then, and I feel like there's something he's not saying. Something he *wants* to say.

But then he turns back and asks, "Could it be your parents?"

I honestly feel like I've been slapped. My head rears back and everything. "*Excuse* me?"

Chafing his palms on his thighs, Miles shrugs. "Calling the photographers. You may not want to be in the papers, but they might. I know your father used to be——"

"I'm going to stop you right there," I say, holding up one hand. I think I might actually be shaking, I'm so pissed.

"You don't know anything about me or my parents if you think for one second they'd try to shove my ass up the ladder with Ellie. I know it makes all of you people feel better to think we're a bunch of gross social climbers because then you don't have to deal with the fact that *maybe* Alex just likes Ellie better than the Flisses and Poppys of the world."

"That is not at all what I——" Miles starts, but I cut him off again.

"I actually thought you might *not* be as big of a douche as you seemed, but you, my friend, are clearly the Earl of Summer's Eve."

Miles's brow crumples in confusion, but luckily the car has pulled into Holyroodhouse now.

I don't even wait for the driver to open the door for me; I step out into the rainy night and don't look back.

I wake up to a thump right by my head. Cracking my eyes open, I see an iPad lying on the pillow next to me, and I scrub at my face, trying to pull myself out of a dream I can barely remember, except that I think Miles might have been in it, and that is just—

"What the hell happened last night?"

That's Ellie, and a supremely pissed-off Ellie if that tone is anything to go by. I've gotten kind of used to that weird museum-guide voice she does around here, so a return-to-form Ellie is both alarming and kind of welcome.

And then her question sinks in.

I sit up in bed. It's bright outside, the light streaming in through the gaps in the heavy velvet drapes, and I wince when Ellie marches over to the window and yanks the curtains open. The clock by my bed says it's just seven, but Ellie is fully dressed in a conservative black sheath covered with a red cardigan, her blond hair in a chignon at the nape of her neck. She even has jewelry on, a pretty little brooch in the shape of a thistle, and a thin silver bangle. *Do* bluebirds help her get ready in the morning?

Oh, right, last night.

I pick up the iPad and see the headline on the *Sun*'s webpage.

"CRAZY FOR DAISY!" it screams, and there's a blurry shot of me outside Seb's club, his hand on my shoulder. Miles and Isabel are nowhere to be seen, and this really looks like . . .

"Okay, this is stupid," I say, looking up at Ellie. She's standing at the foot of my bed, jaw clenched, arms crossed tightly over her chest. "Isabel was with Seb last night, and I went out to get her!"

Walking over to the bed, Ellie takes the iPad from me. "That's not what the internet is saying," she says, and she opens another page, then another, scrolling through a series of links.

"SEB AND DAISY!"

"PRINCE SEBASTIAN: CAUGHT AT LAST?"

"OOH-ER! A ROYAL NIGHT OUT!"

"PRINCESS DAISY?"

I almost want to laugh. It's just . . . dumb. Seb and I had hardly even spoken last night. How can this one picture make people think we're a thing?

I'm still shaking my head in amused disbelief when I look up at El.

That's when I notice she's downright pale, and genuinely upset.

Confused, I push my hair out of my eyes. "El, you know—" I start, but she just waves me off.

"All *I* know is that this is the top story on every news site in Scotland right now, maybe in the whole UK." And then her eyes meet mine. "And the queen got here this morning."

Well, now I'm not laughing. "The queen?" I nearly squeak.

Ellie nods and then, in a gesture I haven't seen from her in years, nervously twists the bangle around her wrist. "She wants to see you."

Chapter 24

"DON'T YOU THINK THAT'S A BIT OVERKILL?" DAD murmurs as we walk down the hall to the parlor where we'll meet the queen.

Mom is on my other side, and she glances across me toward Dad. "Oh, Liam, stop," she says, also nearly whispering. "She looks lovely."

"She looks like something they'd sell in the gift shop," Dad replies, and I frown as I look down at my tartan skirt. It was the most Scottish-y thing I had in my new, Glynnis-approved wardrobe, a plaid skirt in shades of bright red, black, purple, and green. I'd paired it with a sensible black blouse, black tights, and a pair of red ballet flats.

But yes, maybe the matching tartan vest was too much.

Or was it the hat?

Reaching up, I snatch the plaid tam-o'-shanter from my head and hand it to Mom, who shoves it in her handbag.

"I panicked, all right?" I hiss. "I avoided the dungeon over the thing at the race, but this? This could be dungeon material."

"Daisy," Mom chides in the same tone she usually uses for Dad, but Dad just pats my shoulder.

"We'll come visit, love, I promise."

Elbowing him in the ribs, I try to fight off an attack of the nervous giggles as Mom tuts and fiddles with one of her earrings.

The hallway we're heading down is dim, little lamps with apricot-colored silk shades casting pools of light on the ancient carpet, and it's in a part of the palace I haven't visited yet. These are the queen's personal quarters, and they're softer, more feminine than the rest of the palace. She's been queen since she was eighteen, and suddenly I wonder if she redecorated the whole place when she came to power. That's what I would've done. Of course I wouldn't have gone with all this peach and blue. I would've gone . . . purple, maybe. Neon green. To keep people on their toes.

Or maybe I'm focusing on interior design to keep from freaking the freak out.

The one thing I was determined to do this summer was keep my head down and stay out of Ellie's . . . everything. And now I am just all up in a royal mess, and I didn't even do anything fun, which is deeply unfair. If *I'd* been the one fighting with Seb at his club? Fine, I'd take my lumps—I did the thing. But I was just being a good and loyal friend, and now I'm about to be—

"Oh god," I mutter as we come to a stop in front of a pair of double doors. They're heavy and covered in fancy scrollwork with thistles, unicorns, and giant *B*s everywhere.

And behind them is an actual *queen* who thinks I am an evil seductress out to snare her youngest son.

I am going to die.

The three of us just stand there for a second, staring at the doors. I don't know if we're waiting for them to open on their own, or for fancy guys in uniforms to come out and open them for us, but in any case, we're not moving, and neither are the doors.

"I met a queen once," Dad muses. "She tried to put her hand down my trousers." Dad looks over at me and raises his eyebrows. "Surely this can't go any worse than that."

Which means I'm both groaning and laughing as the doors in front of us open and Queen Clara of Scotland rises to her feet from an apricot-colored velvet sofa.

The laugh dies in my throat, my cheeks flaming hot as Ellie rises from a striped chair. Alex is standing behind her with Glynnis to her left, and by the window—

Miles?

Sure enough, there's Mr. "I Think Your Tacky Parents Called the Paps" standing by the window in a nice suit, one hand in his pocket as he turns to watch me and my parents walk into the room. What on earth is *he* doing here?

"Mr. and Mrs. Winters," Queen Clara says, coming to a stop in front of us.

Mom drops into a curtsy and Dad bows. I'm half a second behind, so flustered by Miles being here that I nearly forget I'm standing in front of a queen.

Luckily, I manage to pull it off without too much shaking, and I'm really relieved when I raise my eyes to see that the queen doesn't look particularly "off with their heads." She's still smiling, and she has the same bright blue eyes as Alex and Seb. Her hair was once the same auburn as Seb's, but it's a little lighter now, strands of silver framing her face. Her suit is deep green and simple but gorgeous and tailored within an inch of its life, fitting so well I wonder if it was sewn onto her.

It's not just the distinguished hair and gorgeous outfit that make it obvious she's royalty, though. She's holding her whole body like there's a string attached to the top of her head, and every move she makes is elegant and smooth, like she's spent her whole life practicing.

Ellie is beautiful and graceful, but she doesn't have *this*. I don't know if anyone who wasn't born to wear a crown could have it, to be honest, and when I glance over at my sister, I feel a little bit of sympathy for her. I don't think I realized that this is what she'd be expected to live up to. How could anyone do that?

"Please, sit," the queen says, gesturing to another sofa in the room. This one is covered in peachy silk, but it's striped in deep teal, and I am very aware of how badly I must clash as I sit down on it.

The queen waves a hand again, and a maid in a dark suit carries a tea tray to the table in front of us.

Queen Clara doesn't ask how any of us take our tea. The maid just pours several cups, then hands them to us, the china so delicate I can practically see through it.

"Oh, this is *lovely*," Mom enthuses, holding the cup up for a closer look. "I just bought my first set of china last year so I'd have something to serve tea in when Alex and Ellie visit, but it's not nearly as nice as this. Where did you get it?"

Mom looks up, her eyes big behind her glasses, and I remember that while a good 80% of my personality came from my dad, that nervous talking thing I do?

That's all Mom.

I think I can actually feel Ellie dying from our other side, but the queen just smiles. "I believe this set belonged to my great-grandmother, Queen Ghislaine."

The cup rattles in the saucer, tea sloshing over the rim as Mom lowers it, blinking rapidly, her cheeks turning pink.

"Oh, of course," she says, then gives a forced laugh. "Silly of me. It isn't as though you buy your things from the outlet mall, is it? They don't even have outlet malls here, do they? They're really—"

I reach over, squeezing Mom's hand briefly, and my eyes meet Ellie's. She's still a little pale, and she nods her head a little, probably to thank me. When Mom gets going, it's like a babble bomb exploded everywhere.

"I've seen nicer," Dad says, studying his own cup with a shrug, so awesome, Mom surrendered to Nervous Talking, and Dad is going Surly Rock Star. That only took thirty seconds.

For the first time, I get why maybe Ellie spent so much time keeping the two halves of her life separate. Still, my loyalty is always going to be to Mom and Dad over these people who are only important due to an accident of birth, and I make myself sit up straighter, smiling at Queen Clara.

"It's so nice to finally meet you, Your Grace," I say, and Ellie clears her throat.

"Your Majesty," she corrects, and okay, maybe I blush a little at that, but I keep smiling.

"Your Majesty," I repeat, and the queen smiles back at me.

"It's lovely to finally have you all here," she says, crossing one ankle in front of the other. "I'm only sorry I wasn't here when you first arrived. It seems you've been enjoying your time here?"

She directs that at me, and while she keeps that soft smile, her eyes are suddenly . . . colder, maybe?

Dungeons and beheadings may not be on the agenda, but I bet she kind of wishes they were.

Glynnis steps forward then, an iPad in one hand, a folder in the other, and she leans down to murmur something into the queen's ear.

Queen Clara lifts one hand, waving that off, and then gestures for Glynnis to hand over the folder.

The room is very quiet as she flips through its contents, and I squirm a little on the sofa, my fingers clutching my skirt. I want to twist around and look at Miles, still wondering why he's even here. He hasn't said anything, but I wonder if he's in trouble for taking me to Seb's club last night. I also wonder if Isabel has seen all the news and what she might think.

Closing the folder, Queen Clara fixes me and my parents with another smile. Her nails are painted the same color as the sofa she's sitting on, and they drum against the folder for a moment.

"What a pickle," she says with a little laugh. "But such is life with teenagers, hmm?"

She directs that at Mom, who sits up a little straighter on the sofa and pats my knee. "Our girls have never been much trouble," she says, which, in my case, is kind of a lie, but I appreciate her loyalty.

Queen Clara's smile tightens, like someone just turned

screws on the sides of her mouth. "Given what I heard about An Reis, I'd say Daisy is making up for lost time," she says, and my stomach drops.

Ellie is still sitting in that chair, her fingers laced over one knee. Alex is beside her, and I see his hand drop briefly to her shoulder, squeezing.

"I am so sorry for what happened—" I start, but the queen flicks my words away like they're a mosquito buzzing around her head.

"My brother's wife is the one owed an apology, not me. And in any case, there's now a much larger issue to deal with."

Okay, this is officially kind of dumb. Everyone's acting like there are pictures of me and Seb making out on top of Edinburgh Castle or something instead of a few blurry shots of me coming out of his club.

I nearly say that—okay, I was going to leave out the making-out part—when Glynnis steps forward and says, "I'm sure this all seems a little silly to you, Daisy, but we have to be very careful with the optics right now."

Right. Optics.

Tapping on her iPad, Glynnis continues. "Any kind of rumor of things between you and Prince Sebastian has the potential to overshadow the wedding, plus it causes the kind of gossip we try to avoid."

"Has anyone said that to Seb?" I can't help but ask, and Glynnis glances up at me even as the queen's smile slips.

"Sebastian understands his role, I assure you," she says, and, yup, really gonna be lucky to get out of this room with my head still on my shoulders.

Queen Clara waves her hand at Glynnis. "Montrose," she says, and I wonder if that's some kind of code word to have me dragged out of here, but Glynnis just nods, tapping away again.

"Yes, the Duke of Montrose and his daughter, Lady Tamsin, are expected to join us for part of the summer. Lady Tamsin is a lovely young woman, and we're hoping that Sebastian takes a fancy to her."

Glynnis gives me a little wink at that, and I blink, confused.

But when I look over at my parents, they're just watching the queen, Dad's fingers curled tightly around the handle of his teacup.

"I'm not sure—" I start, and Queen Clara cuts me off.

"One of my sons is marrying an American girl from a frankly questionable family," she says bluntly, and I see Ellie draw herself up tight. Alex's hand is still on her shoulder, but he's standing just as stiffly, and Miles turns from the window to watch all of us.

Mom sighs softly, but Dad just fixes the queen with a gaze that used to hold whole arenas full of people in its thrall. "Be offended if you *didn't* think we were questionable," he says.

The queen ignores him. "Eleanor is a lovely young lady, and we're pleased to have her join the family," she goes on. "But one son following his heart is quite enough. Sebastian can marry whomever he chooses, but he will pick a girl from the *right* sort of family. Perhaps it will be Lady Tamsin, perhaps not, but the point remains that there cannot be even the littlest hint that he may be cavorting with your other daughter, Mr. and Mrs. Winters."

"Cavorting?" I echo. "I literally just went to get my friend from his weirdo posh-people club. And why are we even talking about marriage when he's seventeen?"

The queen's eyes may be the same gorgeous blue as her sons', but they are cold and hard as sapphires when they turn to me. "I don't expect you to understand," she says. "But I *do* expect you to stay clear of my son."

Holding up both hands, I perch myself on the edge of the sofa. "That is not a problem, trust me. I don't want anything to do with him."

Another smile, this one just as tight as the last. "Then we're in agreement," she says, and I hope we're about to be dismissed so that I can go find Isabel at her hotel and tell her all about this particular bit of Banana Pants Crazy, but then the queen once again signals to Glynnis.

"Obviously we need to kill this story as soon as possible," she says, and Glynnis nods, stepping forward again.

"And that's where Miles comes in," she says.

I twist on the couch to look over at Miles, but he's facing away from the window now and very much *not* looking in my direction.

"He was there last night as well, so it's a simple thing to make it clear that you were there with *him*, not Sebastian."

"Oh," I say, turning back around and crossing my ankles. "Yeah. I mean, that's true, so—"

"And once people realize the two of you are dating, this entire mess with Sebastian will be a thing of the past," Glynnis continues with a grin.

"*Dating?*" I don't mean for the word to come out like a

squeak, but it does, probably because my mouth, or brain, refuses to contemplate such an idea.

"Only for show, of course," Glynnis says with a flick of her fingers. "A few pictures of the two of you together, a few hints dropped here and there, and we're back in control of the narrative."

Once again, I turn to Miles, waiting for him to protest, but he's still staring straight ahead, his hands now clasped in front of him, and I realize he already knew about this.

They already talked to him, and he . . . *agreed?*

"This is insane," I say. "I know that everyone here is breathing rarefied air and stuff, but in the real world, no one *pretends* to date someone. I mean, unless it's making up a fake boyfriend so your friends at camp don't think you're a total loser, *that's* a thing, but—"

It's Mom's turn to squeeze my hand now, and my words come to a stuttering stop as the queen continues to look at me.

"It's an easy solution," she says, "that would make me very happy. And I'm sure it would please your sister as well."

The words are mild, but Ellie's eyes are pleading, and then I get it.

She's not threatening to call off the engagement. I'm not sure she even *could.* Alex is a grown man, and for all that they might be shoving Seb at whichever willing aristocratic lady crosses his path, it seems clear that the queen understands Alex is marrying the woman he loves.

But between insulting a duchess and being papped with Seb, I've now screwed up enough for this to be my penance, and if I don't want to make things harder for Ellie, I'll go along with it.

Mom and Dad seem to get it, too.

"It's just a few pictures, love," Mom says softly, and Dad sighs on my other side.

"Like I said, get on the train or be smashed on the tracks," he mutters in a low voice.

Ellie is watching me, her knuckles white, and I can see the violet shadows underneath her eyes, the hollows in her cheeks. I may not get anything about this world she's stepping into, but she wants to be here.

A few pictures.

Pretending to date a boy I don't like very much who also doesn't like me *or* my family.

Not exactly appealing, but not the hardest thing in the world, either. And once it's done, Ellie will be happy and secure on the road to princessdom, and I can put this whole—*everything*—behind me.

"Fine," I say. "Sure. Fake date me up."

And from behind me, I think I can actually feel Miles grimace.

I'd been on lots of dates since Mom decided I was allowed to date (Dad said he didn't deserve to have a say in when we started dating since his rock star past was so debauched, and none of us wanted to ask any more questions about that, Mom included).

My first date had been at the outdoor shopping center just outside of Perdido. I'd gone out with Matt Rivera and also seven of Matt's friends, plus Isabel, so I'm not *actually* sure that counts as a date, but I definitely treated it like one in my head, and the roughly three seconds when his hand had brushed mine as he handed me some pennies to throw in the fountain had gotten a lot of ink in my diary. Then there had been the movies with Daniel Funderburke, the seventh grade formal with Heath Levy, a whole summer of hanging out in various parking lots with Aidan Beck, plus this thing with Emily Gould that I hadn't thought was a date at the time but had seemed kind of date-y in retrospect.

And then, of course, Michael. So many dates with Michael. School dances, movies, driving around aimlessly . . .

Point is, I feel like I have a good handle on dates, but this? This is my first fake date, and I can already tell it's not going to go well.

For one, it is *early*. I mean, like, insane-o early. The time when the only people awake are going fishing or possibly in the grips of an amphetamine addiction. As I follow Glynnis across the gravel courtyard, our footsteps loud and crunchy in the still morning air, I squint against the sun, shading my eyes.

"Is anyone believably romantic at this hour?" I call to Glynnis, and she throws a grin at me over her shoulder.

"The royal family always rides first thing," she says, "so that's when the photographers show up."

I come to such a sudden stop that a little shower of rocks sprays around my sneakers. "Ride?" I repeat. "Please tell me you mean on bikes and not horses. Bikes don't bite last time I checked."

Glynnis just laughs, shaking her head. Her dark red hair glints in the sunshine. "I never imagined you'd be so funny, Daisy!"

"Super serious here," I say while she keeps marching. It really seems a shame that Glynnis doesn't wear a Fitbit because she'd nail her daily steps every day, probably a thousand times over.

Sighing, I follow her toward what I now realize are the stables. I hadn't noticed because the building is so fancy—all heavy stone-and-slate roof—that I'd assumed it was a place where *humans* lived, not horses.

Horses I'd now be expected to get on.

"What is it with you people and horses?" I ask as we step out of the sun and into the dim, grassy-smelling stable.

"We're related to them," Miles says, and my eyes adjust enough that I can see him, standing near one of the stalls. "It's why our chins look like this."

I almost snort because that would be a decent joke if he hadn't actually been blessed by the gods of bone structure, and also if I didn't hate him, but he was, and I do, so I don't.

He walks over to us, hands in his pockets, and I'm relieved that he's wearing relatively normal clothes—a white button-down, jeans, and a pair of brown leather boots. If we'd had to wear those super-tight white pants and velvet jackets, I would've just let the queen call off the wedding and brought shame down on my family. Nothing was worth pictures of my butt in those pants being splashed on the front of tabloids.

I'm wearing jeans and one of the shirts Glynnis picked out for me, a hunter-green blouse that looks like something Ellie would wear. I'm also in boots, but, I can admit, way cuter ones than Miles's. The leather encasing my calves is so soft I've had to resist the urge to stroke my own leg all morning.

We all just stand there for a second, me, my fake boyfriend, and the lady putting this whole thing together.

And then Glynnis claps her hands, smiling at both of us. "So this is easy peasy, lemon squeezy," she says, and I press my lips together to keep from laughing. I risk a glance at Miles, but he's not smiling at all. If anything, he looks bored, but then, I guess he's used to people talking like Dr. Seuss. I remember that girl from the club with her "yar" and drawling voice.

But then I also remember how Miles had broken the space-time continuum for a second by being cute, and that's so weird that I shove the thought away again. I probably hallucinated it, anyway. So worried about Isa that my brain snapped—that had to be what happened.

Besides, he was a massive jerk in the car, and that cancels out any cuteness *and* any potential bonding.

"All the two of you need to do is a lap or two around the park, making sure to smile at each other, maybe laugh occasionally . . ."

"British-people third base," I mutter, and to my surprise, that *does* seem to startle some kind of reaction out of Miles. He doesn't laugh, exactly, but he makes this kind of choked noise that he covers with a cough, and Glynnis looks between the two of us. Her eyebrows are especially intense this morning, so maybe this matters to her more than I'd thought. Those are very serious eyebrows.

"The photographers will get a few shots, we'll see if we can find some of the two of you the other night at Seb's club, and Bob's your uncle, all set!"

"That's it?" I ask, propping one hand on my hip. "They see us riding horses and smiling, and the entire country forgets that for one hot second, they were using the hashtag 'Sebaisy'?"

"That sounds like a skin condition," Miles says, screwing up his face, and then he looks over at me, lifting his eyebrows. "Will we have a hashtag, then?"

" 'Maisy' or GTFO," I reply, and this time he really smiles. With teeth and everything.

It probably causes him physical pain, but it looks nice.

And then Glynnis scowls, pulling her phone out. "We'd decided on 'Diles,' but 'Maisy' is better; just a tick."

As she types away on her screen, I look at Miles again, and our eyes meet. Just like at the club, there's this . . . beat between us. A little moment of understanding that feels weirdly nice, given that it comes from a guy who I'm not entirely convinced isn't a tea cozy cursed by a witch to live as a real-life boy.

"There!" Glynnis says, triumphant as she puts her phone back in the pocket of her smart little Chanel jacket. "Shall we get on with it?"

I can hear the horses in their stalls, nickering and shuffling and being horsey. Now seems like a good time to mention that I've never been on a horse, but I deflect a little.

"Why are we doing this for photographers who are already there?" I ask. "Can't we just, like, call them or something? Isn't that what they do in Hollywood? We could go to lunch, have them take pictures there. There's so much less potential for permanent maiming at lunch. Unless you do that thing with your face," I add to Miles. "I can't be responsible for maiming you if you do that thing with your face."

"What thing with my face?" Miles asks, doing exactly that thing. It's this lifting of his chin and tightening of his jaw that makes him look like he's about to oppress some peasants, and I point at him.

"That thing."

Glaring at me, Miles steps a little closer. "This is just what my face looks like."

"That is unfortunate," I say, and Glynnis claps her hands again.

"All right!" she trills. "The sooner we start, the sooner this can be over."

As she leads me to a stall, she adds, "For something as delicate as this, it's best if we let the photographers come to us rather than the other way around. Things feel much more . . . plausible that way. And given how sensitive this situation is, plausibility is our friend."

"Okay, but horses are not mine," I say.

Glynnis laughs, and I end up on the back of a gray mare named Livingston, which is a weird name for a girl horse, but I don't want to point that out in case she hears me and decides to throw me off.

Miles gets this massive black stallion because of course he does, and within just a few minutes, the two of us are in Holyrood Park behind the palace, riding on horses like people who just fell in love in a tampon commercial.

This is ridiculous.

But it's also really pretty here. If I ignore how scary it is to have a thousand-pound animal underneath me, I can admit that.

The sky is blue and almost cloud free, and the park is green and lovely and nearly empty except for a few people jogging and a girl walking an insanely cute little white dog.

And, of course, the photographers. I see them there at the edge of the park, three guys who all look nearly interchangeable in pullovers, baggy jeans, and sneakers.

To take my mind off them, I make myself smile at Miles and say, "Is this your normal first date, then?"

He sits a lot more easily in the saddle than I do, the reins just draped in his hands while I'm clutching mine so hard my knuckles are white.

"This is actually our fourth date if we're counting that time I walked you back to your room, the race, and the other night at the club," he says, and I sit up taller in the saddle.

"If we're counting those, you're pretty much the worst boyfriend ever."

"Not the first time I've heard that," he says, and I jerk my head around to look at him.

"You've been a boyfriend?" I ask. "To a human girl?"

Shaking his head, Miles moves his reins from one hand to the other. "Let's save that for our fifth date, shall we?"

His horse trots ahead a little, and I give mine the slightest little touch with my heels to make her catch up. To my relief, she does, and I try not to think about how much jiggling those cameras might be catching as I pull even with Miles.

"Is there going to be a fifth one?" I ask. "Can't we just do . . . this and be done with it?"

Miles looks over at me, his sandy hair dipping over his brow, and his eyes are particularly green this morning. Maybe Glynnis chose the park to make him look his most handsome. Who can say?

"I assume they'll want us to do the ball together," he says, smiling broadly for the photographers.

"Ball?" I repeat, giving him the same bright grin, complete with a head tilt. This is some excellent work and better end up on at least one front page. I haven't shown this many teeth in *ages*.

"We're headed up north day after tomorrow," he replies, complete with a little chuckle as he reaches out to cover my hand for just a second with his own. "To Baird House. There's going to be a ball for Eleanor and Alex, and if Glynnis doesn't make us sell this there, I'll eat this saddle."

"Oooh, you might choke, and that would be *so* fun to watch!" I say, tossing my hair over my shoulders.

Another laugh, and I swear there's genuine warmth in his eyes now. It almost makes me wonder if he's done this kind of thing before.

There's a sudden flurry of barking off to my right, and I look over to see that cute little white dog I'd spotted earlier suddenly tearing across the park, filled with bloodlust for a flock of birds on the path right in front of us.

It's a pretty nonthreatening dog, but Livingston doesn't see it that way. Suddenly, my previously gentle and super-chill horse shudders, hooves pawing the earth, and then, as the dog gets closer, my horse loses her mind altogether, giving a panicked whinny and lifting her front hooves off the ground.

Shrieking, I panic, and instead of grabbing the reins I sink my fingers into her mane, holding on for dear life, my entire world becoming a panicked blur of barking, whinnying, my own shrill cries, and the vision of headlines reading, "FUTURE PRINCESS'S SISTER KILLED IN FREAK HORSEBACK ACCIDENT WHILE ON FAKE DATE!"

And then Livingston lowers her hooves back to the ground, still pawing and shuddering, and I see a long-fingered hand shoot out and grab her reins.

Miles.

His horse is right next to mine, our knees bumping as he tries to bring Livingston under control, and I manage to release my death grip on the horse's mane, my hands fumbling to hold on to the reins, the saddle, anything.

I want off this horse *now*.

And suddenly, I *am* off.

A strong arm wraps around my waist, and I'm pulled onto Miles's horse, my backside colliding painfully with the saddle.

Startled, I stare up at him, my hands landing on his shoulders. I'm basically sprawled in front of him, the saddle horn pressing into my hip, and holy crap, did he *just yank me off my horse and onto his?*

He did.

Which is some real next-level romance novel stuff, and I have no idea how to feel about it.

Miles still has one arm around me, his hand holding his own horse's reins, and then he leans over to take up Livingston's reins.

"All right, then?" he asks, like he didn't just pull some major pirate maneuver, and I can only nod.

I guess that's enough for him, because he turns both horses and leads us back toward the palace stables.

I'm still holding on to his shoulders—clutching, really—and behind him, I can see the photographers, can practically hear the clicks as they snap shot after shot of me perched on the front of Miles's horse, my arms wrapped around him.

Looking up at his chin, I study the little glints of golden stubble there and try to think of something to say. My heart is still hammering against my ribs from Livingston's freak-out, but if I'm honest, it might be a little more than that.

"Glynnis is going to implode with joy," I finally say, and Miles huffs out something close to a laugh.

"One down," he mutters, and I have to admit, as far as first— or fourth—dates go, this one is certainly memorable.

Chapter 25

"NO ONE IS GOING TO EXPECT ME TO SHOOT THINGS, right?" I ask for what is probably the third time.

El, sitting across from me in the back of the car, sighs and crosses her legs at the ankle. Ever since the car pulled away from Holyrood Palace, carrying us north up into the Highlands, Ellie has been giving me The Sigh, and also The Side-Eye, and just a *hint* of The Chin Tilt.

All of which is ridiculous given that I am pretending to date a boy for her, so you'd think she could be a little less irritated with me. Especially since I was right—those pictures of Miles carrying me off on his horse like we were in a Regency romance had gone over really, really well. I'd seen at least five different angles of that shot, and even I had to admit they were swoony. The fakest thing ever to fake, but still.

"No shooting, Daisy," Alex assures me now, giving El's knee a pat. "Season doesn't start until August, and not even I can break that rule."

"What would happen if you did?" I ask, leaning forward a

little. "Could they arrest you? Is there some kind of royal im-
munity? If—"

"Daisy!" El snaps suddenly, turning her head to glare at me.
"It's a four-hour drive, and if you ask inane questions the entire
way, I'm going to lose my mind."

Lifting my hands, I settle back into my seat. "Sorry," I mutter, and Alex frowns slightly, looking back and forth between
me and my sister. He must have had these kinds of little blowups
with Seb and Flora growing up, and I almost ask him that before I remember that I'm not supposed to ask questions. All El
wanted was for me to show an interest in all of this, and now that
I am, she wants me to be quiet.

Typical.

Also, to be honest, I'd thought that engaging in a little
friendly chatter would help dispel some of the tension that had
been brewing. I'd thought going along with "the palace's" plan
would make Ellie happy, but clearly it wasn't enough, and I have
to fight the urge to start an argument with her over it. It's just . . .
I gave up the Winchester Mystery House for her, I gave up Key
Con, I gave up my personal dignity after the Horse Incident,
and she's *still* acting like it's all my fault somehow.

But fighting in front of Alex would be bad, so I decide to take
the high road.

My shoulder bag is sitting on the seat next to me, and I pull
it closer, still enjoying how soft the leather is underneath my
fingers. This had been one of Glynnis's things, that I needed
to stop carrying my ratty backpack and have something nicer,
just in case there were photographers. I'd wanted to object on
principle, but then she gave me this lovely bag, all supple and

expensive, lined with a gorgeous green-and-purple tartan, a thistle emblem embroidered on the front, and oh man, I'd been a goner.

I take *The Portrait of a Lady* out of my bag, and Alex smiles, nodding at the paperback in my hands. "Henry James? I approve."

It's for summer reading, and I would much prefer to be reading something with dragons, but I give Alex a smile in return, wiggling the book in his general direction.

"You know we Winters fam, always seeking to better ourselves."

"What's that supposed to mean?" Ellie is sitting up in her seat now, hair falling over her shoulders, which are so tense you could probably crack rocks on them.

"I was making a joke," I fire back at El, and I can sense Alex steeling himself for sisterly drama. But he's a born diplomat, which I guess is a useful skill for him, because he just clears his throat and says, "Has Eleanor told you anything about where we're going, Daisy?"

"North," I reply, waving a hand. "Hinterlands. Mountains. Kilts. Special cows."

El is still looking out the window, but one corner of her mouth lifts, and Alex chuckles. "Those are the highlights, yes. But the actual house we're going to is rather special to our family, mostly because it's *ours*."

I lower my book, raising my eyebrows at him. "Unlike Holyroodhouse, right?"

Alex nods. "Exactly. Things like Holyrood and Edinburgh Castle belong to the people of Scotland. We live in them, of course, but we're only stewards. Baird House is private property. My great-grandfather Alexander bought it back in the thirties so that he'd have a retreat for his family—somewhere they could go and feel like regular people."

"The Petit Trianon," I blurt out, and now it's Alex's turn to raise his eyebrows.

Ellie glances over at me, and I shrug. "I went through a Marie Antoinette phase," I explain. "Not the 'let them eat cake' part—which she didn't even say, by the way—but just . . . you know, the history of it all. The Petit Trianon was this little house Marie used near Versailles, and she could pretend to be a regular person there. Milk goats, feed sheep, do whatever it was she thought peasants did."

Alex chokes on a laugh, turning it into the fakest cough I have ever heard. "Well, yes, but I promise you, we don't go up there to pretend to be peasants."

"Do you wear kilts?" I counter, and Alex nods.

"Wouldn't be allowed into the Highlands if we didn't."

"Then I guess that's good enough," I say with a shrug, and Alex smiles at me. It's a real smile, the kind I don't get from him or El that often, and it's nice. Another reminder that without all this weird royalty stuff, Alex is a good guy who makes my sister happy and seems to like me.

The car keeps heading north, and while I try to read my book, I can't stop staring out the window as the landscape changes. For the first part of the drive, it is all fairly normal. Highways, road signs, fast food places. But eventually the rolling hills get higher, craggier. There's even some snow on the peaks of the higher mountains, and before long, I've practically got my nose pressed to the glass. Now *this* is the Scotland I've been waiting for. Before, when we'd visited, we'd only been in the cities, really. Edinburgh, Glasgow . . . I'd never seen the actual Highlands.

Before long, the car is slowing down, bumping over a long gravel driveway, and as we round the corner, a house comes into view.

The car rolls to a stop, and I take in the building in front of me. I know Alex said it's private property, but I still wasn't expecting something this . . . homey.

That doesn't mean it's a normal house, of course. It's huge, red brick and gravel drive and all that, but it's not as imposing as Sherbourne Castle or Holyrood, not even as intimidating as the big hotel we all stayed in back in Edinburgh. And it feels a lot more isolated than either of those places, too, all tucked up here in the Highlands.

For the first time since I got here, I feel like I can breathe a little, and I take a deep breath. Yes, this is exactly what I need. What we *all* need. A chance to get to know each other in less intimidating surroundings, and without distractions.

Then I step out of the car and see that other Land Rovers have pulled up, and Royal Wreckers are spilling out onto the gravel drive.

Okay, so a *few* distractions, then.

I haven't seen the Royal Wreckers since the bookstore and the club, and now there's much slapping of shoulders as Seb and his boys make their way to the house.

Miles hangs back a little, glancing over at me.

I stare back, wondering if we're supposed to fake things

here, too. I know we have the ball later this week—as much as I'm trying not to think about that—but surely that doesn't mean we have to, like, hold hands and stuff now?

To my relief, Miles follows the others inside, and I'm just about to head that way, too, when another car pulls up, this one nicer and sleeker than the Land Rovers that dropped off the boys. I know it's not Mom and Dad—they're spending a few more days in Edinburgh before coming up for the ball—but I'm still not prepared for the girls who pour themselves out of the back seat.

They are, without a doubt, the prettiest people I have ever seen in my life.

One is tall with dark hair that swings in a shiny sheet over her shoulders as she hefts a gorgeous leather bag, pushing her sunglasses up on top of her head. She's just wearing jeans, boots, and a sweater—sorry, a *jumper*—but she could seriously be on a runway somewhere, all long legs and easy elegance.

The other girl?

Princess Flora.

I've seen her before, of course, online and in magazines, but that still doesn't prepare me for how lovely she is in the flesh. I guess I shouldn't be surprised given how flummoxed I was with Seb, but still, I had no idea she was *this* pretty. She's shorter than the girl she's with, and curvier, her dark gold hair just brushing her shoulders, and when she sees Alex, she drops her bag there in the gravel and gives a very unprincess-like shriek.

"Ali!" she yells, launching herself at her brother, who laughs and squeezes her back, swinging her around.

Ellie is standing next to me, her arms crossed. Her sunglasses are too big for me to really read her expression, but her body language is . . . stiff? Uncomfortable?

And when Alex releases Flora, I see why.

The princess's eyes just barely skim over me and my sister, and then she turns to call over her shoulder, "Tam! Let's get in before the rain starts."

The sky is perfectly clear, almost painfully blue, only a few white puffy clouds drifting by.

As Flora and "Tam"—who I realize with a jolt must be the Lady Tamsin the queen is so keen to throw at Seb—swan past us and into the house, I look over at El, my eyes wide.

"Oh my god, we just got the cut direct."

"Daisy," Ellie says, but I gesture to where the girls disappeared into the house.

"Haven't you read enough Jane Austen to see what just happened?" I ask. "Does she always treat you like that?"

"Flora can be prickly," Alex says, coming forward to slip an arm around Ellie's waist. "But she'll get there."

Even though she's still wearing her sunglasses, I feel like El is looking at me for a second before Alex guides her toward the stone steps into the house.

I stand there while the drivers start pulling our luggage out of the car. Seb a human trash fire, the queen a literal ice queen maneuvering her kids into political marriages, and Flora a total bitch. What else hasn't Ellie told me about this family?

Thirty minutes later, I'm tucked up in a room that's not unlike my room at Sherbourne—super fancy, full of old stuff, and also freezing cold. Oh, and fully tartaned up. My bedspread is plaid, the canopy is plaid, even the carpet seems to have a faded plaid pattern, and if I manage to sleep in here every night and *not* get a migraine, I'll consider it a win.

In a few minutes, I'm supposed to go downstairs for tea, but before I do that, there's something else I need to do.

Flopping on the bed, I pull my laptop out, firing up Skype.

After a few moments, Isabel's face appears on the screen, and I think I actually sigh with relief.

"There you are!"

It's not that I'd been worried that Isa might be mad at me about all that had happened while she was here, but there was a part of me that wondered if she might not want a little break from all things Scotland (and by extension, me). She'd seemed pretty eager to get home last week.

But no, she's smiling there in her room, sitting on the floor by her bed. I can see the edge of her sheets, bright pink with little yellow flowers all over them. She bought them in the kids' section at Target because "everything for adults is so boring."

"Where else would I be?" she asks, bringing up a can of Diet Coke to take a sip.

"I don't know. Away from all things royal? I know the trip wasn't exactly what you'd thought it would be."

She sighs, pushing her heavy dark hair back from her face. "Like, I thought it would be really fun and exciting, but instead it was just kind of a pain? The guards and the photographers, and obviously Sebastian."

I raise my eyebrows. "Yeah, I picked up on that one."

Shrugging, Isa leans back against the side of her bed. "He was weird. I felt like he was acting like the person he thought he was supposed to be, not who he actually was, you know?"

I do. Ellie has started doing the same thing sometimes. I remember how she talked to people at the race, the fake-bright smile, the way she would tilt her head down whenever she was listening to someone, making this intense face I'd seen Alex do a bunch.

So I nod to Isa and say, "They're all weird."

"Even Miles?" she replies, a dimple appearing in one cheek as she smirks at me.

"Of course you saw that stuff," I say on a sigh, and she reaches out and actually flicks the computer screen, like she's hitting me in the head.

"I cannot believe you didn't tell me!" she says, and for a moment, I hesitate. Do I tell Isa it's not real? That it's actually because of everything that happened the night she went to Seb's club with him?

I'd like to say it, but I don't want Isabel to worry, and the truth is, I'm a little embarrassed. I've only been here a few weeks, and I'm already faking a relationship in order to please "the palace." That's . . . not a great look.

I shrug. "It's nothing major, just a summer thing." And then, because I need a change of subject stat, I ask, "Anything with Ben?"

"Ugh, I don't want to talk about him," she groans, and while we're definitely going to have to get more into all that at some point, for now, there's another reason I called her.

"Okay, so if you're not averse to looking at those royal blogs, do you think you could maybe do me a favor?"

"Oooh, reconnaissance?" Isabel asks, dark eyes going wide. "Into it."

I lower my voice. "Princess Flora is here," I tell her, "and she's . . . not exactly mine or Ellie's biggest fan. I don't want to be busted searching for anything on her, so could you—"

"Find out what she's like and report back via secure emails?" Isabel finishes, and I laugh.

"Settle down, Jason Bourne," I reply. "Just . . . see what you can find out, and email it to me. I want your take on it, not just a bunch of links."

Isa gives me a little salute. "On it," she announces. "By the time I'm done, you'll be *more* than prepared for her visit."

I laugh, and we sign off, letting me go back to unpacking. And sure enough, within half an hour, Isa has sent me a rundown of all things Flora.

Really, it's not that different from what I'd expected. Like Seb, she can be a bit wild, but *unlike* Seb, her foibles have ended up in the tabloids. She also just got kicked out of school, so maybe that explains the attitude. There's also a pretty hefty list of former boyfriends.

Then I get to the last line of Isa's reconnaissance:

And just so you know, Dais, one of those exes? Miles.

She's harder to track down than her famous brothers, but Princess Flora of Scotland, currently attending an elite all-girls school on the Isle of Skye, is no less talked about. According to sources, Flora is the real wild child of the family, a title she laughs off when I sit down with her in a coffee shop not far from the flat she keeps in Edinburgh. She's home for a break before heading back to her (unnamed at the request of the palace) school and looking forward to a summer spent "with friends, probably. Somewhere quiet." She tells me she's gotten very used to the solitude there on Skye and that "it's definitely been a tonic for the soul."

Yes, the girl we're used to seeing in front rows in Milan, New York, and Paris (and clubs in Monaco, Marrakesh, and Zurich) is becoming something of a homebody. "I've even taken up knitting!" she laughs, rolling those extraordinary light brown—dare we say gilded?—eyes she inherited from her famous grandfather.

One subject Flora is not keen to speak on, however, is the engagement of her eldest brother, Alexander, to Miss Eleanor Winters of Florida.

"There's just not much to say," she tells me when pressed. "I've only met Eleanor a handful of times. I'm sure she'll be a beautiful bride."

Kind words, but it makes one wonder if the rumours that Flora is less than pleased with her brother's American (and commoner) bride-to-be are true.

In any case, it's a kinder, gentler Princess Flora who departs from the café, bodyguards in tow, a gentle summer drizzle raining down on her—what else?—Baird family tartan brolly.

*Editor's Note—Two weeks after this interview was conducted,

Princess Flora abruptly withdrew from her boarding school on Skye at the insistence of school officials. Neither the school nor the palace have commented, save that this is a "private matter" and that gossip involving the princess, the headmaster's son, and a fire at a local whiskey distillery is "scurrilous and baseless."

(*Prattle*, "Princess Flora: An Intimate Chat," *May Issue*)

Chapter 26

THE MORNING OF THE BALL IS THE FIRST TRULY gross day we've had, weather-wise, since I arrived in Scotland. The sky churns with clouds, rain sheets down the windows, and it seems like there's a rumble of thunder about every three seconds.

Honestly, it seems kind of portentous.

We're all sitting in the dining room, having breakfast, and while Ellie said this is the smaller, informal dining room, it's still massive, and the table seats at least fifty people. It's heavy oak, scarred in places, and I can imagine Highland chiefs sitting here, stabbing their knives into the table to make a point. Dead stags stare down at us with glass eyes, and the eggs on my plate seem kind of unappealing.

Maybe because they're next to a lump of what appears to be coal.

I poke at it, trying not to wrinkle my nose.

"Black pudding."

Glancing up, I see Miles has taken a seat across the table from me, and as he spreads a napkin in his lap, I think about him and Flora again. I haven't asked him about any of that—that's a thing *real* girlfriends get to do, not fake ones—but I have to admit, I'm still . . . okay, maybe curious is a strong word, but I'd genuinely like to know what went on there.

Instead, I ask about the pudding.

"Do I even want to know what's in it?"

"You really don't," he replies, and I sigh, pushing it all the way to the edge of my plate.

"Aw, come on, Monters," Gilly says, cutting into his own black pudding. "Don't scare her off the stuff. It's good for you." He winks. "Puts hair on your chest."

"Exactly what I've always wanted," I answer, and Gilly laughs. He's sitting beside Sherbet. Spiffy and Dons haven't appeared yet, and Alex and Ellie are sitting at the head of the table, heads close together as they talk and ignore the rest of us.

"So," Gilly says once he's cleared his plate of black pudding. "Flora."

Across the table, Miles suddenly gets very interested in his toast. "Flora," Sherbet confirms.

"Should liven things up at least," Gilly says. "She usually does."

Sherbet snorts. "The last time Flora *livened up* a gathering, a suit of armor ended up in the fountain."

Gilly heaves a sigh, his gaze far away. "That was one of my ancestors'. Thought Mum and Dad were going to cry."

Miles is still very industriously eating his breakfast, and I tear a bit of crust off my toast, looking at him.

"So the ball," I say, and he sighs, not looking up from his mushrooms. Honestly, mushrooms for breakfast—who does that?

"The ball," he confirms, and I look over at Gilly and Sherbet, who are still chatting to each other. I wonder if they know about me and Miles, that it's not real, or if we're even supposed to pretend for them.

Playing it safe, I ask, "Are you going to wear a kilt?"

Miles finally looks up then, putting his fork down. "I am, yeah."

I nod, chewing my bit of toast. "Can I make fun of you for that?"

"Could I stop you?" he asks, but he doesn't sound pissed off or irritated. He's just . . . relaxed. Normal. Then he clears his throat, putting his fork down and linking his fingers together on the tablecloth.

"I had the chance to speak to your parents for a little while when they came in last night," he starts, and my shoulders go up a little bit, all the vague sort of camaraderie I'd been feeling disappearing.

Mom and Dad had gotten in late yesterday, just in time for the ball, but I was already in my room when they'd arrived. They'd both come in to say hi, of course, but I hadn't known they'd spent any time with Miles.

"They're . . . really lovely," Miles goes on, and now he's looking at his plate again, fidgeting in his chair. "And funny," he adds. "And . . ."

"Not people who would call the paparazzi on their daughter?" I finish for him, and finally he looks up.

"Not at all," Miles confirms, which sort of surprises me. I thought for sure he'd give me some long-winded defense, making sure to point out how tacky we all are. So what was a landed gentleman such as himself *supposed* to think?

Instead, he just looks into my eyes and says, "I'm sorry. I was wrong. Colossally wrong, really."

I blink at him, feeling like I did that night in the club when I was suddenly confronted with Hot Miles. This is Contrite Miles, which is every bit as discombobulating, and it takes me a second before I shake my head and mutter, "It's okay."

Sighing, Miles picks up his fork and resumes pushing eggs around his plate. "It's not, really. It was one of Seb's valets, a bloke who's worked at the palace for years. They sacked him, obviously.

"Anyway, truly, I'm sorry," Miles says again. "I was an unmitigated ass about the entire thing, especially when the call was coming from inside the house, as it were."

"To be fair, you're an unmitigated ass about a lot of things," I say, and Miles smiles at that, acknowledging it with a tilt of his head, which makes me laugh.

Aaaaand then I look up to see Ellie watching me, her brows drawn together, her big-sister sensors clearly on high alert, and I get up from the table, tucking my head so my hair swings over my face. And when she calls my name, quietly but urgently, I feign a sudden case of deafness.

I spend the rest of the day mostly holed up in my room, trying not to think too much about the night to come. The queen's coming in this afternoon, and I was definitely trying to stay out of her way after our last meeting. I'd done what she'd asked, sure, but it seemed smartest to keep my head down.

The rain clears up by that afternoon, and when Glynnis comes in to help me get ready, I'm staring out the window, liking the way the light moves over the hills, how it is never the same from minute to minute, wishing I was good at painting or even photography so I could catch it somehow. Maybe that's something I could try out next? The pictures on my phone aren't doing it justice, so I finally decide to enjoy the view for what it is.

"Wool-gathering?" Glynnis asks, smiling at me as she hangs the garment bag on the door of my wardrobe.

"In the figurative or literal sense?" I ask, and when she frowns at me, I wave a hand.

"Sheep joke. I get it. What's that?"

Glynnis smiles at me, those shiny teeth practically winking in the sunlight. "Your dress for tonight! Just arrived from the city."

I assume the city means Edinburgh, and when Glynnis unzips the bag, I see that gorgeous tartan gown I'd drooled over in the catalog Glynnis had showed us, back when I was getting my new-and-improved Daisy look.

El remembered.

It feels silly to get choked up over a dress, but this is a really, *really* great dress, and also, it means that El still listens to me a little. Still *sees* me.

"It's perfect," I tell Glynnis.

A few hours later, I'm rethinking that statement. Yes, the dress is pretty. Yes, that riot of deep green and purple and black looks pretty with my hair and makes my skin glow. Yes, I feel a little bit like a princess, and okay, maybe, after I've first put it on, there is some twirling.

Just a *little* twirling.

But after an hour or so in it in a crowded ballroom, the tulle underneath the silk skirt is scratching my legs, and I keep surreptitiously tugging at the bodice, afraid my Facebook-famous boobs are about to steal the spotlight. Plus El let me borrow a tiara, and it is *killing me*. Too heavy, tight on my temples, and I'm very, very aware that I not only have several thousand dollars on my head but also several hundred years of history. This tiara had belonged to some ancestor of Alex's, no one that important—Alex's mom has a firm hand on all the stuff that actually matters, the famous jewels and all that, but this had been some king's aunt's or something like that, and I wonder if her picture is hanging up at Sherbourne Castle.

And if she'd wanted to toss this particular tiara from the tallest tower.

I'm out on the stone patio that overlooks the main patio downstairs, and I'm really considering tossing this heavy piece of silver, diamonds, and amethysts into the pond when I hear Dad say, "Good god, they've gotten to you, too."

I turn around, smiling at my dad. "Actually, I was just thinking about throwing this priceless tiara in the duck pond," I tell him, and he raises his champagne flute of club soda to me.

"There's my girl."

Dad ambles over to my side, and for a little bit, we stand in the soft-purple evening, looking down at the party.

Ellie is also in tartan tonight, although hers is the official

Baird tartan. It's pretty, and the diamonds in her hair sparkle. Once again, it's clear to me that El was meant to be a princess.

"They'll eat her up, these people," Dad muses, waving his free hand to take in all the people milling around on the patio below us.

"I dunno, Dad," I say, leaning close enough to him to bump his elbow. "They don't really look much like cannibals to me."

He glances down at me, that familiar smile tugging the corners of his lips. There are deep brackets on either side of his mouth, and the breeze blows his admittedly scraggly hair back from his face.

Threading my arm through his, I nod down at all those people in their fancy dresses and weird headgear. "They'll learn to love her. Everyone loves El. It's . . . like, her superpower. Intense likability. That and having really shiny hair."

"She even had that hair as a baby," Dad says, frowning. "It was unsettling."

I laugh, but something in the sound must be off because Dad looks down at me. "And you, poppet? How are you holding up in all this madness?"

Dad has always been good at understanding when things bug me, maybe because I inherited his skill at laughing off stuff or covering with jokes. It works with Mom, usually works with El, too, but Dad . . . no, Dad is onto me.

"I'm okay," I tell him, because that's close to the truth. Sometimes I have fun, sometimes I actually *love* it here. Weirdly enough, the first thing that flashes through my mind is the other morning, riding through the park with Miles, and I shove it aside, but not quickly enough to stop a blush from climbing up my neck. Dad probably notices—he notices *everything*—but he doesn't say anything.

"It's like being on another planet," I tell him, and Dad chuckles at that.

"It is," he tells me. "Planet Rich and Famous. The air is rarefied and eventually makes it impossible to breathe."

Then he smiles at me and says, "But you'll both be fine. You have something I didn't."

I raise my eyebrows, waiting for the punch line.

And sure enough, Dad nudges me, winks, and says, "Good parents."

I laugh at that, and Dad looks down at his empty glass. "Off for a refill. You need anything?"

When I shake my head, he gives me another wink. "Don't throw any jewelry into the shrubbery without me, darling."

Dad goes back inside, and I smile as I watch him go. I've missed having my parents around, which is a sentiment that might get me kicked out of teendom, but it's the truth. No matter how embarrassing my dad might be, how distracted my mom always is, they love us. They're easy to be around, and they've only ever wanted us to be healthy and happy. In that way, we're a lot luckier than the royals.

Sighing, I turn back to the balcony. It's still not dark—it won't be until nearly 11 p.m.—but the light is so pretty, all soft and golden, edged in lavender, and the nearby hills are dark green against the sky. It's also chilly, enough that I wish I'd brought a wrap or something.

"There you are," I hear, and I turn around to see Miles coming out of the patio doors toward me, and he's just . . . it's very . . .

"Wow," I finally say.

He is indeed wearing a kilt, but I don't much feel like making fun of it. It's the same tartan as my dress, the purple and green and black, and he's wearing it with a matching bow tie, a white shirt, and a gorgeous black jacket. Even those socks the men wear with their kilts don't look silly on him, and when I glance down, I notice—

"Is that a knife?" I ask, gesturing to the leather hilt in the cuff of his sock, and Miles looks down.

"Hmm? Oh, yes, it's part of the whole look. It's called a *sgian-dubh*, and it's—"

I hold up a hand. "No. No history tonight," I tell him, and to my surprise, he grins, a dimple flashing in his cheek. His curly hair has been tamed tonight, but it still curls around his earlobes, and he looks . . . nice.

Better than nice, but I'm not quite willing to admit that right now.

"No history," he agrees, and then holds out his hand. "But how about dancing?"

Chapter 27

THE BALLROOM IS CROWDED WHEN WE WALK IN, my hand tucked into the crook of Miles's arm, and for a moment, I stare at all the whirling skirts.

"That is just . . . so much plaid," I mutter, and Miles does that huffing sound that, for him, almost passes for a laugh.

"How do you not get migraines looking at so many clashing patterns all the time?" I ask him. There's an older lady glittering with emeralds, her skirt a riot of bright orange, green, and black, and she's standing right next to a woman decked out in diamonds and a yellow-and-blue tartan dress. And that's not even taking into account the kilts on every guy.

"Guess we're used to it," Miles replies.

Then he steps back a little bit, looking down at my dress. I remember the way Seb had looked at me in my bedroom, his eyes sliding from the top of my head to my toes, and how that had made me want to pull a blanket over my head.

Miles's gaze doesn't do that, which makes absolutely no

sense. But maybe it's that he's looking at me sort of . . . admiringly as opposed to just assessing.

"The plaid suits you," he finally says, and I squint at the two spots of color high up on his cheekbones.

"Are you complimenting me?" I ask, and I think those pink patches grow a little bit, which is funny because that implies Miles's blood is not *actually* blue, but red, just like us commoners.

"It's called manners," he says, and then shakes his head, leading me farther into the ballroom but not quite to the dance floor yet.

I'm fine with that, as the current dance is some kind of folk deal involving people standing in a line, switching partners, swinging . . . it all looks a little dangerous to me, but I spot Ellie in the crowd, her golden hair bright and a smile on her face as she switches from Alex to Seb, her skirt billowing as she twirls.

I'm still smiling at El when I glance up and my eyes meet the queen's.

She's standing on the other side of the ballroom, talking to some ancient-looking man in the same bright red tartan the queen is wearing, but she's looking at me, and, seeing my arm in Miles's, she nods slightly and purses her lips in what I think is meant to be approval.

Out on the dance floor, Ellie swings back to someone else, a tall man I've never seen before, and Seb takes Tamsin's hands. He's grinning down at her, and she smiles back, her dark hair flying as he spins her into the next part of the dance, but she keeps looking around, her gaze sliding to the edge of the dance floor.

"Do you know her very well?" I ask Miles, pressing closer to speak into his ear. "Lady Tamsin?"

Miles has been clapping along with the rhythm of the music like most of the other people watching the dancers, and he pauses, his hands still pressed together. He has pretty hands, long-fingered and elegant, probably perfect for pointing imperiously at things.

"Not really," he says, "but the queen has been set on her and Seb for ages."

"Why?" I ask, and he gives another one of those shrugs.

"The Duke of Montrose is one of the richest men in Scotland, so maybe that. They also have a really excellent hunting lodge not far from here, and the queen does like her stag hunting."

Twisting around, I stare at him. "So in this, the year of our lord 2018, she'd marry off her son to get access to *hunting grounds?*"

One corner of Miles's mouth kicks up. "Royalty," he says, and I think of Sherbet, telling me that a monarch could just take anything they wanted out of his house.

"You're all insane," I say, and Miles, to my surprise, doesn't get all huffy and offended. Instead, he nods.

"More or less."

"Monters! Lady Daze!"

Sherbet is heading toward us, grinning, his eyes bright and his face flushed, Galen following in his wake.

When I'd first heard about Sherbet's Greek shipping heir boyfriend, I'd assumed he'd be as blindingly handsome and glamorous as Sherbet. Instead, he's a good head shorter than Sherbet, kind of chubby, and so shy that he blushes any time he has to make small talk.

And Sherbet is totally nuts about him.

"Why aren't the two of you dancing?" Sherbet asks, and Miles nods at him and Galen.

"Could ask the two of you the same thing," he says, and Sherbet laughs, throwing his arm around Galen's shoulders.

"Didn't want to show everyone up, old man," he says, then turns his eyes to the dance floor, where the dance is wrapping up. Seb leads Tamsin away, his head bent low as he talks to her, and Sherbet heaves a sigh.

"So that's on, then," he says, and Miles nods. "Seems so."

Turning his hazel eyes back to me, Sherbet nudges my arm. "We'd all hoped Seb might settle on you since you're such a laugh."

I shoot him a wry look. "I don't think 'a laugh' is what Seb needs."

That makes Sherbet chortle, and he shakes his head, dark hair flopping over his brow. "True, true. But it's good for Monters here, at least!"

He slaps Miles's arm, and I try to keep the surprise off my face. So Miles hasn't told them that we're not the real deal?

The music changes suddenly, going from sedate background music into something wild and raucous.

Sherbet's whole face lights up, and he grabs my hand and Miles's. "Strip the Willow!" he yells, tugging us both toward the floor, and I yell back, "What?"

But it's clear as soon as we're in the crowd that Strip the Willow is a dance, not some kind of potentially perverted Brit slang.

I dig my heels in, coming to a stop. "Whoa, I don't know that," I say, watching as men and women begin to form two lines. My parents are in there, as are Ellie and Alex. Even the queen is in the lineup now.

But Sherbet is not taking no for an answer. "Neither does Galen," he says, "so you can both learn. Me and Monters will teach you!"

Shooting a panicked glance at Miles, I lift my eyebrows and mouth, *Help,* but he only smiles and shakes his head.

"If you can get this, you'll survive anything," he says.

And the next thing I know, I'm standing next to Sherbet, facing Miles, Galen at his side, and my sister a few people down.

What happens next is . . . chaotic.

Strip the Willow is an enthusiastic dance that involves clasping hands, swinging, moving down the line . . . And it's complicated enough that only a few people really know what they're doing, so there's a fair amount of colliding into each other, stumbling, and I'm dizzy within about thirty seconds.

I'm also laughing.

It's hard not to, with the general chaos, the Royal Wreckers stealing partners from each other, the loud fiddle music, and for the first time since I came here, I'm not thinking about people watching me or judging me. I'm just . . . having fun.

Miles's hands catch mine as I'm still laughing, his fingers squeezing, his skin warm, and our eyes meet as we spin.

He's grinning, too, his face shiny with sweat, his hair escaping whatever gel he used to slick it down this evening, and this flutter starts up in my chest that has nothing to do with the dance.

It's so startling that I let go of his hands, which is a bad idea because momentum nearly sends me crashing into the people near us. Luckily the dance is so wild that no one really notices, but Miles frowns a little, a trio of wrinkles popping up between his brows.

"Are you all right?" he asks, and I nod, pressing a hand to my chest.

"Yeah, just . . . you know. A stripped willow, I guess."

He goes to lead me off the dance floor, but I shake my head, lifting my hand to hold it out at him.

"I'm fine!" I call over the music. "Gonna go get some air!"

I pretty much flee the ballroom, Cinderella-style, but at least I manage not to lose a shoe.

Instead of heading for the balcony where Miles *might* catch up with me, and then we *might* be alone in the moonlight, which is too much to contemplate right now, I turn down a dim hallway, pressing one hand against the wall and taking a deep breath.

Okay.

Okay.

I did not just have chest flutters for Miles. Those were heart palpitations caused by the crazy dance and nothing more.

Or this place is finally getting to me. There's a chair against the wall, a kind of spindly little thing embroidered with a nature scene. Shepherdess with her flock, soft-purple mountains, that kind of thing. I sink down onto it, bracing my hands on my knees, the silk and taffeta of my skirt rustling, the tiara on my head suddenly very heavy again.

Running from a ballroom, wearing a freaking tiara. Could I be a bigger cliché at this point?

"That chair belonged to Queen Margaret I," a voice says, and my head shoots up.

Queen Clara is standing in the hallway, hands clasped in front of her, posture as regal and terrifying as ever. She's wearing a much bigger tiara than mine, and I bet it never hurts *her* head. I bet she can't even feel it.

"It's nice," I finally say, because what else *do* you say to something like that?

"No one is allowed to sit in it," she continues, and I bite back a sigh.

Great. Of all the chairs, I accidentally plopped my ass onto the fancy special one.

Rising to my feet, I give a quick curtsy like Glynnis taught me. "Sorry, but there wasn't a . . . sign. Or a rope around it."

"That's because anyone who visits this house should already know about that chair," the queen says, and, wow, consider me dressed down.

There are about a hundred smart-ass retorts fighting to fly out of my mouth, but I keep every one of them in. Antagonizing the queen is not going to help me or Ellie, and while it would feel *very* satisfying, it would not be worth it.

Maybe.

"I'm sorry," I say again, and she watches me for such a long moment that I almost squirm beneath that hard blue gaze.

Finally, she asks, "Have you seen my son?"

"Seb?"

Her nostrils flare. "Prince Sebastian, yes."

I shake my head, fluffing out my skirt. "No. I mean, I did, earlier, dancing with Lady Tamsin, but not since then."

The queen keeps looking at me, hands clenched, her nostrils flaring a bit, but apparently she decides to believe me, giving a crisp nod. "Very well. I haven't seen Tamsin, either, so perhaps they're somewhere getting to know each other better."

With that, she turns and heads back for the ballroom, and I blow out a long breath, ruffling my bangs. If the queen is headed in that direction, I am heading in the *opposite*.

I turn and move farther down the hallway, turning a corner, and groan when I see who's standing at the other end.

"Daisy," Seb says, walking toward me.

Excellent. Just what I need right now.

"Aren't you supposed to be wooing your fair lady?" I say, and he rolls his shoulders, flicking his auburn hair off his forehead in what has to be a trademarked move at this point.

"Can't find her," he says, glancing around like Tamsin might suddenly leap out of the wallpaper or something. And then he turns those very blue eyes on me.

"Actually, this is good timing. I was hoping I might talk to you," he says, walking a little closer. "Alone."

Groaning, I hold up a hand. "No. Your mother is here, and the last thing I need is for her to find us having a little tête-à-tête in a dark hallway."

Seb shoves his hand in his pocket, and if I didn't know better, I'd think he was genuinely anxious about something.

"Later, then," he presses. "Once Mummy isn't around, do you think we might—"

"No," I say again. "I don't." Not only do I not want the queen coming for my head again, but I can't imagine there's anything me and Seb need to talk about. And if it's about Isabel, I really don't want to hear it.

Patting him on the shoulder, I start to move past him. "Now if you'll excuse me, I have . . . girl things to take care of."

I'm hoping that might terrify him into bolting, but instead he just sighs and gestures toward the curve of the hallway. "There's a powder room to the left."

"Thanks," I reply, heading in that direction and feeling very relieved when I hear Seb's footsteps going the other way.

Since I don't actually need the ladies' room, I just wander for a bit, finally spotting a door slightly ajar, soft golden light spilling out onto the carpet. That'll do for a nice hidey-hole, I think, moving toward it and pushing open the door.

Only to come up short as I see that I have found Lady Tamsin. She's standing in the middle of the room, wrapped around another person, the sounds of heavy breathing and lips meeting soft in the quiet room. For just a second, my confused brain wonders how Seb got back to this part of the house without me seeing him.

And then I really *look*.

It's very much *not* Seb she's kissing.

It's Flora.

Chapter 28

A FUN THING ABOUT ME THAT I LEARN ON THIS TRIP:
I really, really hate shooting.

Alex kept his promise—we're not shooting any living creatures, thank god, but we *are* shooting clay pigeons, and it turns out it's not just the killing that bugs me about shooting.

It's the noise.

When I shriek for the third time as my gun goes off, Gilly, my shooting partner for this outing, gives me a look.

"Every time?" he asks, and I scowl, adjusting my cap lower on my head. Oh yes, I have a cap. I have a whole *outfit* made out of tweed, and there are sturdy boots and leather gloves, and honestly, if anyone takes a picture of me like this, I am going to die.

"Sorry, I'm not used to gunfire going off right by my head," I tell him, and Gilly looks at me, puzzled.

"But you're American," he says, and then, before I can reply, he shouts, "Pull!"

A clay pigeon soars through the air.

Gilly pulls the trigger and the pigeon shatters.

I shriek.

Sighing, Gilly lowers the gun, fixing me with his dark eyes. "Lady Daze," he says, "why don't you go see if there's something to drink back at the cars?"

I can't blame him for wanting to get rid of me, but I stick my tongue out at him anyway before gratefully skedaddling over to the cars. There are a bunch of them, old Land Rovers, some jeeps, all of which have seen better days. It must be more of that thing Miles told me about, posh people not needing to show off all the time.

Walking around to the back of the jeep that I know has the drinks and snacks, I kick a loose clod of dirt and grass with the toe of my boot. It's a beautiful day, clouds racing across the sky, and the air smells sweet and smoky. It's also warm enough that I don't really need my jacket, and I shuck it as I round the back of the jeep.

And come face-to-face with Flora and Miles.

They're not standing particularly close or anything, and they seem to just be making small talk as Flora pours lemonade out of a thermos and Miles unwraps a sandwich. She's laughing at something he's said, but when she sees me, her smile fades, her movements suddenly becoming a little stiff and jerky.

She and Tamsin hadn't said anything to me the night of the ball. They'd seen me, Tamsin jerking to look over her shoulder, her eyes wide, her lips swollen, and I'd muttered apologies, backing out into the hallway so quickly I'd almost tripped over my dress. Flora had only narrowed her eyes at me.

I didn't see her at all yesterday, and now I try to act as nonchalant as possible as I pick up one of the other thermoses from the back of the jeep.

"Having fun?" Flora asks me. She's also dressed in tweed, but she's taken off her jacket, too. Her dark golden hair is held back in a low ponytail, aviator sunglasses covering her eyes. Miles has a similar look, although he's also got a cap kind of like mine. They look . . . right standing there together. Flora is clearly not interested in him at the moment, but it's just another reminder that they all inhabit this same world, all travel in an orbit that I can barely understand on a good day.

Then Flora surprises me by saying, "Help me carry these things out to everyone, would you, Daisy?"

Like her mom, Flora has enough authority that you just kind of do what she says without really thinking about it. I scoop up an extra thermos and a stack of little china plates while Flora gathers a handful of wrapped sandwiches and a couple of glasses, tucking the stems between her fingers.

We're about halfway between the cars and the shooting when she says, "You didn't tell anyone."

It's not a question, but I answer it like it is. "No, of course not."

Stopping, Flora turns to look at me, but I can't see her eyes, only my face reflected twice in those giant mirrored aviators.

"Why not?" she asks. "I was a total bitch to you, and you could've run off to tell everyone. Mummy, Seb. The press." She lifts one shoulder. "It's what I would've done."

"You're a princess," I tell her. "It was to be expected."

That makes her smile, or at least sort of smile. One corner

of her mouth lifts, revealing her perfect teeth for just a second.

"It's not all that serious, me and Tam," she tells me. "Just a bit of fun, but given Mummy's current obsession with locking in a bride for Seb, it's really best if no one finds out about us."

I nod, squinting as the clouds move overhead and a shaft of sunlight falls right where we're standing. "So it's that, then," I say. "It's Tamsin specifically, and not that you like girls, that would upset your mom?"

Sighing, Flora turns to walk back down the hill toward all the gunfire. "Oh, she's not thrilled about that."

I frown and walk a little faster to keep up with her. "But it's the twenty-first century," I say, and she stops, laughing as she nods down at all the boys in their tweed, guns at the ready.

"Darling," she drawls, "does anything about this look like the twenty-first century to you?"

"Fair enough," I reply. "This *is* a bit BBC miniseries."

Flora laughs then, and for the first time, I see that there might actually be a cool person beneath the whole haughty princess thing. Is anyone in this family what they seem like?

I follow her to the little table set up right behind everyone, putting down the plate and thermos, and I'm about to turn away when she catches my arm and says, "Daisy."

When I face her, she slides her sunglasses up. Even though we're all outside today, no photographers in sight, her makeup is perfect, hazel eyes lined with gray, lashes thick and black. "Thank you," she says, and then rolls her eyes at herself.

"I can't remember the last time I said that and meant it," she adds. "But I mean it. I appreciate you keeping this between us."

I smile and give her arm the most awkward pat known to

man. "No problem. I'm just glad you don't hate me because of Miles."

Those pretty lashes flutter. "Miles?" she says, and then she gives one of those perfect, trilling laughs again. "Oh, no, I didn't like you because of the entire situation." She waves a hand over me, and I wonder if she means the American thing, Ellie, or my general me-ness.

"But now I see that you're nothing like what the papers made you out to be. If you were after Seb or fame or anything like that, surely you'd try harder."

"Thank you?" I reply. "I think?"

Shrugging, Flora dusts off her hands and looks over the table before reaching for a bottle of champagne and pouring herself a glass. It's only around ten in the morning, so I pass when she offers me a flute, too.

There's another boom from all the guns, more clay pigeons raining down, and while I don't shriek, I do jump hard enough that Flora looks over at me, startled.

"I'm just gonna . . . not . . . be here," I say awkwardly, jerking my thumb back toward the row of jeeps up the hill, and Flora nods.

"Toodles!" she says with a little wave of her fingers.

I wave back, but I cannot bring myself to say "Toodles." I don't even like *thinking* it, to be honest.

When I get back to the jeeps, Miles is the only one there, leaning against the side of one, biting into a sandwich. I perch myself on top of the folded-down tailgate of the jeep and pick up another thermos, turning it in my hands.

"Why aren't you shooting?" I ask him, and he shrugs, folding his sandwich back up in wax paper.

"Not one of my favorite activities," he says. He puts the sandwich down, then shoves his hands in his pockets, and for a second, I think we're just going to sit there in total silence until we actually die of the awkwardness.

"Flora's not giving you a hard time, is she?" Miles asks, pulling me out of my thoughts. I turn to see Flora at the bottom of the hill, joking with Gilly, and lift one shoulder.

"I think we might actually be becoming friends? Or at least not enemies."

Miles makes a little noise in the back of his throat and takes off his cap for a second to scrub a hand over his hair. "She's not so bad, Flo," he says. "Or at least not as bad as she'd like people to think."

I look back at him, wanting to ask about her, about *them*, but before I can, Miles nods at one of the jeeps. "Do you wanna go for a drive?" he asks, and I blink at him.

"With you?"

His lips quirk. "Unless you'd prefer the company of one of the sheep."

That makes me smile in spite of myself.

And then he adds, "Hopefully there will be a good story in the papers about us sneaking off on this shooting trip. Glynnis will be thrilled."

Oh, right. We're spending time together because of how it *looks*, not because we actually want to.

I think of the other night at the ball, that weird little moment that passed between us, and then I grind that thought to dust under my mental boot.

"Good plan," I tell him, hopping off the tailgate. "Let's go be illicit."

I don't know if anyone sees us leave, and as we drive away, it occurs to me that I probably should've told Ellie we were going. But by the time I think of that, the jeep is already rattling over the hills, the wind blowing hard enough in the open top that we can't talk.

The Highlands spread out before us, rolling fields, snow-capped hills, and I take a deep breath, grinning at the sheer *prettiness* of it all. It's wide open in a way that makes me want to . . . I don't know, run around with my arms thrown out or something.

The jeep slows as we approach a fence, and I look at Miles, curious.

He smiles back at me, then nods at the gate.

The jeep rumbles to a halt, and I can't stop the sound of delight and surprise that escapes me. It's embarrassingly close to a squeal.

But there, at the fence, is a shaggy red cow, his massive horns curling up from his head, long hair covering his eyes, and he is the actual cutest.

I hop out of the jeep, approaching the fence carefully, but the cow only munches on grass, clearly not that concerned with me.

"Ellie said you still hadn't seen one," Miles calls, and I turn to smile over my shoulder at him. "I hadn't," I say, and I reach out—*very* cautiously, those are some massive horns—and give the cow a little pat on his head, that long reddish hair rough under my fingertips.

"Hit all the Scottish high notes now?" Miles asks, and I head back to the jeep, dusting my hands off on the back of my pants.

"Just about," I say. "Fancy cows, shooting, wearing plaid, doing folk dances, seeing lots of kilts . . ."

He's still sitting in the driver's seat (and I'm never going to get used to the whole "sitting on the wrong side of the car" thing), smiling at me, and it occurs to me that this—taking me to see a cow, which, okay, not exactly the most romantic of gestures, but still—has nothing to do with papers or tabloid stories. It was just . . . a nice thing to do.

For me.

Which is so bizarre I don't want to think about it too much, lest my head explode.

"Thank you," I say, getting back in the jeep. "I know it must physically pain you to do a nice thing for me, so I appreciate your sacrifice."

He gives a little cough, covering his mouth with his fist and widening his eyes. "Oh god, I think the damage has already been done."

Rolling my eyes, I shove at his arm, muttering, "Shut up," but I'm smiling.

Just a little.

Miles starts the jeep, and we drive away from the fence, the clouds thicker now, the wind a little chillier as we drive down the bumpy ground. I think we're heading back to the house, but Miles makes a turn down a rutted path, the jeep climbing down into a shallow valley, hills rising up around us. A few thin waterfalls trickle down the rocks, and it's so beautiful that once again I wish I had a camera.

And then I wonder if Miles purposely drove this way to show me something pretty, and that thought is so confusing that I tuck my hair behind my ears and yell over the wind and the engine noise, "So what was the deal with you and Flora?"

Miles doesn't say anything, but I see his hands tighten on the steering wheel for just a second.

"Me and Flo?" he calls back at last, and I pull a strand of hair out of my mouth, jolting as the jeep hits a particularly big rut.

"That's what I said!" I yell, and he frowns, deep lines appearing on either side of his mouth.

But before he can answer me, there's a sudden *pop*, and the jeep swerves to the right, making me give a startled cry, my hand flailing out to grab the little handle by my door.

Miles manages to bring the jeep to a stop, putting it in park with a shaky sigh. "Flat tire," he mutters, but I think he's a little relieved that he didn't have to answer my question.

Honestly, *I'm* a little relieved. I shouldn't have even asked him. What did it matter what had happened between Flora and Miles? He wasn't my actual boyfriend, and I'd be gone in a few weeks anyway.

No, this flat tire was clearly a blessing from above, sent to save me from making a mistake. "Thanks," I say in a low voice, shooting a finger gun at the thick clouds above us.

Which was apparently the wrong move because about two seconds later, the entire sky opens up.

Chapter 29

THE RAIN IS DOWNRIGHT TORRENTIAL AS MILES pulls me from the car, and I lift the tweed jacket over my head. Not that it does much good. The rain is blinding, the ground slippery underfoot, but I let Miles lead me over a slight rise, and then, through the rain I see . . . a house? A shed?

He tugs me toward it, and honestly, so long as it has a roof, I don't care *what* it is.

Luckily, the door is unlocked—it's so ancient I'm not sure it even *could* lock—and then we're inside, blinking in the gloom.

Alone.

Look, I want to be cool, okay? I want to put my hands on my hips and make a really bored face, the way Ellie can so easily. I want to radiate nonchalance and make it super clear that while we might have fallen into the most romantic cliché ever—oh, no! We're trapped in a remote location while the heavens rage outside!—we're just . . . colleagues, basically. Not even friends.

"What is this place, anyway?" I ask, looking around and trying to distract myself from our general aloneness.

Not that there's much to look at. It's a little stone hut with a thatched roof, and the only things inside are a fireplace and a built-in shelf holding a few books, some folded quilts, and a truly ancient-looking bottle of some dark amber liquid.

"It's a bothy," Miles says, taking off his cap and ruffling his wet hair, not quite meeting my eyes. "They're all over the place here in the Highlands. Used to be for farmers watching over their sheep, but now hikers use them."

To call it rustic would be an understatement, but I guess if you've been slogging up rainy hills, any place that has a roof would seem like paradise. And when Miles moves past me to get a fire started, I have to admit it's not quite as bad.

There are only a few logs by the fireplace, but there are big bricks of peat, and that's what Miles fills the fireplace with, finding a pack of matches under an upside-down mug on the mantel.

The fire smokes like hell, but it warms the room quickly, and when Miles steps back, wiping his hands on the back of his jeans, he looks really pleased with himself.

"Three years in the Scout Association," he says, and I assume that's the British version of the Boy Scouts.

"Not bad," I admit, crouching down near the fire and unwinding my braid, hoping that will get my hair to dry a little faster.

When I glance up, Miles is studying me with a weird look on his face, and as soon as he notices me watching, he clears his throat, moving away again and going over to the door.

It's still pouring outside, the wind blowing the rain nearly sideways.

"We'll stay here until it clears up," he says. "Then I'll walk back up to the house, either get a new car or get someone to drive me down here."

"Um, yeah, when it clears up, I'll be walking with you," I tell him, fluffing my hair. Most of the time I'm glad I'd decided to grow it out, but right now the hair cape seems like a bad idea. At this rate, I'm going to have a damp head for the rest of my life.

"It's a bit of a hike," Miles says, still looking out the door, hands thrust in his back pockets. He's got one knee cocked, and he looks like a Scottish farmer surveying his land. It shouldn't be cute, but it is, and I bite back a sigh as I turn to the fireplace.

Off-limits, I remind myself. *And snobby and basically a fancy servant, 1,000% devoted to the palace. You want nothing to do with this entire thing, and Miles has a permanent residence in Royal Land. Don't even think about it.*

Maybe if I keep repeating that, it'll be easier to ignore how my pulse is racing.

I can hear the door shut behind me, and even though the wind and rain are still blowing outside, the bothy seems a lot quieter now. My face is hot, and I'm not sure it has anything to do with the smoky fire I'm crouching next to.

Miles goes to the pile of quilts stacked near the fire, taking one and fluffing it out. I'm relieved when a cloud of dust and dead insects *doesn't* come billowing out, but that relief is short-lived because he suddenly crouches down near me, draping the blanket over my shoulders.

"You'll freeze," he tells me, ducking his head. His hair is hanging over his forehead, the rain and the dim light making it look darker than normal, and a fat raindrop slides down and splashes my collarbone.

The rain isn't that cold, but my skin feels too hot, and I jolt, scooting back a little, one hand coming up to clutch the blanket closed in front of me.

Miles lifts his head, his eyes very green and very close to mine.

Tea cozy. Shoe trees. The absolute opposite of your type.

Clearing his throat, Miles straightens up, dusting off his hands on his jeans again.

"It won't last long," he says, then waves at the door. "The rain, I mean. It . . . these things usually burn themselves out in a few minutes."

He drops his arm to his side, fingers flexing, and is . . . is he nervous?

That's almost weirder than me thinking he was cute, so I turn back to look at the fire, ironically hoping to find some chill there.

The rain keeps hammering down, the fire crackles and smokes, and for a moment, I wonder if we're going to sit here in total silence until people eventually find us, dead, smothered by the weight of our own awkwardness.

Then Miles says, "Flora dated my sister."

Surprised, I twist to look at him. "What?"

He's standing near the door again, his hat in one hand, and he thumps it against his thigh a few times. "You asked about me and Flora. That's 'the deal' with us. She was dating Amelia, the palace wasn't ready for that, so they put it out that it was me. That Flora and I were . . ."

He looks over to the window, his hat still tapping against one long leg. "Anyway, that's what happened."

Turning back to me, he tilts his head down, probably because looking down his nose at people makes him feel more comfortable. "I'm obviously entrusting you with something important in telling you that."

I hold up a hand. "Got it," I say. "And I appreciate it."

I'm not going to tell him I already knew Flora was into girls, since I can't tell him about Flora and Tamsin, so I shift against the floor, pulling the quilt in around me.

"So this isn't your first Fake Boyfriend Rodeo," I say, and he glances over at me, brow wrinkled.

"You've done this before," I clarify. "Pretended to date someone for the palace."

In the dim light, it's hard to tell, but I think he might blush as he suddenly becomes really interested in his shoes. "I told you," he says. "The Montgomery family are courtiers. It's what we do. My great-great-great-grandfather actually fought in a duel for Seb's great-great-great-grandfather. Took a sword to the eye."

I wince. "Gross."

That actually makes Miles smile, though, and I'm reminded again that smiling is a good look on him. It takes some of the hardness out of that aristocratic face, makes him look softer and nicer. More boy, less jerk.

"The point is, there are certainly worse things I could be asked to do than spend time with pretty girls."

I am not turning red.

I am *not*.

I turn away to poke at the fire with the iron rod Miles left lying by the hearth. "Are you saying I'm better than a sword to the eye?" I ask, and he chuckles.

The sound is warm and soft, and I swear I can feel it, dancing over the knobs of my spine. Oh my god, this rain needs to end *soon*.

"Maybe not better, but certainly not worse," he says, and then I look at him, which is a mistake.

There's no fighting it this time. Miles is not just cute. He's *hot*.

And he's looking at me in a way I don't understand, or don't want to understand because no, no, no, this is *not* a complication I need right now. Besides, I'm leaving in a few weeks anyway. Why start something that has such a fast expiration date?

Breaking the spell, I stand, letting the quilt drop back to the ground. I chafe my hands up and down my arms as I ask, "So that's why you do it? Family tradition demands that if the palace says jump, you say how high?"

I wait for Miles to scowl at me, but he just leans back against the wall and sighs.

"They're paying my tuition," he says. "Seb's family. They're paying for me to go to St. Andrew's next year."

I don't really know what to say to that. I knew Miles was really loyal to the Bairds—obviously—but I thought it was more about friendship than the whole courtier deal.

"And not just that," Miles goes on, "but the apartment in Edinburgh? That's on their dime as well. Plus last year, my mum was sick—she's fine now—but it was serious for a while. She needed private hospitals, specialists, all that, and I think they paid her hospital bills."

"Miles," I say softly, and he meets my eyes. All of this has come out in the lightest tone, like he's just casually relaying some information, but his gaze is serious.

"I just want you to understand," he says. "I owe them . . . everything. Everything."

Pushing off from the wall, he tosses his hat to the chair by the door. "That's why I was such a prat to you that first night."

"To be fair, you've been a prat basically the entire time I've known you," I say, and Miles gives the littlest smile. His hair is drying a bit in the heat from the fire, and it's curling, turning a deep-gold color, shadows playing over his high cheekbones.

"I have," he admits. "And I'm sorry. Truly."

Swallowing hard, I wave that off. Now is not the time to start becoming friends, not when I've just realized he's super good-looking and there's rain and firelight and just the two of us, miles from anyone.

But I still can't help but say, "It's not like you haven't done a lot for Seb. You keep him out of trouble. Well, as much as anyone can, I guess," I amend, and Miles nods.

"It's a big job for one man."

I look back at Miles. "I'm just saying, yes, they've done a lot for you. But it's not like it's a one-way street."

He's watching me again. He really needs to stop with that because my toes are curling in my boots, my heart jumping around, and my face is burning.

"Thank you," he says softly, and then, maybe feeling as

weirded out as I do, he moves to sit down in front of the fire, taking my discarded quilt and making a little pallet there by the hearth. He sits, drawing his knees up and wrapping his arms around them, and after a second, I sit next to him.

Not too close, of course.

We sit in silence, watching the fire for a while, before I plant my hands on the quilt, leaning back a little. "Do you think Glynnis had someone shoot out our tire?"

Miles laughs, shaking his head. "I wouldn't put it past her. She's a bit mercenary, ol' Glynn."

"Oh my god, *please* tell me you have called her 'ol' Glynn' to her face."

"I have not, as I enjoy having my tongue actually in my mouth and not mounted to her wall."

Crossing my legs, I turn to face him more fully. "I will give you a million dollars if you do it," I tell him, and he looks over, tilting his head to one side.

"A million dollars?"

"A million dollars *or* what I currently have in my wallet back at the house, which I think is, like, five pounds in your weird Monopoly money."

"Tell you what," he says, putting his hands down on the quilt to lean back a little, "I will call Glynnis 'ol' Glynn' if you promise to drink a Pimm's Cup. No, not drink, *chug*."

I screw up my face, sticking my tongue out. "Blargh."

That makes him laugh again, and I'm smiling back when I glance down and realize that our hands are nearly touching on the quilt.

Miles follows my gaze, and his laughter dies.

They're just hands, resting there against the quilt. His, graceful, long-fingered, mine with chipped polish and an octopus ring on my pinky.

The rain is tapering off now, but I can still hear it drumming softly against the roof, and to my right, the fire pops and smokes. Over that, there's the sound of my own breathing, a little faster than it was before, and I hear Miles sigh as the two of us just keep looking at our hands, only the littlest space between them.

We've been closer than this before. The other night at the ball, when we danced, there was a lot less space between our bodies than there is now. Hell, that day in the park, I was basically in his lap.

But those things were for show, and this . . .

This feels *real*.

His hand edges just a little bit closer, his pinky brushing mine, and that—that one tiny touch—sends a shiver of sparks racing through me.

Sucking in a breath, I go to move my hand closer.

The door flies open with a bang, and Miles and I leap apart so dramatically you'd think we'd just been caught together naked instead of touching pinkies. He actually makes a sound, this kind of startled yelp that I'd tease him about had I not cried out, "*Nothing! Nothing!*" when we bolted apart.

Ellie and Alex stand there, still in their tweeds, rain dripping off the umbrella Alex is holding over both their heads.

Alex frowns, but Ellie is looking back and forth between me and Miles, her arms folded over her chest.

"We saw the jeep on our way back, figured you'd be here," Alex says, and Miles nods quickly, smacking his palms on his thighs.

"Yeah, yeah, good thing we were close."

Smiling, Alex looks around. "This place is cozier than I remembered," he says. "And nice work on the fire."

Clearing his throat for what has to be the 8,000th time today, Miles turns to the fireplace, picking up the poker and tamping the flames down, moving ash over the still-smoldering peat. As the fire dies, so does whatever spell this place has cast over me, and I go to stand next to Ellie, putting the past few minutes out of my head.

"You rescued us!" I tell her, my voice bright, and her eyes narrow just the littlest bit.

"Rescued or interrupted?" she asks quietly, and I roll my eyes, gathering up my damp jacket and moving past her to Alex's Land Rover, which, thankfully, has a roof.

Miles climbs in the back seat beside me, and as the Land Rover heads back toward Baird House, neither of us say anything.

And we both keep our hands firmly in our laps.

Chapter 30

I'M NEVER GOING TO GET USED TO ALL THE TEA.

We've been back in Edinburgh for a couple of days now, and lately, everywhere we go, someone has tea to bring us. Sitting down at the palace? Have some tea. Meeting with Glynnis about wedding things? More tea, please. And now, even at the dress studio, there is tea.

I take the china cup from the smiling assistant, careful not to let it rattle in the saucer in case El hears it and snaps at me again. She's been like that lately, quick to criticize anything I do that isn't flawless. There's a part of me that always wants to argue back, but another part wonders if this is just how she feels every day. Watched, judged, found wanting. Maybe it makes her feel better to get to do the same thing to someone else—I don't know.

In any case, the tea cup doesn't rattle even a bit, and I manage not to make a face when I take a sip, even though the tea is way too strong, way too hot, and way too unsweetened for my taste.

Mom and I are in a special fitting area in the back of the

designer's studio. No shops for the future king's bride, of course. We get to go straight to the source, and from what I understand, these fittings are carried out like they're spy missions or something. There were decoy cars when we left the palace this morning, one leaving from the front, the other from a back door near the kitchens. We weren't in either of those, instead leaving about fifteen minutes later through yet another secret staff entrance, and we'd taken just a regular cab, nothing fancy. But all of us had worn hats and sunglasses, me and El in simple ballcaps, my mom in this hot-pink straw thing with flowers that probably drew more attention to her than if she hadn't been wearing a hat at all, but such is Mom.

We still haven't seen El's dress, but that's because she wants to save the surprise. Still, I can see a few sketches pinned to the wall of various wedding gowns, all of them looking fancy enough to be El's, and I squint at one over my teacup.

"Do you have to wear sleeves?" I call out. "Like, are shoulders too scandalous for church?"

From somewhere in the bowels of the studio, El calls back, "It's a surprise!"

"It's a *dress*," I mutter, glad she can't hear me.

Mom can, though, and she reaches out with one leg, the toe of her shoe brushing my calf. "Be nice," she says, and I set my cup on the little gilt-and-marble table next to us.

"I am being nice," I tell her. "See, look." I give her my best smile, the one that looks like I've been shot with a tranq dart, and Mom chuckles, shaking her head.

"You and your father, peas in a pod."

"I'm taking that as a compliment."

"You should." Then Mom leans over and pats my knee, her teacup and saucer balanced in her other hand.

"You've been a real trouper through all of this, darling," she tells me. "I know it hasn't been easy. The papers and the pictures and the ball. That boy."

Right.

That boy.

Miles and I haven't really talked since we got back to the city. We did one quick stroll down the Royal Mile for Glynnis, but both of us had kept our hands in our pockets, and we'd hardly said anything to each other besides random comments on the weather, the shops, anything that was completely neutral and boring.

The headlines over those pictures had read "MILES APART?," so Glynnis is not exactly thrilled with either of us at the moment. But after that day in the bothy, faking things with Miles just felt too weird, and besides, I was heading home soon anyway. The pictures from the park and the ball had done their job—no one was talking about me and Seb anymore, and just yesterday, there had been blurry shots of Seb and Tamsin up in the Highlands, kissing. (The headline there was "SEB LANDS GLAM TAM!," which was kind of a weak offering in my opinion.)

Luckily, I'm saved from having to talk about "that boy" with Mom by Ellie swanning back into the room.

Smiling, El gestures for me to stand up. "Your turn!" she says brightly, and I blink at her.

"For my dress?" I ask, and there's a flash of the old Ellie in her eyes as she smirks at me and says, "What do you think?"

Stupid question, okay, but I wish I'd been a little more prepared for this moment. I'd thought today was all about Ellie, not *me*.

"Oh, how exciting!" Mom says, clapping her hands a little, and I give her a wan smile as I rise to my feet, trying not to wring my hands or fiddle with the hem of my skirt. I look okay today—I'd known better than to wear jeans and a T-shirt to a fashion designer's studio, and had picked out one of the "outfit pods" Glynnis had made for me, choosing a gray high-waisted skirt with a black sleeveless blouse and a gray-and-white cardigan. Bright colors would've been too conspicuous. And trust me, when I'd realized I was picking out an outfit for stealth, I'd had a moment of wondering just when something like that had become so second nature to me. I've only been here a month, after all.

"Angus," Ellie says, pulling me toward the back of the room, behind a heavy velvet curtain. "She's ready for you!"

"I'm not sure that's actually true," I say, but the man she ushers me to is grinning at me. He's got bright red hair, brighter than mine was before I came here, and he's shorter than I am. Wearing a black ruffled shirt and a kilt in neon colors, plus the *sickest* pair of black patent leather boots, he's exactly what I'd expect a famous Scottish fashion designer to look like. He's *not*, however, who I would have thought *Ellie* would pick. Still, his smile is contagious, and when he takes my hands and holds both my arms away from my body, looking me up and down, I don't even feel self-conscious.

"Oh, this will be a *dream*," he says, his brogue heavy, the *r* in "dream" rolling over my ears like a wave.

The space here in the back of the studio is open and bright.

The hardwood floors are ancient and scuffed, and the walls are exposed brick. There's a long table against the back wall, covered in heaps of fabric, and I spot a few sketchbooks. There are also a few dress dummies standing guard, one of which is swathed in the Baird tartan, and I wonder if that's part of Ellie's dress.

And I really wonder what my dress will look like.

Sadly, there's none of that this time, not even a hint of what colors we might be working with. Angus just measures me. And not just one time, either. He runs that tape measure out at least five times, checking and rechecking, making notes in a little notebook at his side. Occasionally he mutters to himself, but between his accent and the music blaring out of hidden speakers, I can't make out what he might be saying.

By the time he's done, I feel like I might as well be one of those dress dummies, but then he turns that bright grin on me again. "Excited?" he asks, and I don't know if he means about the dress or the wedding itself, so I just give him the good old American double thumbs-up. "Super psyched," I tell him, and he laughs, then leans forward to place a smacking kiss on my cheek.

"A dream," he pronounces again. "Just like your sister."

I don't know if anyone has ever called me just like Ellie, and I'm not sure if I think it's a compliment or not, so I shrug it off and say, "Nah, she's got better hair."

Angus laughs uproariously at that, like it's the funniest thing he's ever heard, and his assistant, the lady who brought me tea, also chortles.

Not sure what to do with any of that, I give another awkward smile, then go out to find Mom and Ellie in the sitting room.

Mom is chatting with one of the assistants, and Ellie is finishing up her tea, sitting on the couch opposite from the chair where I'd squirreled myself away. She looks pretty sitting there, all in white, her blond hair caught in a low ponytail and draped over one shoulder. Even the way she holds her teacup is perfect.

The three of us leave the studio amid a flurry of cheek kisses and head down to the car that's waiting in the alley behind the studio.

The car is there, just where we left it, but we pull up short as we see who's standing beside the car. Leaning on it, actually. Seb.

"Sebastian!" Ellie says, moving her purse from one shoulder to the other. "What . . . what are you doing here?"

Seb gives the grin that launches a thousand knickers into the air, and he pushes off the car. "I was looking for Daisy," he says, and I inwardly groan. I have no idea what Seb wanted with me the night of the ball, but I've managed to stay away from him since then, and now it seems like I'm caught.

He winks. "Had some secret best man–maid of honor plans to discuss with her."

Ellie looks back and forth between me and Seb, and I fiddle with the ends of my hair. "Can't we just talk at the palace?" I ask, but he shakes his head, gesturing down the alley.

"We're close to my favorite pub, and it'll only take a second. Don't worry, they know me there. A perfectly photographer-free spot."

That grin again, and I see now why he can get away with most anything. Trespassing, drunkenness, kidnapping . . .

"It'll only take a minute," he cajoles, and I sigh, letting my arms drop to my sides.

"Sure," I say, then turn to Mom and Ellie. "I'll see you back at the palace."

Ellie tugs her lower lip between her teeth, but after a second, she nods, and then looks over at Sebastian.

She doesn't say anything, but he raises his hands, all innocent expression and big blue eyes. "She's perfectly safe in my care," he promises, and I wrinkle my nose at that.

Definitely don't want to be in Seb's *care*.

But I follow him down the alley and toward a heavy wooden door set into the gray stone of a building. "The Prince's Arms," he says, opening the door for me. "Appropriate, no?"

I roll my eyes as I walk past him and into a shadowy interior that smells like smoke, beer, and carpet that's probably three hundred years old.

We make our way to the bar, and the man standing there by the beer taps clearly recognizes Seb, and not just in the princely way. He puts out a hand to shake Seb's. "Been a while, lad," he says, and Seb shrugs.

"Too long. Usual for me, lemonade for my companion, please."

I really don't want lemonade—it doesn't mean the same thing here as it does back home. No sugary tart goodness, it's more like watered-down Sprite, and for some reason, it's the drink everyone seems to be handing me lately. But I don't say anything, and just take my glass from the bartender when he hands it to me.

Seb, of course, has a pint of some cloudy beer, and I wrinkle my nose at the smell of hops and yeast.

He chugs about half of it in one go, and when he sets the pint glass back on the bar, what's left of the lager sloshes around. Seb's eyes follow the motion moodily.

"This is super fun," I tell him. "Is this our version of family bonding? That I watch you get drunk?"

Seb glances over at me then, his ruddy eyebrows drawn down over his blue, blue eyes. He really is stupid good-looking, but it's like I hardly ever notice anymore. I've gotten so used to his face that it's just . . . a face. A good one, sure, but once you know Seb, it's hard not to see the mess behind all that pretty. That has the effect of killing the handsome, let me tell you.

"I wanted to be . . . alone with you," he says, surprising me. I watch him swirl his lager again and shift on the barstool, looking around. There are only two other people in the pub, both of them ancient old men who appear to be having a contest to grow the most outrageous eyebrows. They're sitting in a corner booth, the gilded lettering on the window casting weird shadows on their faces. It's clear that they either don't know who Seb is or don't care, and suddenly I wonder if he comes here because he knows it'll be deserted.

I stab at my "lemonade" with a straw, a creepy-crawly feeling between my shoulder blades. "Why?" I ask Seb, and he bangs his palm down on the bar. The sound startles me, but I realize he's just signaling for another pint, and I roll my eyes. "If it was to see you get day drunk, I've already seen that before—"

"I'm in love with your sister."

Chapter 31

I DON'T KNOW IF THROWING A DRINK IN A PRINCE'S face can get you sent to the dungeons or not, but I risk it.

"What the—" Seb splutters, the remnants of my lemonade dripping down his chin. The bartender doesn't even look up from polishing glasses, but I hear one of the old men at the booth in the corner give a wheezing laugh.

He calls something to Seb in an accent too thick for me to understand, but I'm pretty sure I hear the word "filly," which makes me glad I didn't catch the rest.

"No," I say, ducking in close to keep my voice down as he pulls napkins out of a dispenser.

"What do you mean, 'no'?" Seb looks up at me, lemonade spiking his eyelashes. God, even covered in my drink, he still looks *GQ*-worthy.

"I mean, no, you do not get to put your particular brand of disaster all over Ellie. You're not in love with her—you probably just want to hook up with her. It'll clear up."

"It's love, not an STD," he says, and before I can give in to a full-body shudder of ick, Seb sighs, tipping his head back to stare at the ceiling. "Sorry. I don't mean to get snippy with you. It's just . . . you're the first person I've told."

I'm still trying to process that when Seb gives one of those elegant shrugs he's so good at and reaches into his shirt pocket to pull out a pack of cigarettes. "Well, the first person besides Eleanor, of course."

My hand shoots out, fingers closing around his wrist. "You told Ellie? This isn't some unrequited, pining-from-afar thing?"

Seb shakes off my grip easily enough, lighting his cigarette. "Oh, it's unrequited, most definitely," he mutters around the butt, and I feel an almost-giddy wave of relief. Okay, my sister isn't cheating on her royal fiancé with his teenage brother. That's something, at least.

"What did she say?"

Taking a deep drag on the cigarette, Seb squints at me. "What do you think?"

I snatch the cigarette out of his mouth, stubbing it out in an amber glass ashtray that has probably sat in this pub since the 1950s. "I hope she told you you're an idiot."

He props his head on his hand, elbow resting on the bar. "In so many words. I think castration was also threatened."

I smirk at that. It's been a long time since I've seen Ellie mad, but I remember that when she gets going, she can get . . . creative. And Seb deserves it, really.

Watching me, he leans closer. "So she didn't tell you?" he asks, and I gesture to his lemonade-soaked shirt.

"Um, obviously?"

Sighing, Seb presses one finger to the bar, drawing circles in the condensation from his glass. "I thought she might have, is

256

all. It's why I wanted to talk to you. To see if . . . well, to see if she ever talks about me."

I think about how stressed Ellie has seemed lately, how much she didn't want me around Seb and his friends, and I wonder just how long she's been dealing with all of this. And why *didn't* she tell me?

Because Ellie stopped sharing her secrets with you around the time Alex came into the picture.

That makes my stomach twist, so I ignore it, asking Seb, "What about Alex? That's your *brother*."

"Is it?" he asks, scowling at me. "I had no idea. Look, I know it was stupid, and—"

"And reckless," I tick off on my fingers, "and selfish. And dickish."

"Is dickish a word?" he asks, raising his eyebrows, and I glare at him.

"It is where you're concerned." And then, a little softer, I ask, "Why are you even telling me this?"

Outside it's started to rain, a gentle, soft afternoon shower. It'll be over in a few minutes, but the men in the corner are already grumbling about it.

"I had to tell someone," he says, dropping his eyes from mine to fiddle with the coaster on the bar, pulling up its edges. "Last week, watching them at the house . . . it's been worse than I thought it would be. Plus having Tamsin there, and *knowing* that's what Mummy wants for me . . . She's fit, don't get me wrong, but she's not Ellie." His shoulders heave up and down. "I was afraid I was going to do something even stupider, like announce it at dinner, or—"

"Oh god, don't do that," I say, gripping his wrist. I didn't know you could actually feel the blood drain out of your face, but I'm pretty sure I'm going super pale right now, imagining Seb standing up at the palace, announcing his love for Ellie, ruining *everything*.

"I'm not going to," he assures me. "But . . . haven't you ever had something inside you that feels so big, so . . . " —he gestures around his chest— "so important that you had to say it to someone?"

He really does look kind of pitiful, but my loyalty is to Ellie, and I can only imagine how much *this* particular time bomb is weighing on her. Seb tried to steal a house as a wedding present, after all. There's no doubt in my mind he's impulsive enough to stand up during a royal wedding and do the whole "I object!" thing.

"You don't love her," I say now to Seb. "You just think you do because she's nice and calm and . . . centered."

"Yes!" he says, pointing at me, light in his eyes. "That's what's so lovely about her, that when I'm with her, things just feel . . . quieter somehow. Peaceful. I could use that in my life."

"Okay, but she's a person, not a yoga class, Seb. It's not her job to love you back because she makes you feel all Zen."

Seb takes that in, blinking at me. "It's not," he says, but I think it's a question, not an agreement.

I signal to the bartender that I'd like another lemonade, then turn back to Seb.

"It's not," I say firmly. "And you have to promise me that you're not going to do anything about it. You're going to take your completely gross and insanely inappropriate feelings, and you're going to crush them into tiny bits inside you, and then learn from this, okay? And maybe Tamsin isn't the one for you, but she's here now, so at least *try*. I mean, she seems pretty into you, or at least willing to ignore your general disaster-ness."

He doesn't answer that and instead pushes his pint glass in little circles on the bar. Then he looks up at me and, out of nowhere, says, "I was a wanker to your friend, wasn't I?"

The whole thing with Isa seems like it happened a thousand years ago, so it's hard to remember that it was only a few weeks ago. Still, he was indeed a wanker, so I nod. "Totally."

Sighing, Seb continues to make a circuit with his glass. "I am working on being less of one, I swear."

He sounds so defeated that I almost feel sorry for him, and I reach out tentatively, patting his knee. "You'll get there," I promise. "And one way to do that is to never, ever tell anyone how you feel about Ellie, okay?"

Seb's hair is falling over his forehead in that attractive way that all the Royal Wreckers seem to have cultivated, and he watches me with those very blue eyes that are just like Alex's. "I won't," he says.

"Are we going to be friends now?" he asks, and I roll my eyes as I take a sip of my lemonade.

"We're about to be family," I remind him, and he brightens a little at that.

"Family," he repeats. "I'd like that." Then he shrugs, tossing back the rest of his drink. "Never thought I'd have regular people in my family."

"Okay, see, saying things like that really tips you back toward that whole 'wanker' thing you were trying to avoid."

Grinning, Seb reaches out and smacks my knee. "See, that's what I need you around for. Remind me of wanker-like behavior."

He pays for our drinks, which surprises me since I wasn't even sure he had money on him, and as we make our way to the door, I ask, "Is it really weird paying for things with your mom?"

Queen Clara's face is stamped on all the ten-pound notes, and her father, King James, is on the twenties. One day, Alex could end up on money. Or his kids. It's another reminder that while Ellie may be my sister, everything that comes after this marriage is going to change my family forever.

Seb just laughs, though. "Barely notice it, to be honest."

We step back into the alley, and I take a deep breath. Everything smells like rain and old stone and the exhaust from buses, plus the faintest hint of lemonade still wafting from Seb's shirt.

Seb is in love with Ellie, but Ellie is in love with Alex.

Seb is *supposed* to fall in love with Tamsin, who is actually fooling around with Flora.

Flora pretended to date Miles, who is now pretending to date *me*.

And it *is* pretend.

Totally, totally pretend, no matter what happened in the bothy.

"This is so messed up," I mutter to myself, and Seb surprises me by clapping me on the shoulder.

"Nah, you haven't seen anything yet."

Chapter 32

I HAD THOUGHT THE HORSE RACE WAS THE FANCIEST, most pretentious thing I'd do in Scotland. Maybe the shooting day with all that tweed and the Land Rovers. Or the balls. Balls, super fancy, obvs.

But polo? Polo puts all of those things to shame.

The match is held just outside Edinburgh on one of those magical sunny summer days here in Scotland, the kind that will probably turn to rain by the afternoon, but for now, everything is gorgeous. Striped tents, tables groaning with flutes of champagne and all kinds of tiny finger foods, people wandering around in the brightest, prettiest of outfits . . .

And I hate all of it.

I'm in one of the dresses Glynnis picked out for me, yellow instead of the green she usually puts me in, and all scalloped skirt and fluttery sleeves. No hat today but a fascinator that, thank god, contains exactly zero feathers and only one little piece of netting.

My heels are sinking into the grass, and all I want to do is find a place to sit down. I glance back at the stands and see a beautiful woman in a large black hat striding toward one of the striped tents. She looks like all the women I've seen here: extremely well put-together but also kind of like a purebred Afghan hound.

As I watch, she hails a friend, and then, slowly, almost inevitably, tips over, sinking into the wet grass, one hand still raised in greeting.

The man next to her doesn't even pause, just continues on his way, and I shake my head.

Up in the stands, I can see the queen, standing beside Ellie, Alex, Seb, and Tamsin. The queen is all decked out in blue today, her auburn hair glossy in the sun, and as she chats with Alex, I see Tamsin glance behind her. Flora is there, talking to Fliss and Poppy, and I watch her meet Tamsin's eyes, and see the little smile that passes between them.

Then Tamsin turns back and slips her hand into the crook of Seb's elbow. Seb smiles down at her briefly but then turns his eyes back to Ellie, who is staring so hard at the queen that I know she's purposely ignoring Seb's gaze.

What a freaking mess.

"You're looking a bit bolshy."

I turn to see Miles at my side, his hands shoved in his pockets. He's wearing a white button-down shirt, the sleeves rolled up, his dark tie loose at his throat, and suddenly all the anger goes out of me.

"Bolshy?" I thought I'd absorbed most of the Brit slang there was to learn in the past month or so, but clearly there are still a few things I need to learn.

"Like a Bolshevik," Miles clarifies. "Someone about to start a revolution. I can see it in your face," he tells me now, grinning. "Just like you colonists, coming over here and wanting to cut everyone's head off."

"I could go for a decapitation or two," I confess, and he laughs, his teeth very white against his tan face. I think back to that night at the bothy and my face goes hot.

Maybe he's thinking the same thing because he stops laughing, his eyes darkening a little bit.

Then he steps back a bit, straightening his shoulders. He's tamed his hair with some kind of gel, but it still shines like an old coin, and the green stripes on his tie bring out his eyes.

"Do you know anyone playing today?" I ask, desperate for a safe topic of conversation, and the corners of Miles's mouth turn up. He apparently likes the distraction, too.

"Gilly's riding," he says, turning to gesture at the field. "Spiffy and Dons were going to, but Spiffy fell down some stairs on the Mile last night and twisted his ankle, so Dons decided he'd sit it out, too. They're over there, either charming or horrifying the Earl of Hatton's daughters."

He nods toward a striped tent where, sure enough, Spiffy sits, ankle propped up on some pillows, Dons at his side, two very blond girls standing near them, hands over their mouths either to hide their laughs or to hold back vomit.

Always hard to tell.

"Where's Sherbet?" I ask, letting Miles lead me back to the refreshment area, my hand resting very lightly in the crook of his arm. Even that little touch is enough to have my nerves vibrating, and I hear a few muted clicks as photographers get their pictures.

"Sherbet is off to Greece with Galen for the rest of the summer," he says. "Lucky bugger."

"Because Greece or just because he's not here, staring at ponies?" I ask, and Miles glances down at me.

"Because he's with someone he loves," he says, and my heart does a weird flipping thing in my chest. I know Miles isn't saying he loves me—that would be stupid—but it was clear at the ball that he envied what Galen and Sherbet had. Maybe because he always has to be free in case the palace needs him to pretend to date somebody.

"And also Greece," he acknowledges. "Bloody love Greece. Plus, if I were in Greece, I wouldn't have had to carry Spiffy halfway down the Mile last night, so."

I laugh at that, tilting my head up to look into his face.

And that's when someone calls out, "Give 'im a kiss, love!"

I turn to see a photographer there, camera at the ready, and everything inside me freezes.

We've faked a date, smiled into each other's eyes at the ball, walked down the street like a couple, but a *kiss?*

But to my surprise, Miles is already inching his head just the littlest bit toward mine, his face coming closer, his lips—

I slam my hand against his chest, pushing him back, and for a second, I see his eyes widen.

"I'm—I can't—" I start to say, and then with a muttered "Sorry," I turn away.

Only to smack right into a waiter bearing a tray loaded with champagne glasses.

I hear a few gasps (and more than a few giggles) as probably hundreds of dollars of champagne splashes onto the ground. I get at least fifty bucks' worth on my pretty yellow dress, and I scrub my hand over the growing wet spot down the front of my skirt even as a torrent of apologies spills from my lips.

Leaning down, I attempt to help the waiter pick up the glasses, but then there are more clicks, and then I remember I'm in a dress, it's a windy day, and I've probably just given everyone a clear look at my pink polka-dot underwear.

Great.

So I right myself in a hurry, stepping past the waiter and all those glasses, and catching a brief glimpse of Miles out of the corner of my eye as I practically sprint away.

Where am I going?

I have no idea. Just away from here, away from all those eyes and lenses, and *definitely* away from Miles.

There's a barn at the far edge of the field, and even though everything involving me and horses has been a total nightmare on this trip, I march toward it, putting as much space between me and the polo field as I can, as quickly as I can.

When I step into the barn, I realize that it's not actually a barn at all, but a fancy garage. There are cars parked in here, gorgeous, sleek, expensive cars, and I walk between two of them, letting my fingers drag over the cool surface of a Rolls-Royce as I take a deep breath.

That was certainly a freak-out for the books, and I wait to hear Glynnis or Ellie come in after me, chiding me to get back out there and smile for the cameras.

But it's not Glynnis or Ellie suddenly casting a shadow from the doorway.

It's Miles.

He's just . . . standing there. His hands are loosely clenched at his sides, his chin is tilted down a little, and he's breathing hard, like he ran to catch up with me.

"I'm sorry," I say, and I am surprised to hear how shaky I sound. I'm surprised at how shaky I *feel*. Miles opened the door wide when he walked in, and now in the sunlight I can see dust motes floating in the air between us. "I couldn't do it."

Crossing my arms, I cradle my elbows in my palms and go on even as Miles moves closer to me. "I get that that's part of this whole fake dating thing, but a kiss is . . . a kiss is special. Maybe not to you, but it is to me, and I didn't want—"

And then whatever I might have said next is cut off by Miles's mouth on mine.

He kisses me, his hands coming up to hold my face, and for a second, I'm so surprised that I don't kiss him back. I just stand there with my arms still crossed, my eyes open.

But then he tilts his head, deepening the kiss, his hands warm on my cheeks, fingertips slightly calloused, and my eyes are drifting shut, my arms coming to drop first to my sides, then lifting up to clutch at his shirt there at his waist.

For a boy I'd once thought was made mostly of tweed, Miles can *kiss*.

We stand there in the barn, wrapped up in each other, and I go up on tiptoes, wanting to get even closer to him. Wanting to press every part of my body against his as I finally, *finally*, give into everything I've been trying not to feel since that night in the bothy.

When we finally pull apart, I sink back on my heels, staring at him with wide eyes.

"Wow," I say softly, and he smiles. It's the smile I saw that night at Seb's club, the one that first clued me into the fact that Miles might be more appealing than I'd thought.

"A kiss is special to me, too," he says, his voice so low and rough that I swear I can actually *feel* it moving over my skin, and I shiver.

"You're special to me," he adds, and my fingers flex on his shirt.

He's Seb's best friend, as much a part of this world as the horse races and the tiaras and the plaid.

But he's also funny and kind once you get past the stuffiness, and cute, and he kisses like it's his *job*.

"So what do we do now?" I ask him, the words surprisingly loud in the empty barn.

"You smile!" a bright voice says, and we turn to see Glynnis in the doorway, the photographer right behind her.

Chapter 33

"THIS IS EVEN BETTER THAN A KISS NEAR THE FIELD," Glynnis is saying, moving toward us with her hands spread open wide, like she's framing a shot. "We'll have Fitzy here shoot from behind one of the cars so the entire thing will feel a little sneaky, a little private."

I don't point out the irony in purposely posing for "private" pictures, but then my brain is still too scrambled from the kiss to say much.

Miles, however, doesn't seem to have that problem. As Glynnis goes on, talking about angles and how many pictures and "hand placement," he steps forward, one arm still around my waist.

"No."

Glynnis pauses, her fingers opening and closing in the air like Miles saying no has just caused some kind of system shutdown.

Then she gives a little laugh. "Oh, Miles," she says, waving him off, "I know it's a bit embarrassing to be caught like this, but I promise, it won't take but a moment, and then—"

"No," Miles says again. "I don't want pictures of this. *This*"—he gestures between the two of us—"isn't for the papers."

My chest aches with a mixture of pride and swooniness as he stands there, chin lifted, jaw clenched. All the things that used to make Miles seem so annoying and snobby are actually *really* appealing when they're being employed to protect my honor.

Glynnis's eyes are wide now, and she makes a disbelieving sound. "Of course it's for the papers," she says. "That's the entire reason the two of you were spending time together."

Gaze hardening, she props a fist on her hip. "And given that the *Sun* has pictures of Sebastian and Daisy leaving a pub together through a back door earlier this week, we really have no choice here."

Ugh. I should've known we weren't as stealth as Seb thought we were.

I open my mouth to explain to Miles that there was nothing illicit about that pub visit—well, there kind of was, but it wasn't between me and Seb—but he's still looking at Glynnis.

"Don't care," he says, and then he slips his hand in mine, squeezing.

"I covered the arses of a lot of members of this family," Miles goes on, "and I haven't minded it. But not this time. Not with Daisy."

And then he walks past Glynnis, tugging me after him.

As we walk back out into the sunshine, hand in hand, I practically gawp at him. "Did you just tell the royal family to get screwed?"

That muscle in his jaw ticks, but I think it's because he's holding back a smile this time.

"I think I did?" he asks, and, yup, definitely a smile.

One that is immediately captured by a camera as a series of clicks go off, and I lift our joined hands between us, shaking them slightly.

"It was a little bit for naught, though," I say. "Definitely a grand gesture, and I was very impressed and kind of turned on, but . . ." I shake my head and laugh.

Tilting his chin, Miles looks down at me, and his fingers flex in mine. "It's still different," he says. "We can't keep people from taking pictures, but we *can* not pose for them. Not fake anything, not use this"—he tugs at our hands—"for anyone else's benefit."

I nod, but even as I do, I'm thinking of those prom pics that nearly made it onto *TMZ*, the way I'd started getting hyper-aware of someone taking my picture. How I'd thought Ellie could keep her life here separate from mine in Florida, and that people would eventually forget about me.

They won't if I'm dating one of the Royal Wreckers, even if he *is* the least wreckish.

Miles frowns. "What is it?" he asks, but before I can reply, Seb is there, his jacket flapping open, his hair windblown yet weirdly perfect, his eyes shining, and his breath . . .

Stepping back, I place a hand over my mouth. "Oh my god, did you fall into a vat of whiskey?" I ask him, then glance around. I know Seb can be a mess, and Miles knows Seb can be a mess, but the general public has been spared a lot of his messitude.

"Did you know that Tamsin and Flora were shagging?" he asks me bluntly, raking a hand through his hair.

"What, no!" Miles says, startled, and sadly my "No, I didn't" is just delayed enough to sound pretty weak.

Miles looks down at me, pulling back. "Wait, *do* you know something about that?"

"Not the shagging part," I admit, tucking my hair behind my ear. "But just the general, you know, them-ness of them."

I turn and look at Seb, acutely aware that there are photographers nearby and that he is super, super drunk. In public.

"But why is that a big deal?" I whisper. "You don't even like Tamsin."

"I might, though," he fires back. "I might decide to like her, who can say?"

Rolling my eyes, I mutter, "And this is the most eligible bachelor in Scotland. Be still my beating heart."

I can see Dons approaching, also three sheets to the wind, listing slightly, and I tug on Seb's arm. "Hey," I say softly. "Why don't we go somewhere quiet and talk about this? Somewhere not quite so public and . . . exposed."

But Seb shakes me off. "No," he says, and Miles steps forward, putting his hands on Seb's shoulders. "Mate," he starts, but Seb steps back from him.

"Don't 'mate' me," he says, and I wrinkle my nose.

"Word choice," I mutter, but Seb—who has managed to keep his disastrous life private for all this time—is now on a roll.

"It just doesn't make any bloody *sense*," he says plaintively. Throwing one hand out at me, he all but cries, "You didn't want me, and you picked *Monters* of all people."

I open my mouth, but Seb just waves off anything I was about to say. "Oh, don't give me that 'it's just for show' thing.

The two of you have been making sex eyes at each other since day one."

My face flames hot, and I make a startled noise. "Have not!" I reply, and Miles is spluttering, too.

"Daisy and I only . . . *recently* realized th-that we—"

"Oh, stuff it, Monters," Seb says, placing his hands on his hips. "I'm not blind. But then Daisy's friend calls me a wanker, now Tamsin prefers Flora, and am I *not* the good-looking one? Am I *not* on a million bleeding bedroom walls all over this country? I just . . ." He shakes his head, and I look over at Dons, who is giggling into his cider.

"Who let him get this drunk?" I ask.

Dons shrugs. "Sherbet's not here, Spiffy's laid up with his ankle, Gilly's on the field, Monters has been too wrapped up in you to notice what Seb is up to, sooooo . . ." He pokes at his own chest and grins brightly. "Me! I did!"

Laughing, he slaps Seb on the back. "But it's good! Man deserves to let his hair down."

I don't point out that Seb is not so much letting his hair down as letting his feelings spew out his mouth, but then I don't have to because Seb keeps going.

"And Ellie," he says darkly, and now I step forward, grabbing his jacket and not caring *who* might be taking pictures.

"Seb, no."

"Ellie loves Alex. Boring, stupid Alex. I!" He lifts one hand, nearly smacking me in the face. "I am the interesting brother. I b-bought her a *house*."

"You tried to steal a house from a farmer, and also you're seventeen," I remind him.

"But I love her," he replies, and then from behind us, I hear, "What?"

Great. Greatgreatgreat. Exactly what this moment needs.

Alex and Ellie stand there, clearly worried and confused. They're holding hands, and I think for a second of the tableau we must all make standing there. Me clutching Seb's jacket, Miles right beside me, Dons giggling his stupid drunk ass off.

Seb's chest rises and falls underneath my hands as he takes a deep breath, and I hope—I *pray*—that he's not—

"I'm in love with Eleanor," he announces, and we all freeze for just a second.

And then Alex—sweet, noble, quiet Alex—rears back and punches Seb right in the face.

Which is when things go crazy.

A ROYAL BRAWL!

Shocking pictures out of Scotland today as Prince Alexander and Prince Sebastian took sibling rivalry to a new—and physical!—level. While the younger Prince Sebastian's crowd has certainly had run-ins with the press and they're no stranger to throwing punches, the prince himself has always stayed above the fray, and his older brother is usually a model of restraint. However, it appears something sparked off a row during the McGregor Charity Polo Match. Rumor has it the two were fighting over a relationship between Prince Sebastian and Daisy Winters, younger sister of Alexander's fiancée, Eleanor. Daisy was said to be dating Sebastian's friend, Miles Montgomery, seen in these photos just to the right of Miss Winters, but sources tell us tension has been building between the friends for some time now.

(*People*, "Royal Watch")

AHAHAHAHAHAHAHAHAHA!!!!!!

DID YOU GUYS.

EVER THINK.

WE'D SEE PRINCE ALEXANDER THE BORING.

THROW A PUNCH.

AT HIS BROTHER????

I did not, Crown Heads. I did not see this coming, and god bless us, every one. God bless YOU, Daisy Winters, because from what I hear, this whole thing was over her. She's apparently caught in an honest-to-god love triangle with Seb and Miles Montgomery, and it finally erupted into an ACTUAL BRAWL! Look at that right hook Alex threw! Seb is IN THE DIRT! Poor Ellie is totally traumatized, looks like, can't see Daisy's face, but I bet she's LOVING IT because hot, royal guys throwing punches over you is THE DREEEEE-AAAAAAAAAAAAAAAAM. In any case, this is the best day of my life. Please forward all my mail to me in heaven, thank you.

(*Crown Town*, "BEST DAY EVER")

Chapter 34

I HAD THOUGHT THE MEETING AFTER SEB'S CLUB
had been rough, but it's nothing—*nothing*—compared to the
post–polo debacle conference.

This time we're not in a sitting room but at an actual table,
this long slab of polished mahogany that's been cleared of everything. Dozens of Alex's ancestors glare down at us from the
wall, and I remind myself that I could always cut them out of
their frames with those special knives.

*Like you guys never did anything super embarrassing and scan-
dalous,* I think as I look at a painting of a guy in a poufy white
wig. *At least no one ended up decapitated.*

I look at Queen Clara's face where she sits at the head of the
table.

Yet.

"I don't think I have to tell everyone what a disaster this is,"
she starts, and Seb, still holding an ice pack to his jaw, mutters a
series of pretty filthy words.

Alex is still flexing his fingers, his knuckles a little swollen, but his other hand is clutching El's firmly as she sits at his side, and that makes me happy to see. No matter what went wrong today, they're still good.

Which is kind of a miracle, really.

Miles sits across from me, and every once in a while, he gives me a little smile, but mostly he studies the table, his fingers drumming, his brow wrinkled. He's the one with the most to lose here, though, so I can't blame him.

I'm sorry, I mouth when he looks up at me again. Glynnis is still going on about "optics" and "getting ahead of the story," and I already know where that kind of talk leads. At this rate, I'll probably have to marry Miles on the top of the Scott Monument to make people forget about *this* story.

Miles only shakes his head in reply, one corner of his mouth kicking up.

I'm sorry, he mouths back, and I wish we could sit next to each other like Ellie and Alex are.

"Daisy, are you listening?"

I snap my head up, looking at Glynnis, and am about to guilt-ily confess that no, I wasn't, and await whatever public shaming ritual she devises for me when Ellie suddenly stands up, her hand still in Alex's.

"I'd like to speak to my sister alone if that's all right."

Queen Clara, sitting at the head of the table, waves a hand. "Of course," she says, "as soon as we're done—"

"We're done now," El says, and she sounds every bit like a queen, her chin high, her shoulders back.

The queen actually sits back in her chair a little, clearly stunned by this show of backbone.

So am I, actually, but Ellie just turns her gaze on me and signals for me to get up. Once I do, and walk over to her, she says, "Change into something comfortable and meet me by the servants' entrance in ten minutes. We're going for a walk."

And that's how I find myself just a few minutes later, following my sister up a volcano.

Okay, it's not an *active* volcano, and these days Arthur's Seat is really just a big hill behind Holyrood Palace, a place where people go to eat their lunch on nice days. I was surprised when we just walked out the door, no car, no bodyguards, El in track pants and a T-shirt, her hair in a ponytail, face hidden by giant sunglasses.

I follow her up the rocky path now, trying not to let on just how hard I'm breathing, especially when there are little kids practically frolicking up the hillside in front of us.

The sun is doing its normal thing of sliding in and out of the clouds, making the light shift and change over the green grass and gray rocks. Turning on the path, I look back down at the city, getting smaller beneath us. I can see Holyrood Palace and the Scott Monument, shooting up in the sky, but it suddenly feels very far away. Hard to believe a place like this could exist in the middle of the city. The breeze is strong, smelling like growing things and the distant ocean without a hint of exhaust or the cold smell of stone buildings.

Seeing me stop, El comes to a halt, too.

"I come up here a lot when we're in Edinburgh," she tells me, and I nod at her big sunglasses.

"Do you always ditch the bodyguards?"

El flashes a grin, surprising me. The biggest disaster of my trip so far, and she's *smiling* at me?

"Whenever I can," she confesses, and I find myself smiling back.

We don't say much more as we continue to make our way up, and there's a fine sheen of sweat on my skin that cools rapidly in the wind. My hair is blowing all over the place, and as we go to sit down on a grassy flat space, El pulls an extra ponytail holder out of her pocket and hands it to me.

I thank her, wrangle my hair, and we sit. Nearby, there's a guy on a chair playing a cello, and I stare at him, wondering how he managed to haul that thing up here.

Ellie doesn't turn around but clearly knows what I'm looking at. "He's here a lot," she says. "It's nice."

The music *is* nice. It's also nice to sit here with my sister, just the two of us. We're quiet, the wind blowing our ponytails, rippling through the grass, filling up all the silent space between us.

"I'm sorry," Ellie says finally, and I turn to her, surprised. "What?"

She's not looking at me, her gaze focused below us. I wonder what she's thinking, if she's looking at the city and thinking how pretty the view is, or imagining a day when she'll be queen of this country.

"I've asked you to do so much, Dais," she says on a sigh.

"Go here, go there, don't do this, don't do that. Don't spend time with Seb's friends, but *now* spend time with Seb's friend because it'll make the queen happy, and that's all I care about these days."

She turns to me then, golden ponytail brushing her shoulder. "I've been the worst big sister ever. I'm very aware of that."

"I saw a thing on the true crime channel about a girl who tried to kill her younger sister with a blender," I tell her, shrugging. "You have competition, is my point."

El laughs at that, and then, shocking me, she leans over and rests her head on my shoulder. "It's all just so mad. I love Alex so much. I do."

"I know you do," I tell her, laying my cheek on her sun-warmed hair.

"But everything that comes with him scares the shit out of me," she says. "And I feel like two different people all the time. Maybe even three. I want to be your sister, and Mom and Dad's daughter, and just . . . *me*. But I want to be Alex's wife, too. And being Alex's wife means being a princess."

"A duchess, technically, settle down."

She laughs again, then lifts her head to look at me. I can't see her eyes behind her glasses, but I feel her gaze on me.

"I'm trying so hard to be everything to everyone that I feel like I'm actually screwing it up. I haven't been a good sister to you, I basically told Mom and Dad they embarrass me, and Alex . . ." She heaves a sigh. "I didn't tell him about Seb because I thought it would upset him."

"With good reason," I remind her. "Alex punched Seb in the face."

A sudden smile splits her face. "He did, didn't he? So unlike Alex," she muses, turning her gaze back to the city. "It was hot."

"Okay, gross," I laugh, nudging her with my elbow.

She nudges back, and a brief silence falls again. I wonder if we're done when she says, "I have to do this. Be this. And for me, the gains outweigh the losses. But you didn't choose this, Dais, and I never should've made you play along with any of it. I have Glynnis for that, and the Flisses and the Poppys of the world, but I just . . . I want you to be you. I *like* you. And I've missed you, Daisy."

It's not the most eloquent of speeches, but it still makes my throat go tight, and I nearly shove her with a "Shut up" just to shove down any inconvenient sisterly feelings.

Instead, I put my arm around her. "I love you, El," I tell her, and she gives a slightly watery laugh.

"Now who's being gross?"

But she puts her arm around my waist, and we sit up there on top of the world, watching the city for a long time.

When we get back to the palace, Alex is waiting for us, his face relaxing in a grin when he sees Ellie, and honestly, I'm not even that grossed out when they kiss. I'm just relieved.

When they part, Alex turns to me and reaches out to ruffle my hair. "At least we made your last week here an exciting one," he says, and I smile back, stepping back from his hand.

"I definitely feel very royal now that I've witnessed punching and paparazzi," I reply, then look around.

"Is Seb still here?" I ask, and Alex's grin fades.

"No, I think he's nursing his wounds and his pride at his club with the rest of his friends."

That makes sense, and I'm glad I'm not going to have to run the risk of bumping into him for a little bit.

And then, from behind Alex, I see Miles coming down the back stairs, hands in his pockets.

Glancing over his shoulder, Alex clears his throat and takes Ellie's hand. "We'll let you two chat, shall we?"

Ellie gives my arm a last squeeze, and then she and Alex are gone, heading down the narrow hall off the main foyer, leaving me and Miles standing there.

"Are you getting beheaded?" I ask him, and he laughs, shaking his head.

"No, so far my neck seems to be in the clear," he says as he reaches up to loosen his tie. He's still smiling, but I can see how tense his shoulders are, and I remember that for all the joking, Miles could be in real trouble with the royal family here. His apartment, his school, even medical stuff . . . that's all been on the Baird family dime, and what if this one stupid thing with me today put all that at risk?

It's not worth it. *I'm* not worth it.

Ellie and I have made things right, so there's really only one thing left to do here.

"Look, Miles," I say, stepping back from him. "I really appreciate what you did today. Standing up for me, not letting Glynnis use . . . whatever this is." I gesture between the two of us. "Oh, and also the kiss, that part was definitely A-plus, well done, you," I add, giving him a thumbs-up.

The tips of his ears turn pink, and a dimple appears in one

cheek as he tries not to smile, which is really very unfair right now.

Which is why I have to rip this Band-Aid off, and fast.

"But it's not like there's any chance of this actually going anywhere."

That hurts to say more than I thought it would, and when he looks up at me, his brows drawn together over those green eyes, I feel like something is squeezing my chest.

"I'm going back to America and regular high school," I hurry on. "And you're going to, I don't know, some university where people wear striped ties and spit at poor people."

"That place actually rejected me," Miles says, and I give a slightly forced laugh, shaking my head.

"Ugh, don't do that," I say. "Don't be funny when I'm try-ing to—"

What am I trying to do? Break up with him? We were never really a couple, and one kiss doesn't change that.

I move closer and lift my face, brushing the quickest of kisses on his cheek. Just over his shoulder, I can see the bust of one of Alex's ancestors, and in the distance, I hear the steady tick-tick of the grandfather clock in the hall.

"It was never real," I tell Miles, backing away. "It was just . . . part of summer in this bizarre-o world. And it's messed up enough for you already, so let's just call it a day, okay?"

Miles watches me, and it's like I can see that invisible suit of armor he wears half the time building itself back up. All the warmth slips out of his eyes, his jaw tight, his shoulders stiff.

"If that's what you want," he finally says.

It's not, not really, but what can I say? One kiss and a weird summer of fake dating is not worth screwing up his whole life for. And it's not like there's a future for us anyway. For all I know, we both got carried away faking a romance and just tricked ourselves into thinking it was the real thing.

But when he turns and walks back up the stairs, never looking back, the sudden pain in my heart feels pretty freaking real.

Chapter 35

IT'S SO HOT BACK IN FLORIDA.

There's a part of me that loves it, that wants to soak in the sun, the vaguely salty air, the bright colors. And for the first couple of days, I do. I shake off my jet lag lying on a blanket in our backyard, watching tiny lizards run over the palm fronds. I slather myself in sunblock and let the smell of coconut remind me that I'm home now, and that everything that happened in Scotland is in the past.

Of course, it can't really stay in the past—the wedding is still very much on and will be in Scotland in December. Then I'll have to go back and face everything I left behind. Ellie and I are fine, so at least that's good, but I'll still have to deal with Alex's family. With Seb.

With Miles.

That's the one that still hurts. I hadn't talked to him before I left, and even though I have his email—thanks to Sherbet—I don't want to risk it. The whole thing had been such a mess, and it seems like it's better to leave it alone. Maybe now that I'm gone, Miles can repair his relationship with "the palace," and by the time I come back in the winter, it won't be a big deal anymore.

That's probably wishful thinking.

Isa told me that it was all over the blogs, and I haven't ventured out of my house since I got back, afraid to suddenly see my face on all those magazines.

I guess it's impressive, how the palace spun the story of what happened at the polo match, and from everything Isa told me, the stories had Glynnis's fingerprints all over them. There was no mention of Seb's declaration of love to Ellie, and now Alex had punched him because he'd besmirched my honor or something. A total misunderstanding was turned into me being some kind of scarlet woman, breaking up the Royal Wreckers, and while Miles and Seb had definitely not been fighting over me—well, not *really*—I guess the end result is the same anyway.

For those first few days I'm back, I mostly just sit either in the backyard or in my room, checking in with Isa (and, yes, asking her to check the blogs for me), too afraid to go out. The paparazzi have never bothered us here in Perdido, but that was before I became a story, and every time I lie out in the backyard, I tense for the clicking of shutters. I won't even wear a bathing suit when I lie out, just in case.

It's on day four of my self-imposed hermitdom that Dad comes into my room wearing one of his loud shirts and a pair of long cutoffs. His gray hair is a mess, and he's got his sunglasses perched on top of his head with his regular glasses balancing on the end of his nose.

In other words, typical Dad.

"C'mon," he says, and I look up from my laptop, frowning. "What?"

"No more of this," he replies, gesturing around my room. "Baptism by fire, here we go."

He wants me to go out.

I scoot up the bed, pulling my knees to my chest. "Nope. No baptisms, no fire, no outside."

But when Dad is in one of these moods, he can't be talked out of it. "You can't live in this room forever, Daisy Mae," he reminds me. "Eventually you're going to have to go to school, or maybe get another job so that you can pull your weight around here. Can't raise a moocher, you know."

"Mrs. Miller said I could have my job back at the Sur-N-Sav," I say in a low voice. "But I don't . . ."

"You don't want to see yourself on magazines, I suspect," Dad finishes, then quirks an eyebrow at me. "Or *perhaps* you don't want to go back to your former life of unglamorous servitude now that you've tasted the finer things."

That irks me as, I guess, Dad had thought it would. "That's not it," I tell him, and he shrugs.

"Prove it, then. Let's go to the Sur-N-Sav right now and tell Mrs. Miller in person that you will be donning the smock this week, shall we?"

Which is how I find myself back in the land of linoleum and cheap bread just fifteen minutes later, wincing as we pass the rows of magazines by the registers. Isa isn't working today, but Bradley, one of the kids from my school, is, and when he sees me, he gives me a wave. Nothing else, no look or weirdness, just a wave.

I'm beginning to think things might actually be normal after all when I see the first cover.

"CRAZY FOR DAISY!"

Seriously, why is that their favorite headline?

It's me at the polo match, before everything went wrong, standing with Miles, and there's a little inset picture of Alex punching Seb.

My stomach drops, and my knees are weak, everything inside me suddenly feeling liquidy and queasy, and I nearly turn and bolt out of the store.

But Dad stops me. "Now wait just a tick," he says, and ambles up to the stand.

"Dad," I say, trying to keep my voice low, but there's a clear edge of desperation to it.

Dad either doesn't hear it or chooses to ignore it. "Now then," he says, flipping through the pages, "is any of this true?"

It's not what I'd been expecting, so I only stare at him, confused, and shake my head.

"None of this happened, then? Prince Sebastian was not desperately in love with you, only to lose you to his best friend?"

Now my face is turning red, and I'm glad the store is fairly empty. "No," I say in a whisper. "You know that."

"I do," Dad agrees. "Well, most of it. Not sure how much I really want to know about all this if I'm being honest. Your mum knows the truth. Ellie does. Isabel does, I'm sure."

I tug at the hem of my T-shirt. "Still not sure where you're going with this, Dad."

He puts the magazine back on the rack, then places both his hands on my shoulders, looking into my eyes. "Is there anyone at all, anyone who matters to you, who thinks any of these stories are true?"

The Sur-N-Sav is fairly quiet except for "Lost in Love" playing over the speakers and the occasional beeping of the scan belt and the squeaking of wheels on the carts. And the answer to Dad's question suddenly seems so easy.

"No," I say. "There isn't."

Dad shrugs his bony shoulders. "Then there you have it." Jerking his head back toward the magazines, he adds, "This is a bonkers world your sister has entered, and you can't stay out of it because she's family. Even when you're here, even when things seem normal, they never really will be. But *you*"—he squeezes my arms slightly—"you can stay as normal as you want, my Daisy Mae. So long as you remember that all that matters is the truth as you know it, and as the ones who love you know it."

I'm suddenly really afraid I'm going to start crying in the middle of the Sur-N-Sav, and then I may never get *any* of my dignity back. "Thanks, Dad," I manage, and he pulls me in for a quick hug.

I leave that afternoon, my green apron back in my hand, and as we make our way out of the store, I don't stop to look at the magazines even once.

Two weeks later, I'm wearing that apron, at my usual register, and while there are still two magazines with my face and name on the cover, I'm not quite the hot story I was. Luckily for me, Seb got caught making out with some model at a party. Normally, that would've just been, like, a Thursday for Seb, but this particular supermodel was dating Declan Shield, and when he went after Seb at a fashion show the next week, there was an all-out brawl. "PRINCE AND ROCK STAR BRAWL OVER VICTORIA'S SECRET ANGEL" beats whatever I had going on by a mile.

And there are a few times I look at the new covers with Seb's face on them and wonder if he did it for me. Maybe not. Maybe he just liked the chance to finally be himself, hot mess that he is, but we *had* gotten to be friends.

Kind of.

That's probably crazy thinking, and this is just normal Seb behavior, but still—the timing is good.

My line is busy today, so I don't even have time to look at magazines anyway, especially when some lady comes in with a massive coupon binder. I've just helped her load her roughly 500 boxes of Kleenex into her cart when I hear, "Is there a special on something called 'Cap'n Crunch'?"

The voice makes the hair on the back of my neck stand up, and I whirl around to see Miles standing there.

Miles.

In the Sur-N-Sav.

His hair is shorter now, not even touching the collar of his shirt, and he stands there, his arms full of . . .

I take a closer look at the stuff he's pulled off the shelves, and a smile spreads across my face, so broad it actually hurts.

"There's not right now," I tell him, "but I think there's a coupon for peanut butter."

He drops his purchases all on the belt with a sheepish shrug. Not just peanut butter, but Cap'n Crunch, Goldfish crackers, two bottles of ranch dressing . . .

"American grub," he tells me very seriously. "So I can blend in."

I'm so busy staring at him, wondering why he's here—knowing why he's here, but wanting to hear it anyway—that I nearly miss that last bit.

And then I look up at him, eyebrows raised. "Blend in?" I echo, and Miles nods, tucking his hair behind his ear.

"The more I thought about next year, the less some, let's see, how did a charming American girl put it to me? Ah, yes, some 'stick-up-its-ass university where everyone wears striped ties and spits at poor people' seemed to fit." He smiles a little then, just the one side of his mouth quirking up. "Figured I might take the risk my ancestors never did and explore the colonies a bit."

I shake my head, suddenly very aware of Isabel leaning over her own register and *very* happy there is no one in my line but him. Miles. Here in Perdido, Florida, wearing a jacket even though it is roughly a million degrees outside, his hair a mess from the humidity, smiling at me. A real smile from a real boy who, it seems, might really like me.

"Seb's family—" I start, but Miles shakes his head.

"It's fine," he says. "Or it will be." That dimple flashes in his cheek. "Turns out I don't really like living my life at other people's beck and call. Apparently the courtier genes skipped me."

291

"Or maybe you were just under a bad influence this summer," I suggest, and his eyes move over my face in a way that makes my heart flip-flop.

"Could be," he agrees softly. "In any case, after you left, I kept thinking about you. About the summer. About how little I was actually faking anything when it came to you. So." He lifts his shoulders. "America it is. For a little while at least."

"You might need a guide," I say. "Someone to show you the ropes. Make sure you don't get in over your head."

With a sigh, Miles leans against the belt. "That's presumptuous," he tells me, even as he reaches out to cover one of my hands with his. "Only a real ponce would make an offer like that."

I lean closer. "I happen to like ponces."

He leans closer, too, enough so that I can feel the warmth of his breath on my mouth as he replies, "As do I."

And then we're kissing at my register at the Sur-N-Sav, no hiding, no sneaking around. Full-on *snogging*, as he would say, right there in front of everyone.

Okay, so everyone in this case is Isabel and the one old lady in her line, but still. So I lean even closer, awkward with the conveyor belt between us, but hey—

"NO BOYS!"

The cry is muffled but still *very* loud and accompanied by a frantic knocking sound.

I pull back and look up toward the window of Mrs. Miller's office. She stands there, one fist propped on her hip, the other rapping the window. "NO BOYS!" she shouts again through the glass, and Miles looks up at her, brow wrinkled.

"Is that the norm here?" he asks as I waggle my fingers at Mrs. Miller.

"In America, no, but at the Sur-N-Sav, yes."

He looks back at me, green eyes bright. "Then can we leave the Sur-N-Sav, please?"

I glance back up at Mrs. Miller, who's turning away from the window now, purple smock fluttering, and probably on her way down here to lock me in a chastity belt or set Miles on fire.

Still, I grin and pull Miles back to me, my fingers twisted in the collar of his shirt. "In a minute," I promise, and then we're kissing again.

Maybe not in a palace or a bothy or a Rolls-Royce, but there's no place else I'd rather be.

ACKNOWLEDGMENTS

THANK YOU TO EVERYONE AT PENGUIN FOR LETTING me write my spin on a Princess Book! Thanks especially to Ari Lewin, whose guidance helped me turn this into the book I wanted it to be.

Thanks to my wonderful agent, Holly Root. This is book #10 we've worked on together, and I hope we have 10,000 more. (Okay, maybe like 30 more, writing is hard.)

To everyone on Twitter, specifically Stacey Kade, who went, "YEAH, DO THAT!" when I talked about wanting a book about a girl who gets famous when her sister marries a prince. Those immediate cheers and "I would read that" responses made this an actual book as opposed to This Cool Idea I Had for Five Minutes.

Thanks to Jennifer Lynn Barnes, Ally Carter, and Carrie Ryan, who plot busted like the pros they are with me and, more important, coined the term "Hot Tub Prince Harry." I still can't believe they didn't let me call the book that, ladies.

To all my readers, whether this is the tenth book you've read from me or the first, I love and appreciate you more than I can say. I hope you've had fun!

And as always, thanks to my family, without whom none of this would be nearly as fun.